"When you crack open a Chapman book, you are guaranteed pure reading pleasure."
—*Romantic Times*

Praise for *New York Times* bestselling author Janet Chapman's charming Highlanders series

SECRETS OF THE HIGHLANDER

"Liberally spiced with mystery, this story has warmth and genuine love that make it the perfect antidote for stress."
—*Romantic Times*

ONLY WITH A HIGHLANDER

"A mystical, magical book if there ever was one. . . . A perfect 10!"
—Romance Reviews Today

"This time-traveling Highlander series has been a pure joy to read, and this book is no exception."
—*Romantic Times*

"An excellent addition to her entertaining Highlander series."
—*Booklist*

TEMPTING THE HIGHLANDER

"Chapman breathes such life and warmth into her characters, each story is impossible to put down."
—*Romantic Times*

WEDDING THE HIGHLANDER

"A series that just keeps getting better. . . . This is Chapman's most emotional, touching and powerful novel to date."

—*Romantic Times*

"Exciting . . . Janet Chapman writes a refreshingly entertaining novel."

—The Best Reviews

LOVING THE HIGHLANDER

"Janet Chapman has hit another home run with *Loving the Highlander*. It's a fresh take on time travel, with both humor and drama. She's a keeper."

—*New York Times* bestselling author Linda Howard

"The characters are lively, intriguing and full of passion."

—*Romantic Times*

CHARMING THE HIGHLANDER

"Splendid. We can expect great things from Janet Chapman."

—*The Oakland Press*

"Time travel, tragedy, temptation, along with desire, destiny, devotion, and, of course, true love, are all woven into Janet Chapman's romance."

—*Bangor Daily News*

"Terrific . . . A real gem of a story!"

—*Romantic Times*

. . . and for her captivating contemporary romances

THE STRANGER IN HER BED

"A thoroughly enjoyable tale of a modern-day knight and his feisty ladylove set in the rugged mountains of Maine."

—*Booklist*

THE SEDUCTION OF HIS WIFE

"A charming story of love, growth and trust."

—*Romantic Times*

"Chapman presents a cast of rugged characters in rural Maine who enact a surprisingly tender romance."

—*Booklist*

THE DANGEROUS PROTECTOR

"One thing that Chapman does so deftly is meld great characterization, sparkling humor and spicy adventure into a perfect blend."

—*Romantic Times*

THE SEDUCTIVE IMPOSTOR

"Chapman's skills as a storyteller just keep getting better. Utilizing warmth and humor, she makes this thrilling romantic tale both funny and scary."

—*Romantic Times*

"One of the best books I've read in a long time. . . . A fun, sexy read!"

—*Old Book Barn Gazette*

Also by Janet Chapman

The Man Must Marry
Secrets of the Highlander
The Stranger in Her Bed
The Seduction of His Wife
Only with a Highlander
The Dangerous Protector
Tempting the Highlander
The Seductive Impostor
Wedding the Highlander
Loving the Highlander
Charming the Highlander

Available from Pocket Books

JANET CHAPMAN

Moonlight Warrior

POCKET **STAR** BOOKS
New York London Toronto Sydney

Pocket Star Books
A Division of Simon & Schuster, Inc.
1230 Avenue of the Americas
New York, NY 10020

First Pocket Star Books paperback edition May 2009

Cover design by Min Choi
Cover art by Chris Cocozza

Manufactured in the United States of America

10 9 8 7 6 5 4 3

ISBN-13: 978-1-4165-9487-1
ISBN-10: 1-4165-9487-6

To Ella Lavoie Byram
(1913–1995)
I used to look into your eyes and wonder where you were;
now I realize you were taking shelter in the hearts
of those who loved you.
You're still in our hearts, Mama.

Chapter One

Kenzie Gregor politely smiled down at the tiny prattling woman, nodding occasionally. He had no idea what she was saying, as he didn't recognize the language. Stealing a quick glance around the bank lobby, he arched a questioning brow at Father Daar, sitting in one of the chairs against the side wall. When his companion merely shrugged, Kenzie was forced to turn his attention back to the woman.

She appeared quite spry for her advanced years, considering how quickly she'd jumped up from her chair when he and Daar had walked in two minutes ago. Her white hair was coiled on top of her head in a loose bun held in place by two knitting needles.

Kenzie darted another desperate glance around the lobby, hoping to discover whom the woman belonged to. The man at the teller's station, engrossed in his business transaction? The couple sitting at the desk on the far wall, signing papers?

The woman tugged on his sleeve. "Please look at me, young man, when I'm speaking to you," she said, her firm command softened by her smile.

English! "I'm sorry, madam. But I did not understand what you were saying before."

She launched into her foreign tongue again.

"Can ye not see she's touched in the head, Gregor?" Daar said from the sideline. "It's an omen, telling us we shouldn't be here. Handing over all our money to someone else to look after surely makes ye as crazy as the old woman."

Kenzie took hold of the woman's arm when she turned to advance on Daar, and shot the old priest a warning glare. "I promised Matt I would open a bank account the moment I found a town I wished to settle in. Writing checks is how money is exchanged in this time, and I intend to fit in here in Midnight Bay."

"Fine," Daar said in a huff. "Then your brother can just write ye another fat check when the bank suddenly *misplaces* our money. I can't exactly conjure up more coin now, can I?"

"Mom?" came a woman's voice from Kenzie's left. "Oh my God, Mother," she said, rushing toward them.

Kenzie immediately let go of the old woman and clasped his hands behind his back.

The younger woman stepped between them. "I told

you to stay in that chair," she whispered, trying to lead her mother back to the row of seats. "You can't just walk up to strangers and start bothering them."

The older woman pulled free. "I wasn't bothering him, was I, young man? I was merely telling him to do business with the bank over in Oak Harbor," she said, projecting her voice to the whole lobby of onlookers. "And explaining how the people running *this* bank are trying to steal a widow's only means of support right out from under her."

"Mother!" the young woman quietly hissed, glancing at the back office as she led the woman away once again. "You're not helping matters. I'm trying to get us a new loan." She nudged her into one of the chairs. "Please just sit here and don't speak to anyone."

The moment the young woman turned to give Kenzie an apologetic smile, her mother jumped to her feet and rushed back to take hold of his arm—which she squeezed. "My, but you're a big, strong man. Are you married?" she asked, glancing at his left hand.

The younger woman turned a lovely shade of pink.

"Eve, come introduce yourself, so this handsome young man will no longer be a stranger."

Kenzie smiled at the beautiful daughter, and gave a slight nod when her crystal blue eyes met his. She immediately dropped her gaze, her short blond curls framing a flawless complexion that was now bright pink.

Thoroughly enchanted, Kenzie held out his hand, suddenly having an overwhelming need to touch her.

"Kenzie Gregor," he said, careful to keep his voice soft, as she appeared as delicate as a fawn. "It's a pleasure to meet you, Miss . . . ?"

"This is my daughter, Eve Anderson. She moved home with me two months ago. I'm Mabel Bishop. Are you moving to Midnight Bay, Mr. Gregor, or just passing through?"

Kenzie dropped his hand when it was obvious Eve Anderson had no intention of taking it. "Father Daar and I are planning to settle here," he said, nodding toward his companion.

Mabel turned to Daar. "I am *not* crazy," she declared. "I merely get confused sometimes, and it was very unkind of you to refer to me so."

Just then a man emerged from the office. "Eve. I need you to sign the new loan application before I submit it for consideration." He nodded to her mother. "Mabel. You're looking especially fine today."

As Mabel Bishop sat down with a harrumph, pointedly ignoring the man, Eve walked into the office behind him.

Kenzie sat down between Mabel and Daar.

She immediately turned to face him. "So, Kenzie, what is it you do?"

"Do?" he asked.

"For a living. What sort of work are you planning to do in Midnight Bay?" She gave a desolate sigh. "There's not much here, I'm afraid. Just a few clam diggers and lobstermen. The cannery closed quite a while back, and our one industry in town, the lumber mill, has been laying off workers."

"I'm in the process of buying a farm out on the point. I've had thoughts of opening an animal sanctuary. I enjoy working with animals."

Mabel's silver eyebrows arched. "You're wealthy, then?"

Kenzie ignored Daar's snort behind him. "If ye mean do I have enough money to get by, I suppose you could say that."

Mabel leaned closer. "Then I should warn you, Kenzie, that every unattached female in Midnight Bay will be showing up on your doorstep, casserole in hand, the minute word gets out that a wealthy man has moved to town." Her eyes sparkled. "Your being handsome won't hurt, either. Nor will that charming Scottish accent of yours."

Daar snorted again, and Mabel gave him a glare.

"Will your daughter bring me a casserole?" Kenzie asked, having absolutely no idea what a casserole was, but quite intrigued by the idea. "I did not see a ring on her finger."

Mabel gave a small laugh. "Sorry, but you'd probably starve to death waiting for Eve to show up on your doorstep. She swore off men when she divorced two months ago." Her expression turned sad. "It'll be years, I'm afraid, before she'll ever trust another man."

"Your daughter was married?" Kenzie remembered how delicate she'd looked. "Was she forced to divorce him because he abused her?"

Mabel looked surprised, then laughed. "Oh, good mercy, no. Parker wouldn't have dared lay a hand on her. Eve might appear all soft and feminine, but only a suicidal idiot would mess with her. No, Parker ran off with all their savings and their neighbor's wife after Eve suggested I move down to Boston to stay with them."

Mabel suddenly stood up as Eve walked out of the office. "Welcome to Midnight Bay, Kenzie. And you, too, Father Daar," Mabel said, giving the priest a cursory nod. Her eyes sparkled again when she looked at Kenzie. "We'll be neighbors—Eve and I live out on the point. And if you need a nice woodstove to heat your new place, come to our store and we'll fix you right up. It's Bishop's Hearth and Home, just across Main Street."

Kenzie had stood when she had, and he took her extended hand and gave a slight bow. "It was wonderful to meet you, Mabel. Thank you for the warm welcome. And the warning about the casseroles," he added with a wink.

He held out his hand to Eve, who had taken her mother's elbow. "It was wonderful meeting you, too, Eve. I look forward to shopping in your store."

She gave him a small nod as she stepped away. "Yes, do stop in, Mr. Gregor. We sell the most efficient woodstoves on the market." She glanced at the office she'd just left, then back at him. "Or once we get them in stock, maybe we could interest you in a new wood-pellet stove," she said, ushering her mother from the bank.

Kenzie walked to the large window, clasping his hands behind his back as he watched the two women walk across the street.

"Aren't we buying our farm from a gentleman named Bishop?" Daar asked, coming to stand beside him.

"Alvin Bishop," Kenzie confirmed, watching Eve and her mother enter one of the shops, the weathered sign over the door stating it was Bishop's Hearth and Home. "He could be Mabel's brother-in-law."

"Mr. Gregor?"

Kenzie turned to the banker Eve had been talking to earlier. "Mr. Johnson?" he asked, shaking the man's hand. "Did Chelsea send down the paperwork from Bangor?"

"Yes, she did," Mr. Johnson said, leading the way to the back office. "Your lawyer had everything overnighted. It helped that you and Alvin Bishop used the same law firm. Alvin mentioned Mrs. Rand is related to you?"

"My brother married her sister. Chelsea's actually the one who saw the Bishop farm advertised in the Bangor newspaper and called me last week."

"Alvin should be along soon," Mr. Johnson said, gesturing to the chairs in front of his desk as he took his seat behind it. "He also lives in Bangor, and he called earlier to say he's running late. It seems there was a bad accident on Route One this side of Ellsworth, and traffic was backed up. I'm sorry you had to wait, Mr. Gregor. The woman who just left didn't have an appointment; she simply showed up."

"Eve Anderson. Mabel implied they're having money problems? How long has Mabel been widowed?"

Mr. Johnson appeared startled. "Ah . . . Nathan's been gone almost six months now. But I can't discuss Mabel's financial situation with you, Mr. Gregor. Our bank has a very strict privacy policy, and I assure you, *your* business with us will remain equally confidential." He leaned forward. "You mentioned on the phone that you have some funds you wish to deposit? We can take care of that before Alvin arrives, so your account will be in place when you write him your check. It will take just a few minutes to verify the transfer of funds."

Kenzie reached in the inside pocket of his leather jacket and pulled out the check Matt had given him over a month ago. "It's from a Maine bank. Matheson Gregor is my brother. There shouldn't be any problem," he said, setting the check on the desk.

Mr. Johnson picked up the check, read it, and snapped his gaze from Kenzie to Daar, then to Kenzie again. "Of course, Mr. Gregor. And the balance, after you've purchased the Bishop farm? Will you be leaving the rest on deposit with us?"

Kenzie leaned back in his chair and propped his right foot on his knee. "That would depend on whether or not ye took care of Mabel's problem to her daughter's satisfaction."

"Excuse me?" Johnson's gaze darted nervously to a stack of papers on his left. "But what . . . um . . . are you a friend of Eve's?"

"I'm a friend of Mabel's."

The banker slid an account document toward Kenzie. "But I've known Mabel most all my life, and I've never heard her mention you. If you would just sign here, Mr. Gregor, to open your account with us."

"I only met Mabel today." Kenzie pulled the pen Matt had given him from his pocket, still leaning back in his chair, and nodded toward the papers on the banker's left. "I'm not sure I wish to do business with a bank that is trying to take away a widow's means of support." He dropped his foot to the floor and reached for his check.

The banker immediately leaned back, taking the check with him. "I was only able to get a three-month extension on Mabel's business loan, but I give you my word, Mr. Gregor, that I will do everything in my power to persuade the main office to give Eve a working line of credit to expand their business."

Kenzie smiled, clicking the pen to make the ballpoint appear, and quickly signed his name. "Then I look forward to our doing business, Mr. Johnson." He slid the signed document toward him. "Make the transfer. I'm eager to go explore my new land."

Kenzie settled Father Daar on the sheltered knoll overlooking the ocean so that the old priest was facing the late April sun. He placed a blanket over Daar's legs before walking back to the truck for the basket of food.

"I cannot believe we have to spend five more nights outdoors when we just paid a king's ransom for a warm, dry house," Daar muttered.

"Which is occupied at the moment," Kenzie said, setting the basket beside him. "You saw that someone was still living there when Alvin Bishop showed us the farmhouse after we signed the papers. And you heard him ask if I'd give his tenants five days to move out."

"I heard ye say *you* don't mind waiting," Daar said, opening the basket and scanning its contents. "I did not hear anyone ask me if I minded." He grabbed one of the sandwiches and glared at Kenzie. "Nor did I see my name on the deed beside yours. Considering all the trouble your blackguard of a brother caused me last year, I believe I'm entitled to a portion of that check."

"You've taken a vow of poverty, remember?"

Daar harrumphed and bit into his sandwich.

Kenzie sat down beside him and rummaged through the food basket. "This is good land," he said. "It has nearly four hundred acres and is surrounded by ocean on three sides, which will afford us plenty of privacy. And turning it into a working farm will be a good disguise for our true mission. The farmhouse seems sturdy, sitting high on a bluff overlooking the Gulf of Maine, though the barn is in need of repair." He pointed at the ocean. "The deed claims we also own those small islands. I'm sure William will find one of them to his liking."

"Speaking of William, where is the accursed beast?" Daar asked, before stuffing the last of his sandwich in his mouth.

"Holed up in a nearby pine grove," Kenzie said. "He'll join us after dark." He lowered his own sandwich to his lap. "I'm worried that William's not adjusting well to this century. Maybe the ocean air will give him some comfort by reminding him of his old homeland."

"Not that you gave any thought to *my* comfort," Daar said. "The damp air makes my bones ache."

"The salt breeze will do you good as well, old man."

"I miss my cabin. TarStone Mountain has been my home for nearly forty years, and until you bullied your way into my life, I was perfectly content to die there."

"You're many years away from dying, priest. So, what do ye think of Mabel Bishop and Eve Anderson?" Kenzie took a bite of one of the sandwiches he'd had the waitress make up for them at breakfast.

"I think the daughter left no doubt she isn't interested in you," Daar said with a scowl. "Don't think I didn't notice the way ye were looking at her." His scowl intensified. "Ye best not be entertaining any notions of being attracted to her. Women have a sneaky way of diverting a man's attention from his true work." The old priest's face suddenly softened. "I know ye returned to being a man only a few months ago, Kenzie, but ye must fight any romantic notions of getting involved with a woman in this modern time. Helping displaced souls become human again is going to demand your full attention."

"I am well aware of my duties," Kenzie countered. "I just wanted to touch the lass, to see if she felt as soft as she looked." He sighed. "Ye needn't worry, old man. Mabel said Eve doesn't trust men after what her husband did to her, so it matters not if I find her attractive."

"Mabel Bishop is crazier than a loon." Daar shot Kenzie a reproachful glare. "And ye had no business sticking your nose in her money problems. The whole point of us moving to this godforsaken coast was to remain anonymous. We haven't been in town one day, and ye already started throwing your weight around to rescue some crazy woman ye just met."

"I was testing Matt's theory that the pen he made me would prove to be mightier than my sword, even when I don't use the magic he placed in it," Kenzie said with a shrug, not at all contrite. "It does appear that in this age, ink is a rather powerful weapon. Instead of having to hold a sword to his throat to get Johnson to help Mabel and Eve, withholding my signature got him to give me his word to help them get credit to expand their business."

Daar was back to glowering at him again. "And if that hadn't worked, you'd have gone to the truck and gotten your sword, I've no doubt. What's a casserole? Do you suppose it's something to eat?"

"I have no idea." Kenzie looked over to see Daar holding a large muffin. "I thought the older a person gets, the less of an appetite he has," he said with a chuckle. "I've never met anyone who worries so much about his next meal before he's even finished the one he's eating. Yet you're so thin, a good wind would carry ye off. Why do you eat as if every meal might be your last?"

Daar stopped with the muffin halfway to his mouth. "God's teeth, I'm eighteen hundred years old; every meal *could* be my last. And you were once an eleventh-century highland warrior who never knew where your next meal might come from. How many battles did you fight on an empty belly?"

"All of them, if I wanted to win. A full belly would have slowed me down." He gestured toward the basket of food. "But this is the twenty-first century, not the eleventh. And here a person can't travel five miles without passing a store or diner." He snorted. "You and William suffer from the same affliction. That beast is going to eat himself to death."

Daar set the muffin back in the basket with a sigh. "I visited Ireland once in the ninth century, about the time William would have been living there." The aged priest puffed up his chest. "I was at the peak of my powers, and the council of drùidhs asked me to go straighten out some old witch who had gotten too big for her britches."

Kenzie gaped at him. "Is there a reason you're just telling me this now, after I've spent months trying to help William? Could it have been the same witch who cursed him? Why didn't ye tell me you knew her?"

Daar shrugged. "I'd just as soon forget what happened in Ireland." He shot Kenzie a defensive glare. "And because it matters not. My powers are gone, Gregor. I can't help you with William any more than I can light a candle without a match, now."

"But I'm only just discovering my own abilities. And though you may have lost the magic, ye still have the knowledge. Do ye think I asked you to come here with me because of your cheery disposition? What happened to the hag?"

"You're a bigger blackguard than your brother," Daar growled. "I only agreed to come with you and William because Pine Creek had too many wizards and too many damn bairns being born." That said, he gathered the blanket around him and lay down, his back to Kenzie.

"Ye left because you were bored to tears, now that you don't have the power to interfere in everyone's lives." Kenzie sighed. "I'm sorry if I hurt your feelings. We're a good fit, you and me, both of us being outcasts of sorts. And living on TarStone as a panther for the last three years . . . well, I'd have gone hungry many nights but for the meat you left out for me."

"I tossed out those leftovers for the raccoons."

Kenzie chuckled. "Aye, even when the wee bandits were taking their winter sleep. So what happened to the old—" Kenzie suddenly got to his feet. "Do ye hear something?"

Daar sat up, canting his head. "It's only the breeze."

"Someone is calling out." Kenzie walked to the crest of the knoll and scanned the shoreline to the west. "It coming from this direction. There! I see a woman." He leapt onto a boulder for a better angle, and watched a wave nearly knock the woman off her feet as she scrambled up onto an island. "It's Eve Anderson! She's waded out to one of the islands, and she's calling her mother."

"I knew those two were going to be trouble," Daar muttered, standing up. "Women always are."

"The tide is coming in, and she'll be trapped." Kenzie jumped off the boulder and ran toward the island. "Bring the blanket. We're going to need it."

Chapter Two

Eve clung to the rocks as another wave washed over her. The moment it passed, she found a toehold higher up on the granite ledge, climbed out of the frothing surf, and ran toward the center of the island, hoping like hell she'd guessed right.

"Mom! Are you here? Mom!"

Dammit, she hadn't noticed when her mother had left the house. She had brought Mabel home from the store as soon as Alvin Bishop had left, and started calling lawyers to see if he had the right to do what he'd done. She needed to get an alarm for the door so she'd know when her mother was wandering off.

Except in five days, they wouldn't have a door to put the alarm on, would they? The bastard had sold her home right out from under her mother—who was here, thank God.

"Mom! The tide is rising, and we're going to get trapped!"

It was a small island, only thirty acres, and Eve knew it well. She and her mom had come here often for picnics, when Eve returned every summer after getting married six years ago.

"Why are you all wet?" Mabel asked from the bench that overlooked the Gulf of Maine. She gave an involuntary shiver. "Evangeline, it's too early in the year to go swimming. This is Jens's fault. Your father had you playing in the tidal pools when you were three."

"I remember, Mama," Eve said, taking her mother's hand. "Let's go back to the house and you can make me a cup of tea to warm me up. But we have to hurry. The tide's coming in, and we're going to have to wade to shore."

"Oh, dear. I've spent the entire day daydreaming again, and now I'm late getting dinner ready for Nathan." Mabel stood up and started down the path. "Maybe I can throw together a can of soup and whatever I have in the fridge. Nathan won't even realize he's eating leftovers."

They were just approaching the water-covered gravel bar when Kenzie Gregor strode out of the ocean and rushed toward them.

Mabel stopped in her tracks. "A tourist. I bet he wants to camp on our island. Tell him the state park is several miles farther east."

"Mr. Gregor!" Eve said in surprise.

"I heard you shouting. Is Mabel okay? The tide's coming in," he said, giving them a quick visual inspection.

Her mother eyed him curiously. "How do you know my name, young man? Did I have you in school?" She waggled her finger at him. "I don't care how big you've grown; I'm still Mrs. Anderson to you."

Kenzie gave Eve a concerned glance, then smiled contritely at Mabel. "Forgive me, Mrs. Anderson. I forgot my manners. But you can be thankful I've grown big. I'll carry you to shore."

He swept Mabel into his arms, then turned to Eve. "Stay here. I'll come back for you."

Eve stepped past him onto the rocks. "I'll lead the way. There's only a narrow gravel bar. One wrong step and you'll be swimming."

Eve guessed he must have muttered something inappropriate, for she heard her mother say, "Your mouth could use a good washing with soap, young man. Be careful!"

"I won't drop ye, I promise."

Her mother shrieked, and Eve turned to see a rogue wave soak them both.

"Don't worry, I've got her," Kenzie said. "Keep going."

The distance to shore had grown to about twenty yards, and though the water was only up to Eve's waist, the waves were building as the breeze picked up. She was definitely beginning to feel the cold—likely because this was her second soaking in only ten minutes.

Eve braced herself for the wave she saw coming just as her mother gave another scream, this one ending in a woof of expelled air. An arm of solid muscle wrapped around Eve's waist, and she was lifted off her feet and tucked up against an equally solid torso. She craned her neck to see Kenzie Gregor had hefted her mother over his shoulder so he could carry Eve like a football as he fought the swirling tide with another muttered curse.

Eve felt a lecture coming on. Big, strong, take-charge men *always* lectured tiny women in these sort of situations. And didn't she have a string of ex-boyfriends and one ex-husband to prove it? Just because she looked like some fragile little Kewpie doll, men always tried to take care of her—even though she was perfectly capable of taking care of herself.

Heck, if she weighed what Kenzie Gregor did, the waves wouldn't have been a problem. The man felt more solid than the granite he scaled as easily as if he were carrying two sacks of feathers.

He set her on her feet, carefully set her mother down, then tossed his heavy leather jacket at Eve.

With a swift economy of effort, Kenzie Gregor had her mother wrapped up in a blanket and was already striding away with the wet, shivering woman in his arms. "My truck's just over the hill. We'll take ye home," he said, disappearing into the stunted spruce trees.

The priest who had brought the blanket took hold of Eve's arm and started to follow. He was obviously trying to help her, and Eve stifled a snort. It was all the old man could do to walk up the knoll himself! His outdated cassock certainly wasn't helping matters, as the rising wind tangled it in his cane.

"I'd not say a word on the ride home, if I were you," he said, his sharp blue eyes reproachful. "Gregor doesn't much care to have his commands ignored. Ye should have waited on the island like he told ye to."

Eve sighed, helping him over a rough spot. She had no intention of saying anything to Kenzie but thank you. When they reached the large SUV, it was running, her mother sitting in the front seat and Kenzie standing with the back door open. Eve started to help Father Daar into the backseat, but Kenzie nudged her inside.

The blast of heat coming out of the floor and ceiling vents nearly took her breath away. Eve leaned forward and touched her mother's shoulder. Mabel didn't acknowledge her, but simply stared out the windshield. Father Daar climbed in next to Eve.

Kenzie got behind the wheel, tucked the blanket more tightly around her mother, then looked back at Eve. "She seems to be in a daze. Should I drive to the nearest doctor?"

"No. She'll be fine. She . . . she does this sometimes. I just need to get her into some dry clothes and into bed. She'll be okay after she has a nap."

He looked at Mabel again, leaning forward to see her eyes. When he still got no response, he put the truck in gear and slowly eased onto the dirt path toward home.

A heavy knot had formed in Kenzie's stomach the moment he pulled up in front of the sturdy white farmhouse, and by the time he was sitting at the table, looking around the well-maintained kitchen, he wanted to roar.

He had bought Mabel and Eve's home.

"They don't look as if they're preparing to move," Daar said as he fiddled with the large wood-burning cookstove that took up a good portion of one wall. He turned, his eyes troubled. "We're in a mess, aren't we, Gregor? Alvin Bishop sold us Mabel's house."

Kenzie finished buttoning the shirt he'd gotten out of his truck along with a full change of dry clothes. He'd dressed right there in the kitchen, while Eve gave her mother a warm bath upstairs and put her to bed. "It's beginning to look that way. Why would the man do such a thing to his brother's widow?"

"Because Alvin Bishop is a bastard," Eve said, walking into the kitchen.

Kenzie stood up. "I wouldn't have purchased this farm if I had known it was Mabel's home."

She walked to the sink and started filling a container with water. "It doesn't matter, Mr. Gregor. If you hadn't bought it, someone else would have. From what Alvin told us, when he came with the eviction notice, the farm has been for sale for five months." She dumped the water in the coffeemaker. "He put it on the market less than a month after his brother died."

"Are there not laws that allow a widow to keep her home?" Kenzie asked.

Eve glanced briefly at Father Daar before returning her troubled gaze to Kenzie. "There are—if my mother had actually been married to Nathan."

"They weren't married?" Daar asked, frowning in confusion.

Eve's face reddened. "My father died in a paper mill accident ten years ago. Mom later fell in love with Nathan Bishop, and they started living together six years ago, when I moved to Boston. If she had married Nathan, she would have lost her widow's benefits, and she couldn't afford that. So she and Nathan pretended they'd gotten married when they went to Bangor one weekend, and she came home calling herself Mrs. Bishop."

She smiled sadly. "You have to remember what generation my mother is from. Having been a well-respected schoolteacher in town, she simply couldn't bring herself to live openly with a man." She turned back to the counter and got several mugs down from the cupboard. "We'll be out of here in five days, Mr. Gregor, and then the house is all yours."

"Where will ye go?"

She stilled, not turning around. "We can live at the store until I find a place."

Kenzie gazed around the kitchen, taking in all of Mabel's possessions and feminine touches. "But this is her home," he whispered, the knot in his gut becoming so heavy that he had to sit down.

"She'll simply have to adjust to a new home."

"What is wrong with Mabel?" Daar asked, coming to sit beside Kenzie. "She seems to get confused a lot, and starts talking in . . . I believe it's French, though not any dialect I recognize. Does she have that disease that afflicts old people?"

Eve turned, and Kenzie sucked in his breath at the distress he saw in her eyes.

"It's not Alzheimer's," she said, "though a lot of the symptoms are the same. The blood vessels in her brain are slowly leaking. And whenever there's a new leak, more tissue is killed. I started noticing symptoms last year, when I came for my summer visit. She seemed to have lost her sense of time. Six hours could have been six minutes to her. She grew worse over the winter, after Nathan died. One moment she's in the present, and the next she thinks she's eighteen years old, living in Quebec with her parents. She regresses to French because she didn't learn English until she went to teacher's college in New Brunswick. She met my father when she came to visit a school friend from Midnight Bay," she finished, turning back to pour coffee into the mugs.

Kenzie stared down at the steaming mug she set in front of him, unable to look her in the eye. Dammit it to hell, he felt two inches tall. "Does Mabel understand that she's lost her home?"

"She was quite lucid when Alvin told her."

"Is that why she went to the island?" Daar whispered. "Was she so distraught, she intended to throw herself in the ocean?"

Kenzie snapped his head up. "No! You must persuade your mother that we'll work something out. I'll not put Mabel out of her home!"

Eve Anderson looked more amused than shocked. "Mom would never do something like that," she assured them. "No matter how confused she might get, it's simply not her nature. She went to the island to sit on her bench and watch the sea, because that's her favorite place on the farm."

Kenzie sighed in relief. "Will ye give me tonight to decide what to do about this?"

"There is nothing to decide. Knowing Alvin, he made you pay a small fortune for this farm, and it's legally yours. I would appreciate it, though, if you could give us more than five days to move. If I can find a reasonable rental in town quickly, we won't have to stay at the store."

"You may have as long as you need."

Daar choked on a swallow of coffee and shot Kenzie a glare.

"But I wonder if I might ask a favor of you," Kenzie added. "Would it be possible for Daar to stay in the house with you and your mother? He promises to be a undemanding houseguest, and he'll even help with some of the chores."

Daar started choking again, and Kenzie reached over and lightly pounded his back. Eve eyed them both skeptically.

"It was our intention to camp out on the knoll for the next five days," Kenzie continued. "But if it's to be longer, I'd feel better knowing Daar will have a warm bed."

"You were going to camp out?" she asked, her eyes widening. "But it still gets below freezing most nights."

Kenzie shrugged. "I enjoy brisk weather. Daar, though, claims it makes his old bones ache," he said, giving her a wink.

She immediately started building a fire in the cookstove. "I have no problem with Father Daar staying here." She suddenly turned back to them. "Could you both do one more thing for me?"

"What would that be?"

"Please don't mention my mother's illness to anyone in town? She's a proud woman, and if people start pitying her or treating her differently, she'd be crushed."

Kenzie stood up. "Mabel's secret is safe with us. I'm going to get Daar's things out of the truck, then go make camp." He stopped at the door. "Thank you, Eve, for helping me work out this problem."

She gaped at him. "*You're* thanking *me*? But you're the one being generous."

Kenzie shrugged. "The arrangement serves me as well as it does you. I enjoy sleeping outside, but I was not comfortable leaving Daar alone in a strange house. This way he gets a roof over his head, and I get the stars over mine."

Chapter Three

◈

Eve hefted a large piece of beech wood onto the splitting table, then nodded at her mother to push the lever. The ram slowly descended, and the engine's powerful hydraulics pushed the heavy, T-shaped wedge through the sinuous fibers. The moment the wood split into four pieces, her mother reversed the lever and the wedge lifted free. Eve tossed the fallen pieces onto the conveyer belt, watched them travel up into their delivery truck, then picked up another sixteen-inch log.

"Did I get married?" Mabel asked over of the sound of the idling engine.

Eve dropped the heavy wood onto the table and blinked at her mother. "No. What makes you think that?"

"Did you get married, then?"

"No!"

"Then who was that man at our supper table?"

Eve sighed. "He's a priest, Mama. His name is Father Daar, and he's boarding with us for a little while." She positioned the wood under the wedge. "We're almost done with this load. We'll deliver it to Mrs. Simpson tomorrow morning, before we open the store. Push the lever."

Mabel didn't move. "Priests live in rectories."

"Father Daar is retired. He's traveling the Maine coast, staying with charitable people willing to take him in."

"Eve, we can't take in strays, even clergy. We're broke. We had to drive all the way to Ellsworth the other day to go the food pantry."

They'd driven to Ellsworth because if they'd gone to the local food bank, everyone in town would have known exactly how bad their situation was. "Father Daar can't weigh as much as I do, Mama. How much food could he possibly eat?"

"He ate three pieces of chicken tonight! I planned to use those last two pieces for our lunch tomorrow."

"But just think of all the heavenly points we'll get for taking in a priest. How's that saying go? 'Be kind to a stranger, as you might be entertaining an angel?' "

Mabel snorted and pushed the lever. The process repeated itself, and Eve tossed four more pieces of split wood onto the conveyer belt. When they landed in the truck, one of the pieces fell over the side onto the ground.

"We've got a full load." She shut off the engine,

bringing blessed silence to the farmyard just as the sun disappeared behind the trees to the west. "That takes care of Mrs. Simpson. Tomorrow we'll start splitting Jonas Thompson's wood."

"Don't forget to collect the balance from Betty Simpson. She only paid for one cord up front, remember?" Mabel said. She stood up, then rolled the piece of oak she'd been using as a seat over to the pile of unsplit wood. "And Jonas owes us for one cord. He paid for three, but upped it to four at the last minute."

"I remember."

"Have you found us a place to live yet? Doesn't Betty have a house that she rents out to summer tourists?"

Thrilled that Mabel seemed to be back in the here and now, Eve made a comical face. "Do you really want Betty Simpson as a landlord? Besides, the cottage is probably already booked for the season."

"I don't want to live too far out of town," Mabel said. "What about that handsome young man we met at the bank this morning? Kenzie, wasn't it? Maybe the place he's buying has a house on it we could rent. Several of the old farms in this area have second homes for hired hands. We don't need anything big."

Feeling like she was tiptoeing through the twilight zone of her mother's mind, Eve decided to be honest with her. "Kenzie Gregor bought *this* farm, Mama."

"He did? Then where is he? Wait—that explains Father Daar! He was with Kenzie at the bank. Is that really why he's living with us?"

"Yes. And Mr. Gregor is camped out on the knoll by your island."

"Why?"

"He gave us more time to find a rental, but asked if Father Daar could stay with us until we move out."

Mabel beamed brightly. "Kenzie is a real gentleman, isn't he? He didn't want people in town to talk, so he's staying out of the house. I knew I liked that boy the moment I met him."

"Do you remember that he carried you through the surf this afternoon?"

Her mother looked at her blankly. "Why did he do that?"

"You'd gone to the island to watch the ocean, and got stuck when the tide came in."

Mabel's eyes darkened with sadness. "It's getting worse, isn't it? I'm losing whole blocks of time now."

Eve hugged her. "It'll be okay, Mom. I'll keep you safe."

"But where will it end?"

"I don't know." Eve leaned away and looked her in the eye. "The doctors can't predict that sort of thing. I can only promise that I'll be here for you, no matter what."

"But I don't want to be a burden. You have your own life to get back on track. You should be finding someone to love and have babies with, not babysitting your crazy old mother."

"Seventy-four is not old, and you are not crazy. You're just ill. And the last thing I need right now is a man. I love you, Mama, and there's no place I'd rather be than here with you. Besides," she said, taking off her gloves. "We're an excellent team. The two of us will make Bishop's Hearth and Home a success again."

"Oh, Eve. Even if we had *two* fully functioning brains, we would still need a miracle. Nobody around here has any money to spend. And those who do already bought stoves from us over the last six years. There are no more customers to sell to."

"Then we'll get creative. As soon as I get that new line of credit, we'll expand our market by selling those fancy new wood-pellet stoves that have become so popular. And for added insurance, we'll come up with something else to sell." Eve gave her mother a reassuring smile. "You love baking. Maybe we could change our sign to Bishop's Hearth and Home and Bakery, and start selling bread and homemade jam to the tourists."

"Nobody's going to pay for my bread, Evangeline. We sell firewood. That's been our only reliable source of income for the last five years."

"But Kenzie Gregor owns the farm now, so we don't have access to any trees. And even if we did, and even if I *am* strong—Eve flexed her muscles in a prize fighter's pose—I don't think I'd last very long running a chainsaw."

"I agree."

Eve swung around with a gasp to find Kenzie Gregor standing beside the woodpile.

"You might manage to cut down the trees, but limbing

and sawing the logs into stove lengths would likely do ye in," he continued, his golden eyes lit with amusement. He looked at the truck full of wood, then walked up to the splitter and ran his fingers along the wedge. "What is this machine?"

"It's a wood processor," Mabel said. "You lift the wood onto the table, split it into four pieces, then the conveyer belt carries them up into the truck."

Kenzie turned and smiled at Mabel. "You're looking none the worse for your adventure, Mrs. Anderson."

"It's Mabel to you, Kenzie," her mother said. She held out her hand. "And I believe thanks are in order. Eve told me you carried me through the surf earlier, when I foolishly got stuck on the island. My sincere thanks, young man."

He took her hand and gave a slight bow. "Your daughter was already doing a fine job of rescuing you. I just happened along and thought you might prefer a ride as opposed to wading."

Eve barely stopped herself from rolling her eyes. Kenzie Gregor could charm a snake charmer. Her mother was blushing!

What was his game? Strangers did not pay small fortunes for prime oceanfront farms, then sleep outdoors. Was he a throwback to the age of chivalry, or did he have some sort of agenda?

Eve gestured to the pile of unsplit wood. "Some of this wood belongs to Jonas Thompson, because he already paid for it. But I suppose the rest belongs to you now, since it was cut on your land. The processor and truck, however, are ours. As soon as we find a new place, we'll get them out of your yard."

He looked at the woodpile. "Who cut all this wood?"

"My husband, Nathan. He died right back there," Mabel said, pointing to a stand of hardwood at the end of the overgrown pasture. "He had a massive heart attack. I didn't even realize anything was wrong until it got dark and he didn't come home."

"I'm sorry for your loss, Mabel," Kenzie said softly.

"Thank you." She shook her head. "I told Nathan he was too old to be logging wood, but apparently I'm attracted to stubborn men. My first husband, Jens, was just as bullheaded."

"Daddy was not bullheaded."

"No?" Mabel said, a gleam lighting her eyes. "Then how come you took six years of martial arts instead of dance classes, like I wanted you to?"

Eve felt her cheeks heat up. "Daddy knew dancing lessons wouldn't help me as an adult the way self-defense classes would."

Mabel turned her gleam on Kenzie. "Jens made sure every boy who came calling on Eve knew she could beat them up. From the time he realized she was going to end up a petite, blue-eyed, curly blonde, he started driving her all the way to Ellsworth for karate lessons."

"I would say Jens was a very wise man," Kenzie said, his own eyes gleaming. "I have a friend in Pine Creek who has seven daughters, and he taught each of them to defend themselves."

Mabel snorted. "I bet those girls didn't intimidate every boy who came calling."

"Oh, I don't know," Kenzie drawled. "Greylen's youngest daughter certainly gave my brother a merry chase. In fact, Winter is seven months pregnant and she's still causing him fits. Now honestly, Mabel, would ye want your daughter to be with the sort of man who would let a wee lass intimidate him?"

Eve knew her cheeks were blistering red, but if Kenzie thought he could bait her, he was going to be disappointed.

Mabel, apparently, wasn't so sure. She gave Eve a cautious glance, then suddenly rubbed her arms. "My, but it's getting chilly. Let's go in and make a pot of tea. Kenzie, would you like to join us for some blueberry pie?"

"Ye left Daar inside with a pie?" He headed for the house. "I doubt there's any left, if it wasn't hidden. I will fill your cupboards with groceries tomorrow."

"What was that all about?" Eve hissed as soon as he was out of earshot.

"What was what all about?"

"Don't play innocent with me. Why in God's name would you even bring up my karate lessons?"

Her mother stepped closer. "I think Kenzie likes you, and I simply wanted to warn him how . . . off-putting you get sometimes. I like Kenzie, and I don't want his feelings to get hurt. That's why at the bank, when I noticed how he was looking at you, I warned him you were newly divorced."

Eve opened her mouth, then snapped it shut. What could she possibly say?

Her mother hooked an arm through hers, and started for the house. "Are you sure you don't find him even a little bit attractive? Doesn't he remind you of your father?"

Eve pulled them to a stop. "You're not dying, Mama. Not for many, many years. So don't try fixing me up with someone who will take care of me after you're gone, just so you can die in peace."

Mabel stepped away. "That doesn't mean you have to live like a nun in the meantime. A wonderful young man has all but been dropped in your lap, and if you don't take advantage of that, the other eligible women in town certainly will."

Eve snorted. "We don't know anything about Kenzie Gregor. Some of the worst serial killers in history were handsome charmers. For all we know, he bought this remote farm so he'd have a place to bury the bodies."

Mabel started them toward the house again. "You've been living in the city too long, Evangeline, and have grown cynical. You only need to take a long, deep look into his eyes to see that Kenzie is a gentle giant. He told me he wants to open an animal sanctuary. And he takes very good care of the old priest. Not all men are like Parker. That man might have put on a good face, but I never did trust him."

"And you're just telling me this now? Why didn't you say something six years ago?"

"Like what? That I knew you had fallen in love with a jerk? Eve, you were so excited about moving to Boston and getting a teaching job down there, and it all happened so quickly. You'd only known Parker six weeks when you announced your engagement. I honestly hoped I was wrong, because I wanted you to be happy. And you were."

"For a year," Eve said with a sigh. "Then Boston began to feel more desolate than Midnight Bay. Parker was always working late or flying off someplace on business. That's why as soon as school broke for the summer, I came home for a two-month visit." She snorted again. "Which certainly left the door open for Pauline to cozy up to my husband."

They went up the porch steps, and walked into the house to find Kenzie Gregor standing at the sink, doing the dishes they'd left in order to finish splitting the wood before dark.

Eve decided then that the man wasn't a serial killer. He was much, much scarier than that.

Chapter Four

"Is it true?" Maddy Kimble asked Eve after pulling her to the front of the store so her mother wouldn't hear them. "Did Alvin Bishop really sell Mabel's farm?"

The cherub-faced brunette was Eve's closest friend in Midnight Bay, and the fact that she'd run half the length of Main Street on her short lunch break was exactly why Eve loved her.

"It's true. Alvin put it on the market less than a month after Nathan died. And he didn't even have the decency to tell Mom he was selling, so she could start looking for another place to live! He came to the store yesterday, right after signing the papers, and told us we had *five days* to move out."

"That bloodsucking bastard."

Eve couldn't help but smile. Maddy might look

angelic, but she could make a sailor blush when she got riled. They'd gone to the same school, though Maddy had been a few years younger, but it wasn't until Eve had moved back two months ago that they'd become close friends. Maddy was a nurse and worked down the street at the retirement home.

"Do you know who bought it?" her friend asked. "I heard it was some gorgeous hunk of a man and an old priest. Susan said the guy looks strong enough to stop a train, and that he's got piercing gold eyes that nearly made her faint when he came to her window. She also said he's got a Scottish accent to die for, and that he's richer than God."

"Susan thinks any man who's not married is to die for. And she's not suppose to talk about *anyone's* bank balance."

"Like she's going to worry about that if she can make herself look important," Maddy scoffed. "She's only a teller, but she acts like she owns the damn bank." Maddy stepped closer. "So have you met him yet? Is he as gorgeous as Susan claims? Do you think he might give you and Mabel more time to find a place to live?"

"He told us to take as long as we want to move. He's been charming Mabel with some knight-in-shining-armor act, and she's falling for it. And he's definitely gorgeous, if you're into giants with deep golden eyes and bodies that make Atlas look like a wimp." She lifted her chin. "Which is exactly why I refused to even shake his hand when we first met in the bank. I'm not about to fall into that trap again."

"Oh, Eve," Maddy said softly, shaking her head. "Not all men are like Parker."

"It's only smart to learn from my mistakes. And if Parker taught me one thing, it's that rich, handsome men from away can't be trusted. I tell you, Maddy, Kenzie Gregor is weird. Nobody's *that* nice. He doesn't know us from a fence post, yet he appears more concerned about my mother's welfare than I am. And the old priest is even stranger. He has to be in his nineties, but his eyes are totally sharp. And he acts like he just stepped out of the Middle Ages, too, and wears an old wool cassock."

"He's probably more comfortable in traditional clothes. Old people cling to the familiar."

"He's staying with Mom and me until we move, and I didn't sleep a wink last night. I expected to hear chanting coming from his room downstairs."

"Where's the gorgeous giant sleeping?"

"He's camping out down by the ocean. He claims he *likes* sleeping under the stars in freezing weather. See what I mean? They're both odd. Mom and I were splitting wood last night, and I think Kenzie was standing next to the barn the entire time, watching us. I turned around and he was suddenly— There! That's him!" Eve said, pointing out the window. "He's just pulling into the Shop 'n Save. That's his SUV."

"He really is richer than God." Maddy leaned over one of the displays to get a better look. "That truck must have cost a fortune. Holy hell," she muttered, all but pressing her nose up to the glass. "He *is* gorgeous! And he looks deliciously normal to me: black leather jacket, short hair, tight jeans, and shoulders broad enough for a woman to cling to." She sighed. "I wonder if he owns a kilt?"

Eve pulled her away from the window. "Stop acting like you're sixteen."

Maddy turned her big brown eyes on Eve. "The answer to your prayers just might have moved into town, and you're too bitter to see it."

"I do not need a hero to ride in here and save me."

"Then can I have him? I've been praying for a man like that for years." She gave a fierce scowl. "You can be damned sure that Susan's going to go after him."

"She can have him. Or you can. But first, ask yourself: if he's so rich and handsome and charming, what's he doing in Midnight Bay? This place is so depressing, even the salmon won't return to the river. Nobody would *choose* to live here."

"Thank you very much, Miss Sunshine," Maddy snapped.

"You know damn well you're only staying here to run interference between your brother and mother. The moment Rick heads off to college, you're heading to Portland."

"Not anymore. I've decided I can't leave Mom all alone. Besides, moving her precious granddaughter two hundred miles away would kill her." Maddy glanced toward the black truck parked across the street. "So I guess my knight in shining armor will have to come to Midnight Bay to find me."

"Hello, Maddy," Mabel said, stepping out of the back office. "How is Amos today?"

"Hello, Mrs. Bishop. I'm sorry to say that Amos died last night."

"Oh, dear. How is Gertrude taking it?"

"I think she's relieved, actually. It was hard for her to see him like that."

Mabel nodded. "I guess I should be thankful Nathan went so quickly. It's sad to watch a loved one waste away." She looked at Eve. "I have to go see Gertrude."

"Of course. We'll stop by her house on the way home."

"No, I want to go spend the afternoon with her. Gertrude's my friend."

"But I can't just close the store."

"I can take the delivery truck."

Eve's gut tightened. She didn't want her mother driving anywhere alone. "But what if you get confused again? You might end up in Canada," she said, softening her words with a grin.

Mabel puffed up. "I don't need to be watched every minute of every day. I'm not an invalid yet, young lady."

"My mom's going to visit Gertrude, Mrs. Bishop," Maddy piped up. "How about if I ask her to stop by and pick you up?"

Mabel gave Eve a scowl, then walked back to the office. "Thank you."

"She's right, you know," Maddy said gently. "You can't watch her twenty-four/seven. You'll burn yourself out."

"But I never know when she's going to go off to la-la land. It happens in the blink of an eye. Yesterday she wandered out of the house and got trapped on one of the islands when the tide came in. If Kenzie Gregor hadn't come along and carried her to shore, I'm not sure I could have gotten her across by myself."

Maddy perked up. "Your gorgeous knight showed up exactly when you needed him, and he carried your mother to shore? Just like in a fairy tale?" She sighed again. "Oh, Eve, do you have to be hit by a bolt of lightning?"

"He did the dishes last night, too," Eve snapped. "And I bet he writes poetry, and gives fantastic back rubs and foot massages. God, you're worse than my mother!"

Maddy blinked at her.

Eve took a calming breath. "I'm sorry. It's just . . . I have a lot on my plate right now. If losing our home and possibly this business isn't bad enough, now I have to worry about Mom wandering off."

"I'm sorry, too." Maddy touched her arm. "I'll stop teasing you about Kenzie Gregor. Before yesterday, when was Mabel's last bad spell?"

Eve shrugged. "A week ago. It's not that it happens often, it's just that I can't predict when. And sometimes she seems perfectly lucid but does strange things. I've had to resort to shutting off the circuit breaker to the range when I'm not using it. She puts stuff in the oven and doesn't set the timer, then forgets it's there until we smell something burning. And several times, I've caught her talking to people who aren't there. When I ask her who she's talking to, she just smiles and says her imaginary friends."

"Actually, Eve, that's not unusual for dementia patients," Maddy said gently. "They're usually living in some random old memory at the time, and are conversing with a long-lost family member or friend." She glanced at her watch. "I have to get back to work. How about if Sarah and I come over this evening and help you start packing?"

Eve gave her a hug. "I'd like that. And thanks for volunteering your mother to drive Mom to Gertrude's."

Maddy opened the door and stepped onto the sidewalk. "I'm going to check with Social Services at work, to see if you can get someone to come in a few days a week to watch Mabel. You need some time to yourself."

"Mom would never go for that! She's too proud."

"Then we'll rally her friends to drop by for a visit so you can slip out for a few hours."

"That would be wonderful. I'm still trying to clean up the mess from my divorce. Everything I own is sitting in a storage container in Ellsworth. I have to start going through it."

"Any bites on your house in Boston?"

"Not yet. I hope it sells soon, or I'm going to have to turn it over to the bank. Paying the mortgage ate up the last of my money."

"Thank God that you had your teacher's retirement fund to cash in, and that Parker couldn't get his hands on it. Okay, I really gotta go," she said. "I'll see you around six?"

"Make it seven. I have to split wood right after supper."

Maddy made a disgusted face. "I had my fill of splitting wood in my teens. When I got my first job, I offered half my paycheck to Daddy if he would scrap the woodstove and use the boiler. But with three kids for free labor and a hundred acres of forest, he said wood was cheaper."

"It did wonders for your figure in high school. Didn't you have to beat the boys off with a stick?"

Maddy snorted. "Too bad Billy Kimble had such a hard head. I wouldn't have spent three years married to the bastard. God, I was stupid when I was eighteen."

"No, you were pregnant."

"That's the only thing I don't regret. Sarah's the best thing that ever happened to me." She reached in her pocket and pulled out her cell phone. "I'll tell Mom to pick up Mabel. See you at seven," she called out, walking down the sidewalk backward as she dialed. "And I'll have Sarah bring her math homework so Mabel can help her with it."

Eve noticed a tall figure coming out of the Shop 'n Save with a grocery cart, and ran back into her store. She peeked out the window and watched Kenzie Gregor open the back hatch of his truck and start loading in groceries. A bag boy followed, pushing a second cart.

Holy hell, he'd bought enough food to feed an army!

* * *

The first thing Eve noticed when she pulled into the dooryard that evening was the huge pile of split wood sitting where the delivery truck was usually parked. Then she noticed Kenzie Gregor standing next to Father Daar, using his shirt to wipe the sweat off his naked chest as he watched her drive in.

"Oh, my," Mabel said. "Will you look at that?"

"He split all the wood."

"Not the wood—the *man*. Just look at that body."

"Mom! You're old enough to be his mother!"

"Age has nothing to do with anything. I can still appreciate a good-looking man when I see one." She shot Eve a coy smile. "Then again, maybe I was referring to the priest."

"Mother!"

Mabel barked out a laugh and climbed out of the truck. "Oh, loosen up, before your face freezes in that expression."

Eve shut off the truck with a sigh. Sometimes she felt older than her mother.

Someone rapped on her window, and she looked over to find Kenzie smiling at her, buttoning his shirt with one hand as he motioned with the other for her to roll down the window.

Only she couldn't, because the crank was missing. She opened the door, causing him to step back. "I can only pay you fifty dollars for splitting that wood," she said as she slid out.

His smile vanished. "A good meal is all I would ask for," he said, turning and walking away.

Eve wanted to kick herself. When had she turned so bitter that she couldn't accept help without being suspicious?

Maddy plucked another dish out of the rinse water, then stepped back to the window to watch Kenzie tossing wood onto the conveyor belt.

"I swear, if you sigh again, I'm going to dump dishwater on you," Eve said. "The man puts his pants on one leg at a time, just like every other man."

"But he sure fills them out nicer than most," Maddy said, giving an exaggerated sigh as she came back to the sink for another dish. She nudged Eve's hip with her own. "Susan wasn't telling tales. I pretty near fainted when he shook my hand."

"Which you shoved at him like a love-starved teenager," Eve said, nudging her back with a laugh. She nodded at the window. "But do you see why he annoys me? He's out there doing *my* job, while I'm in here doing dishes like a good little woman."

"The no-good, rotten bastard," Maddy said, walking back to the window. "Omigod—he took off his shirt and is wiping his chest!"

Eve darted a glance toward the living room, where her mother was helping Sarah with her homework, and dragged Maddy back to the sink. "Can you get your mind off sex for just one minute? Honestly, I don't like being indebted to him. He split all my firewood for free, and stocked our cupboards with enough food to feed a nation. And now he's loading the truck for tomorrow's delivery. I don't like it."

Maddy folded her towel and set it on the counter. "You know what I think? I think you're attracted to Kenzie Gregor, and *that's* what bugs you about him."

"What?"

"The man is making you crazy. I remember when Parker rented Betty Simpson's cottage that summer. You took one look at him and trampled over all of us other women."

"I did not."

Maddy laughed. "You were like a guided missile aimed right at Parker's heart. The poor jerk didn't know what hit him."

"What does Parker have to do with Kenzie Gregor?"

"Your tracking system locked onto Kenzie the moment you met him."

"You're insane."

"No, I'm right." Maddy grabbed Eve by the sleeve and pulled her to the window. "So maybe it's time for *you* to be honest, Miss I-think-she-doth-protest-too-much. What do you see when you look at Kenzie Gregor?"

"A stranger with an unknown agenda."

"Really? Because I see a man who just might be handsome and charming and nice enough to heal my friend's broken heart," Maddy said softly.

"You've been reading too many romance novels," Eve

growled, turning away from the window. "And Parker didn't break my heart, he just made me wiser. Besides, I've only been divorced two months; it's too soon to be jumping into a new relationship."

"You told me your marriage had died several years ago, so that's not an excuse."

"Is there a reason we're having this discussion at all? Kenzie Gregor isn't attracted to me. We've just stuck together because of circumstances."

Maddy rolled her eyes. "Have you *looked* in a mirror lately? He's not out there chopping up your wood for the fun of it; he's trying to burn off his lust."

"Maddy!"

Her friend laughed. "I'm not saying you should fall head over heels in love with the guy. I'm just trying to make you see that there *is* life after Parker. Get over the cheating bum by indulging yourself in a hot, sweaty, burn-up-the-sheets affair."

"You don't think it's a little immoral to use one man to get over another?"

"Kenzie Gregor is a *male*, and we both know what simple creatures they are. Keep his belly full and his lust sated, and he won't mind helping you get over Parker one bit. I promise."

"My God, you're serious," Eve muttered, utterly floored.

The door suddenly opened and Father Daar and Kenzie walked in. Eve ran into the back room. Maddy was two seconds behind her, her hand over her mouth to keep in her laughter.

"You are *so* bad," Eve whispered, fighting to contain a giggle. "You're going straight to hell, and you're trying to take me with you!"

"But what a ride it'll be!"

Kenzie stuck his head in the door. "I'm done for the night, and Daar has gone to bed. Is there anything you ladies need from me before I head out?"

"No!" Eve blurted before Maddy could suggest something outrageous.

Kenzie lifted a curious brow. "Okay, then." He smiled at Maddy. "I look forward to meeting your husband. Does he fish? I would like to ask a local fisherman about what bait to use in the stream."

"I don't have a husband. I divorced the no-good bastard six years ago."

"Forgive me. I just assumed . . ." He cleared his throat. "You've done a fine job of raising your daughter. She's a delight."

"She's nine going on sixteen."

"Are you all set for the night, Eve?" he asked.

"All set."

"Good night then," he said, turning and walking out.

The moment they heard the screen door shut, Maddy sagged against the old chest freezer with a sigh. "*Please* have an affair with Kenzie Gregor. For me?"

"You're the one who won't stop sighing. *You* have an affair with him."

"I can't. I make a complete fool of myself whenever I get within ten feet of a handsome man." She covered her face with her hands and shook her head. "I can't believe I blurted out my divorce to him like that."

Eve patted her shoulder. "There, there," she crooned.

Maddy spread her fingers and peeked at Eve. "But you could handle having an affair with him." She dropped her hands and smiled. "And I'll just live vicariously through you."

"I am not having an affair with Kenzie Gregor."

"Why not?" her mother asked, walking into the room. "If I was forty years younger, I'd certainly have a go at him."

"Mother!"

"You're making that face again, Evangeline."

Eve headed into the kitchen. "Hey, Sarah. Did you get all your homework done?"

"Who's that old man sleeping in your front bedroom?" the girl asked in a whisper. "He dresses funny."

"That's Father Daar, and he dresses that way because he's a very old priest."

"His cane is cool," Sarah continued. "Is Kenzie Gregor your boyfriend?"

"No, he's our landlord until Mom and I find a new place to live. Mr. Gregor bought this farm."

"You could come live with us. Uncle Rick is graduating this year and leaving for college in August. You can have his room." Sarah made a disgusted face. "But you're probably gonna have to fumigate it first. It stinks really bad."

"Thanks for offering, sweetie, but I think Mom and I

have too much furniture to move in with you and your grammy. We're going to need a house all to ourselves."

"Samantha Graves is moving to Idaho as soon as school gets out. Maybe you could live in her old house."

Eve glanced at Maddy, since they both knew the Graveses were moving to go live with Mr. Graves's parents because he'd lost his job at the lumber mill. She smiled at Sarah. "I'll check into it. So, young lady, if you've finished your homework, I believe pie is in order."

Sarah ran and sat down at the table. "It's not blueberry, is it? Grammy made me help her put up so many blueberries last summer, I hope I never see another blueberry again as long as I live."

"Sarah Jane!" Maddy scolded. "Mind your manners. You'll eat whatever kind of pie they have."

"I believe I saw some chocolate chip cookies in the pantry," Mabel said, opening the pantry door. "Come on, Sarah. We'll have our treat in the living room, so we can watch *America's Funniest Home Videos*. Eve and your mother have some packing to do."

"You know, maybe Sarah's onto something," Maddy said when they were alone again. "The bank foreclosed on the Graves house, and they're not going to be able to sell it anytime soon in this economy. You could see if the bank would rent it to you."

"It'll be seven more weeks before school's out and they move. I can't expect Kenzie to camp out for another two months. Besides, have you driven by the Graves house lately? If the inside looks half as bad as the outside does, the place should be razed. It's a dump."

"What about the Taylor farm? Old man Taylor died last fall, and the house has been empty ever since. His son lives in Vermont, I think. You could contact him and see if he'd rent it to you."

"That's a great idea. I'll call the Town Hall Monday and see if they'll give me his address." Eve looked around the kitchen and sighed. "Where should we start?"

"Boxes would help."

"There's some in the attic. You're not afraid of spiders, are you?"

Maddy grabbed the flyswatter hanging by the door, shouldered it like a rifle, and saluted. "You lead the way, and I'll back you up. If any crawly critters try to jump you, I'll knock them into tomorrow."

Chapter Five

"Is the dark-haïred woman as handsome up close as she is from a distance?"

Kenzie dropped another log on the fire and looked over at William. "When did you see her?"

"When she arrived. Is she comely? What color are her eyes?"

"They're brown. And yes, she's a handsome woman."

"She has a child, so I suppose she also has a husband," William said with a sigh.

Kenzie chuckled. "She told me she divorced the *no-good bastard* six years ago."

William sat forward, his back bristling. "He abused her?"

"There seem to be any number of reasons a woman can get divorced today, William. And at first glance, I doubt Maddy would put up with any sort of abuse from a man."

"Maddy? It must be short for something . . . Madeline, maybe? What's her daughter's name?"

"Sarah. She told me she's in the third grade, and that she's going to the fourth grade next fall because she got straight A's—whatever that means."

William went silent and stared into the fire.

Kenzie glanced over at the beast, bolstered by William's interest in Eve's friend. Maybe a bit of lust would pull him out of his depression.

As long as William didn't try to *do* anything about it.

"You mustn't wander too far afield, especially during the daylight hours," Kenzie reminded him. "You should be okay here on the farm, but don't go near town, day or night. The last thing we need is for someone to see you."

"I'm being careful. Did you bring any pie with you?"

"Nay. I left it for Eve to feed to her visitors."

William leaned back against a tree. "Maddy," he said, as if trying out the name. "Maddy and Sarah." He chuckled. "The wee lassie didn't stop talking from the time she got out of the car to when she went inside."

Kenzie looked at him sharply. "Just how close did you get to the house?"

"I was in the barn. Don't worry, Gregor, I can avoid being seen when I want. I once snuck five dozen warriors into an enemy's keep in broad daylight."

"This isn't the ninth century, and since you're no longer a man, you don't exactly blend in anymore."

"So," William said, dismissing the warning, "there seem to be plenty of single women around here." He glanced at Kenzie, his large dark eyes reflecting the firelight. "I noticed you stopped working long enough to watch Eve Anderson walk into the house. When was the last time ye had a woman, Gregor?"

"It's been a few years."

William snorted. "More like a few *hundred*. You should bed the blonde; you seem attracted to her. Though she doesn't appear all that enamored with you," he added with a chuckle. "She does have some fire in her, though. She might actually give you a good ride—assuming you don't break her in half."

"You're a crude bastard, Killkenny. It's no wonder that old witch turned you into the monster ye are."

"Christ, Gregor, you're a highland warrior. Would you have me believe you didn't indulge in the soft flesh of your enemy's women after a battle?" he scoffed. "You Scots populated half my village with your bastards."

Kenzie gave William a warning glare. "For someone who traveled centuries to ask for my help, ye have a strange way of going about it. You never mind about Eve Anderson. And Maddy, too, for that matter. Stay away from those women."

"You can't have both of them."

"I don't *want* both of them."

"Just the blonde?"

Kenzie stood up and looked William level in the eye. "My intentions are not the issue here—*yours* are. If I catch you anywhere near Maddy or Eve or any other female, I will dispatch your slimy soul to hell myself."

William also stood. "You can't, Gregor. You've given your word to help me."

Kenzie stepped closer. "I only promised to help you lift the old hag's curse and become a man again, Killkenny. I never said anything about your being alive when it happens."

William stepped back, tripped over his tail, and nearly fell. "At this point, death would be a blessing!" he snapped. "Christ's blood, when are you going to make it happen?"

Kenzie sympathized with William's impatience. Having lived a multitude of lives as several different animals for nearly two centuries—thanks to his drùidh brother's fateful decision when Matt had found him mortally wounded on a long-ago battlefield—he was very well acquainted with William's frustration.

But at least he'd always been a natural animal, not a mythical beast. He'd been a panther when he'd come to this modern time three years ago, which had made it somewhat easier to blend in—whereas William would stick out like the monster he was.

"It'll happen when you stop fighting your curse, William, and learn from it instead."

"I've spent centuries trying to figure it out! You're my last resort, Gregor. I was told that you could make everything right again!"

Kenzie sat back down and said nothing.

William stood stiffly, his powerful muscles humming with tension, his massive wings twitching with anger. He finally sat down with a snarl, coiling his tail around him.

"It doesn't work that way, Killkenny," Kenzie said softly, staring into the flames. "I have no magic wand to turn you back into the man you once were. You were urged to come find me because I can help displaced souls like yourself find your *own* paths back."

"But your brother did it for you. Why can't he do it for me? He's Cùram de Gairn, the most powerful of all wizards."

Kenzie gave a humorless laugh. "Matt didn't do a damn thing. It was *me,* William. I had the power all along to choose my fate. For two hundred years I believed Matt had caused my misery, when it was my own doing. When Tom finally explained to me that blaming someone else for my situation only prolonged it, the change simply . . . happened."

William sat up. "Who is this Tom fellow? Maybe he can help me."

"Thomas Gregor Smythe," Kenzie said. "He's Matt and Winter's grandson."

William snorted and leaned back. "He isn't even born yet. You must have dreamed him."

"If you traveled forward twelve hundred years to get here, why couldn't Tom have traveled back to this time?"

"Because he isn't born yet," William repeated.

"Then that would mean you and I are long dead, my friend."

"Goddammit, Gregor, I don't know how the blasted magic works! I just know that if I don't get home soon, *as myself*, I'm not going to have a home to return to. If my enemies haven't stolen it from me already, you can be damn sure my friends will."

"You're not going back, William," Kenzie said gently. "Once you return to your old self, you won't be able to breach time again. *This* is your home now. Just as I must, you too must live out the rest of your natural life in this century."

William recoiled in horror. "Are you saying I'm *stuck* in this accursed place?"

"No, William. You still may choose to return to your time."

"As the monster I am!"

"Yes." Kenzie shrugged. "But you could still learn your lesson back in the ninth century, and become yourself again in your own time."

William leaned forward, his ears twitching with eagerness. "Then teach me what I need to know *here*, and I'll go back and use it *there*."

Kenzie just stared at him.

"What?" William snapped when the silence stretched between them.

"I'm trying to decide if ye truly are as dense as you appear, or if you're just so damned stubborn ye simply refuse to get it."

"Get what? You've spent the last four months talking

in circles, Gregor. Just teach me what I have to know and I'll go back and use it!"

"And you continue to let my words go in one of your ears and out the other. Once knowledge is gained, Killkenny, then ye *know* it. The moment you unlock the secret, the change begins, and it'll be too late for you to go back. So either resign yourself to remain here until ye die, or take your chances on going back and figuring it out on your own."

William grabbed his head with a groan. "Christ, my head aches. I need a drink."

"We've already established that modern ale doesn't agree with you. Why don't ye go take a refreshing swim in the sea?"

William lifted his head just enough to glare at him.

Kenzie settled back onto his bedroll with a chuckle. "Then go enjoy the freedom to roam that the night gives you. I'm going to sleep. I have to start building stalls in the barn tomorrow. Matt and Winter are coming to visit next week, and they're bringing horses."

"*War* horses?" William asked, suddenly sounding interested.

"Are there any other kind?"

"You'd be surprised at the number of pansy beasts I saw on my flight down to the coast. There were a few nags I was tempted to have for dinner, just to put them out of their misery."

"Go away, Killkenny."

Kenzie nestled deeper into his bedroll, turning his back on William. Silence settled over their campsite but for the crackle of burning wood, until he heard the whisper of air moving over leathery wings. As large as a horse yet as silent as an owl, William disappeared into the night.

Kenzie knew he still wasn't alone. "I'm too tired to-night for one of our philosophical chats, Fiona."

The red-tailed hawk perched on a branch overhead cooed softly.

"Aye, we'll visit tomorrow. Good night, little sister."

Eve had gone past panic to hysteria. She couldn't find her mother anywhere. She had awakened early, and while her mom was still sleeping, she'd taken a shower and started breakfast. But when she'd gone back upstairs to wake her up, all she'd found was an empty bed.

She'd searched every square inch of the house as well as the barn and shed, and even her car and the delivery truck. Now she was standing in the yard, yelling for her mom at the top of her lungs, frozen in place. She couldn't bring herself to go search the woods or shoreline, immo-bilized by the horrifying image of her stumbling across her mother's lifeless body.

"Eve. Eve!"

Someone had hold of her shoulders and was shaking her.

"Leave me alone!" She pushed at the broad chest in front of her. "I have to find Mom!"

Kenzie let go of her shoulders and cupped her face in his hands, forcing her to look at him. "Breathe, Eve. Look into my eyes and take slow, deep breaths," he said calmly. "Come on. Look at me."

She finally made eye contact.

"Your mother's fine, Eve. Do you understand? She took a morning stroll down by the sea, and is on her way back right now. She's fine, I promise."

Eve shuddered violently.

Kenzie wrapped his arms around her and gently cupped her head to his chest. "I didn't speak with her," he continued, his soothing voice matching his steady heart-beat. "I didn't want to intrude on her pleasure. Mabel appeared quite herself, so ye needn't worry. She had a bag of bread with her, and was spreading crumbs for the birds."

He kept up the gentle chatter, but Eve stopped listening and simply felt the cadence of his voice. She couldn't stop shaking, and her heart seemed determined to thump out of her chest.

"Keep breathing, and it will pass."

She was beginning to feel light-headed as the heat of his embrace worked its magic. Her muscles slowly relaxed to the point she felt boneless, and she sagged against him.

"There ye go," he whispered into her hair. "You're okay, little one. Everything's going to be okay."

Eve tried to remember the last time a man had held her like this; asking nothing, only offering his strength until she could regain her own.

"Good morning, Kenzie, Evangeline," her mother said brightly. "Isn't it a wonderful day to be alive?"

Eve gasped and tried to step out of Kenzie's embrace, but her knees buckled and he pulled her back against him with a soft laugh.

"Easy, now. She's already up the steps and gone into the house. Give yourself a minute. Ye try to go running off, and you're going to fall flat on your face."

Eve buried her hot cheeks in her hands, unsure which horrified her more: that mother had just caught her and Kenzie embracing, or the reason she was in his arms.

"Ye had a fright," he said, rubbing her back. "And it drained all your strength."

She looked up at him, stricken. "But why did I panic like that? What if she'd been in danger?" She started shaking again, and dropped her head to hide her shame. "I couldn't have helped her. I was completely frozen."

"But she wasn't in danger. She just went out for a walk."

"But what if she *had* been?" She stepped away, locking her knees to steady herself. "She could have been drowning, while I just stood in the middle of this yard, screaming like an idiot."

"Ye would have found your wits soon enough."

"You can't know that!"

"I do know," he said calmly. "I've experienced what you just did enough times to know that when it really matters, we get it together and do what needs to be done. Especially if someone we love is involved."

He took her hand and led her over to an old farm implement, urged her to sit down, and sat down beside her. "Eve, ye can't possibly watch Mabel every minute of every day. Nor should ye even try. She's not a child."

"But you saw what happened the day we met. She got trapped on the island."

"And if you hadn't found her, what would she have done?"

Eve blinked. What *would* her mother have done? "She might have tried to wade across the gravel bar by herself and drowned."

"Ye told me Mabel has a strong will to live. And when people get confused, their instincts usually take over. There's an equally good chance that Mabel simply would have waited until the bar was exposed again."

Eve leaned away in surprise. "Are you saying I should ignore the fact that she's losing her mind, and go about my business as usual?"

"No, I'm merely suggesting that you might remember that, even confused, Mabel's mind is still that of a mature woman. Everything your mother has seen and done in her lifetime is in her head somewhere, even if it sometimes gets jumbled a bit. I'm just asking that ye keep that knowledge in the back of *your* mind the next time she goes missing. Even if ye can't immediately find her, the odds are she will be fine." He smiled gently. "And if you coddle Mabel too much, she might feel smothered and deliberately start sneaking off."

Eve couldn't believe her ears. This guy was actually lecturing her on taking care of her mother? Who the hell did he think he was?

Eve stood up. "Thank you, Mr. Gregor, for your pearls of wisdom. If you will excuse me, I have to go to work now."

Chapter Six

Eve stopped the empty delivery truck in front of Bishop's Hearth and Home, shut off the engine, and looked at her mother. Though she was loathe to admit it, something Kenzie had said this morning had her wondering if she might be creating more problems than she was solving.

"So, do we have a deal? You'll tell me when you're going out for a walk?"

"And if you're in the shower?" Mabel asked, staring out the windshield, not at all happy with the conversation.

"Then leave me a note." Eve touched her mother's arm. "I'm not trying to take away your independence, Mom. I'm just worried about you."

Mabel sighed and patted Eve's hand. "I know,

Evangeline. And I'm sorry for scaring you this morning." She suddenly brightened. "Although it certainly warmed my heart to see you in Kenzie's arms. Now be honest, was it really so hard to let a man comfort you?"

"It cost me a ten-minute lecture."

Mabel laughed and got out of the truck. "It's a small price to pay," she said when Eve walked around the truck to join her. "Trust me, there'll come a day when you'll *wish* you had someone who cared enough to lecture you. What I wouldn't give to have Jens or Nathan back, telling me how to fix my problems."

"That's where you and I differ, Mom. I prefer to fix my own problems."

"You do take after your father." Mabel stepped onto the sidewalk, but stopped and looked across the street. "I wonder what's going on?" she asked, pointing at the group of men gathered around the back of a pickup.

Eve could see that the tailgate was down, and it appeared a large, dead animal was holding everyone's interest.

"Somebody must have shot a bear."

"That looks like Johnnie Dempster's truck." Mabel nudged Eve toward the street. "Go see his trophy, and ask Johnnie how much it weighs."

Eve gaped at her mother. "Why would I want to go see a dead bear?"

"To be sociable," Mabel said, exasperated. "You've been back in town two months, and I can count on one hand the number of young men you've spoken to. Go on. Go admire Johnnie's bear, and at least pretend you're interested."

Eve handed her mother the store keys and walked across the street. If she didn't go fawn all over Johnnie Dempster's dead bear, she wouldn't hear the end of it all day. Only once she got there, she couldn't get close enough to see it, much less tell Johnnie what a great hunter he was. There were so many men crowded around the back of the truck, all unusually silent, that a person would think Johnnie had shot Bigfoot.

Eve shouldered her way into the crowd, pushing past Barry Simpson, the Shop 'n Save manager, only to have him grab her arm and pull her back.

"You don't want to get any closer, Eve," he said. "It's not a pretty sight."

She frowned up at him. "I've seen dead bears before, Barry. My dad used to hunt."

"This one wasn't shot," he said, pulling her farther away from the truck. "It's all mangled to pieces."

"Did it get hit by a truck?" she asked, craning to see.

"No, it was eaten."

She snapped her gaze to Barry. "Eaten? But what would eat a bear? They're at the top of the food chain."

Barry shook his head, his brow furrowed. "That's the question of the day. We've called in the state biologists. Hopefully they can tell us."

"Coyotes can't bring down a bear, can they?" she asked, inching her way back toward the men. "Unless the poor thing was sickly," she speculated.

"Don't look, Eve," Barry warned, reaching for her.

Eve spun around to avoid being caught again, and ran directly into a rock-solid chest that felt all too familiar.

"And just why are ye so determined to see a dead animal?" Kenzie asked, taking hold of her shoulders. "Are ye wanting nightmares?"

She tilted her head back to look up at him. "Did *you* see the bear?"

"Yes."

"And are *you* going to have nightmares?"

His eyes took on a sudden gleam. "Probably."

"Well, Mr. Gregor, I'm not the squeamish type. My nightmares tend to run more toward being *smothered*."

He nodded, the gleam intensifying. "I could see where that might be an ongoing worry for someone your size."

He guided her out of the way as a dark green pickup pulled in beside Johnnie Dempster's truck. Two state biologists got out, and the crowd parted.

Eve got a clear look at the bear and instantly spun away. Kenzie immediately ushered her toward the gathering crowd of women across the street. Maddy and Susan were standing with Mabel and several other women, watching what was happening in the Shop 'n Save parking lot.

Susan's eyes narrowed, her gaze darting from Eve to the man walking beside her, his hand at the small of Eve's back.

"What's going on?" Maddy asked.

"Something ate a bear," Eve said with a shudder,

stepping onto the sidewalk. "Half of it was gone, and what's left is . . . it's not pretty."

Maddy wrapped her arm around Eve. "Why on earth did you go over there?"

"Because I am a good daughter."

"That's just terrible," Susan interjected, and when Eve looked up, she realized Susan wasn't talking to her. "What could eat a bear, Mr. Gregor?"

Kenzie smiled at Susan, but Eve knew he didn't have a clue who she was.

"I'm Susan Wakely," Susan said, pulling back her jacket and sticking out her chest to expose the tiny brass name tag pinned on her ample bosom. "I waited on you at the bank the other day."

"Yes, of course. Mrs. Wakely," Kenzie said with a nod.

"It's *Miss* Wakely, but please call me Susan." She stepped closer to him, her expression horrified. "How terrible for that poor bear. I can't imagine what could have eaten it. And to think I walk home from work every evening, all alone, right past a very dark section of woods."

Eve stifled a snort.

Maddy wasn't nearly as circumspect.

"You would be wise to find another way home," Kenzie said. He looked at Eve. "If you will excuse me, I'll go see what the biologists think happened to the bear. I'll tell you tonight when you get home," he said, turning and walking back across the street.

Dammit, he hadn't really said that in front of everyone!

Susan glared at Eve. "What did he mean, 'I'll tell you tonight when you get home?' Is he *living* with you?"

"Of course not. He bought the Bishop farm, and is letting Mom and me stay there until we can find a rental."

"Where is *he* staying?"

"He's camping out down by the ocean."

"I saw him first! You had your chance with Parker and blew it. So back off and give someone else a chance for once."

"Oh, for the love of— This isn't a contest, Susan, and Kenzie Gregor is not some prize."

Maddy took hold of her arm. "It's no contest because Eve's already won. But Parker's someplace in Brazil, last we heard. Why don't you go look him up, Suze, and give him our regards," she said, dragging Eve toward the store. "That witch," Maddy continued once they were inside. "Doesn't she know that poor-little-frightened-me act doesn't work on real men? I wanted to puke when she batted her false eyelashes at him."

"But why did you have to say that I had *won* in front of half the women in town? Now everyone's going to think I'm chasing after Kenzie."

"Good, let them. Did you ever consider that maybe we just did the man a favor?"

"How?"

"If everyone thinks you and Kenzie are a couple, all the women in town will leave him alone. Can you imagine what it must be like to be rich and handsome and single? By pretending you already got him, you're actually saving him."

"That has got to be the most outrageous thing to *ever* come out of your mouth. And besides, it's a big fat lie."

"It won't be, as soon as you have your affair with him."

Eve gaped at her.

Maddy opened the door. "I've got to go to work. Sarah and I will come over again tonight, and I'll bring Mom this time. Then maybe you and I can head over to Oak Harbor and find you a sexy new outfit. It's hard to get an affair going when you dress like an elementary-school teacher."

"I *am* a teacher. And I don't need a new outfit, because I am not having an affair!"

"Of course you are, silly. Not for yourself—for me. See you at six," she said, disappearing up the sidewalk.

Eve stepped out of the store and searched the thinning crowd for her mother, but she didn't see her anywhere. Dammit, now where had she wandered off to?

She ran inside to check the back office, and was just heading back to the front of the store when her mother walked in.

Eve took a calming breath, determined not to let her panic show. "You didn't go see the bear, did you?"

"No, I was over at Ruthie's. I left you a note."

"You did? Where?"

"On the counter," Mabel said, picking up a piece of paper.

"Oh, I hadn't looked there. What's interesting at Ruthie's?"

"I asked her to order a book for me."

"But Mom, we really don't have money to buy books right now. We need to watch every penny."

"Books are not a luxury, Evangeline; they're as necessary as food."

"I know the Anderson motto," Eve said with a sigh. "It wasn't an expensive book, was it?"

"I have a few dusty old dollar bills tucked away," Mabel said, setting her purse behind the counter and walking back to the front door. "I'm going to the library. Feel free to call and check on me."

Eve glowered at the door Mabel softly closed. Dammit, not smothering her mother was driving *her* insane!

Kenzie finished pounding the nail in the board William was holding, and straightened with a scowl. "Mind telling me what possessed you to go after a bear?"

"I was needing a good fight, and the only thing I could find around here to give me one was that mangy old bear." He made a disgusting face. "It was so tough I nearly choked to death."

"From now on, when you feel the need to take out your frustrations on something, you come see me."

"I was looking for sport, not a slaughtering!"

Father Daar handed Kenzie another board. "You're such a dumb beast, Killkenny," Daar said with a laugh. "'Tis Gregor who'd be slaughtering *you*!"

Kenzie shoved the board at William, poking the beast in the stomach hard enough to make him grunt. "Killing that bear created a problem for us, because now everyone in town is asking what sort of animal could have done such a thing. The least ye could have done was bury the remains. The townspeople are concerned there's something vicious living in the area."

"There is," William smiled darkly. "Me."

Kenzie straightened from nailing the board. "When people are afraid of something they don't understand, their first instinct is to hunt it down and kill it."

"They can try," William drawled. He snapped his tail in agitation, sending a cloud of dust through the stall. "Men of this time are weak-kneed, soft-boned pansies, Gregor. They'll be keeping their doors locked and hiding under their beds instead of scouring the woods for bogeymen."

Kenzie blew out a defeated sigh. "Ye have a bad habit of underestimating people, William. Did ye not see the rifle Jack Stone was carrying the night he came after you on Bear Mountain? And do ye not understand the concept of a firearm? All it would take is a single bullet between your eyes, and Midnight Bay's bogeyman would be dead." He pointed his hammer at him. "You hunt to eat, not for sport, and you leave no evidence the next time. Your arrogance is a threat to us, Killkenny. If you're discovered, Daar and I will be the ones paying the consequences."

William's wings twitched, and he looked away.

"What?" Kenzie said. "Goddammit," he growled when William didn't answer. "What in hell have you done now?"

"The old woman saw me this morning," William muttered. "I didn't speak to her, I swear. I was sitting on a rock, drying my wings after a swim in the ocean. I didn't know she was there until I heard her gasp."

"Then what did you do?" Kenzie asked ever so softly. "Did ye dive in the ocean, or fly off?"

"I flew off," he said, hanging his head. He looked back at Kenzie, his huge dark eyes defensive. "I didn't think; I just reacted."

"You've done it now, you accursed beast!" Daar said, pointing a gnarled finger at him. "Mabel will tell Eve what she saw." He looked at Kenzie. "We have to pack up and leave right now. We'll go back to TarStone, where we'll be safe."

Kenzie grabbed Daar by the sleeve when he turned to leave. "Hold on a minute. Let me think."

"The old woman is crazy, isn't she?" William said. "Nobody will believe her."

"He's right," Kenzie said, looking at Daar. "There's a good chance Eve will think her mother is merely confused." He glared at William. "If you had dove in the ocean instead of flying off, Mabel might have thought that the morning light was playing tricks on her, and that you were just a large seal or something. Ye can't fly when it's daylight, William."

"I still say we should go back to TarStone," Daar said. "I don't like the energy around here. I feel trouble brewing."

"I feel it, too, old man. But the sort of trouble brewing

would find us no matter where we go. No, *this* is where we belong." Kenzie handed William the hammer. "See if you can do something constructive for a change, will ye? These stalls need to be finished by this afternoon so I can get the pasture fence repaired. Matt and Winter are arriving day after tomorrow."

"Where are you going?" Daar asked.

"Back into town. Maybe I can get an idea of what Mabel thought she saw this morning." He took off his tool belt. "Try to work together, you two. But if that's too much of a stretch, at least try not to kill each other."

Eve sat behind the counter of Bishop's Hearth and Home with her chin propped in one hand and absently wrapped a curl around her finger. She let it spring back into place with a sigh, and frowned down at the list of products she thought about selling.

It was a painfully short list. People in these parts were so self-reliant—what they couldn't make for themselves they usually bought at the big box stores in Ellsworth. She was even rethinking her plan to sell pellet stoves, because most everyone could step out their back doors and cut their own firewood. Why pay for bags of manufactured wood pellets?

She needed to find something unique, something most people couldn't or wouldn't bother to make for themselves. But that required capital, and if Mr. Johnson didn't give her a new line of credit, she might as well hand him the keys to the store.

All she needed were a few measly thousand dollars, but she couldn't even scape up a few hundred. Parker had cleaned out their joint savings account, and she'd been forced to cash in her retirement fund to keep her Boston home out of foreclosure when she discovered he'd stopped making payments four months prior to disappearing.

Apparently the bastard had been planning his escape for quite some time.

How could she have been married to a man for six years and not know what a self-centered, unconscionable jerk he was?

She felt so dumb. Especially considering she'd had two women friends in Boston who'd found themselves suddenly divorced. As they'd cried on her shoulder and she had sympathized with them, she'd secretly wondered how they could have been so blind. There had to have been signs that their marriages were failing; had they been living in desperate denial, hoping things would get better?

But then it had happened to *her*.

Too embarrassed to cry on anyone's shoulder, she had run home to her mama with her tail between her legs, utterly humiliated—and with the added indignity of being broke.

And then to discover Mabel had been hiding her own financial crisis . . . well, Eve had spent nearly two weeks mired in despair. That is, until the Nordic blood in her veins had finally surged to the front, and that despair had turned to anger.

Her pity party over, Eve had become determined to build a new life for herself and her mother here in Midnight Bay, afraid that taking Mabel back to Boston might make her mother's illness worse. If only she'd known Bishop's Hearth and Home was on the brink of bankruptcy, she would have used her retirement money to save their business instead of her house. But since that was water over the dam, she'd spent the last month trying to come up with a plan.

Preferably one that didn't involve a knight in shining armor riding to her rescue, having learned the hard way that armor tarnished, happily ever after was a pipe dream, and handsomeness and charm were often masks worn by men with agendas.

So . . . why wasn't her head communicating that wisdom to her heart? Why did it always seem to beat a little faster whenever Kenzie Gregor stepped into view? And why did her eyes seem to lock on him as he puttered around the farm?

Why wasn't she *immune* to his handsomeness and charm?

"Because you're alive, Evangeline, not dead," she growled, grabbing her pencil and crossing wood-pellet stoves off her list of ideas. "And because Maddy put the idea of having an affair with him in your head!"

Eve took a calming breath, then crossed off selling fabric and yarns, since Mabel had reminded her last night that there was a wonderful fabric store over in Oak Harbor.

That left tutoring, baked goods, and day care.

She crossed out day care, figuring there were enough stay-at-home moms who were already taking in children to supplement their family income.

Eve tapped the pencil to her teeth. Maybe they could tutor *and* have a bakery: her mother loved baking bread and pastries, and with her own teaching degree, she could open a summer school for local kids who needed a bit of help with their schoolwork.

The door suddenly opened and Eve plastered an expectant smile on her face at the prospect of a customer—only to have Kenzie walk in.

"Eve," he said with a nod, stopping in the middle of the store to look around. "I never realized there were so many different kinds of woodstoves, in so many different sizes."

"That's because some people use them for heat, and some just want the ambiance of a wood fire."

He walked up to the counter, a discernable gleam in his eyes. "I prefer a campfire under the stars."

"To each his own. What can I do for you, Mr. Gregor?"

"I realized that I got so distracted by the bear this morning, I forgot to ask if you would go out to dinner with me tonight."

"Are you asking me for a date?"

"Yes. I would like to take you to a nice restaurant."

"Why?"

He shifted uncomfortably.

Eve was instantly contrite. Dammit, she didn't want to be a bitter divorcée. "I'm sorry, that was rude of me. I . . . um, I have plans with Maddy tonight."

"Tomorrow night, then?" he quietly offered.

Eve hesitated. This was her chance to prove to everyone—most especially herself—that Parker hadn't scarred her for life. She could go on a date with a handsome man and simply enjoy herself, couldn't she? It didn't mean she was looking for happily ever after, or for an affair. It was just a *date*.

"I'd be uncomfortable leaving Mom alone all evening."

"Daar will be with her."

Eve shot him a crooked smile. "Please don't take this the wrong way, but Father Daar is older than God. He can barely watch himself."

"I have something I wish to discuss with you, and dinner would be . . ." He stopped, then suddenly blew out a breath. "Here's the thing. For the last four months, my sort-of sister-in-law has been after me to go on an actual date with a woman."

"As opposed to with a man?"

He scowled.

Eve smiled and folded her hands in her lap. "Sorry. So why is your sort-of sister-in-law bugging you to go on an date?"

"Because it's . . . been a few years for me."

At first she thought he was using the worst come-on line on the planet, but he looked so uncomfortable, she began to rethink that. There was also the fact that her heart wasn't just beating a little faster, it was practically racing at the prospect of spending an evening alone with him. Hell, she should accept if only to put them *both* out of their misery.

It would certainly make Maddy deliriously happy.

And there was the added bonus of pissing off Susan.

"Exactly how many years?"

"I've lost count." He shifted from one foot to the other. "So can I call Camry and tell her I have a date tomorrow evening? Because I'm fairly sure that if she doesn't hear from me soon, she'll show up in Midnight Bay without warning."

"Camry?"

"Camry MacKeage. My brother is married to her sister."

"Okay," she said, feeling quite empowered by her decision not to let Parker turn her into a victim. "You can tell your sort-of sister-in-law you've got a date. That is, if Maddy can watch Mom tomorrow night."

"Thank you."

"You're welcome. So what is it you wish to discuss with me over dinner?"

"Our living arrangement."

Damn. He was getting tired of sleeping under the stars and was going to kick them out. "Is it about to change?"

"Not if you accept my offer of employment."

Eve pretty near fell off her stool. "You're offering me a job?"

"It's really no more than what you've been doing, with a few added duties."

Now there was a word she loved to hear from a man. "What sort of duties?"

"I would appreciate it if you could wash my and Daar's clothes when you wash your own. And if you could pack us a lunch before you leave in the morning, it would certainly make my day easier. It seems I just get working on something and have to stop to cook lunch. Small duties like that. It shouldn't take up much of your time."

"You're offering me a job as your *housekeeper*?"

He stiffened. "It's honest work."

"I didn't mean to imply that it wasn't. You just surprised me, is all."

"It's my intention to make An Tèarmann into a working farm again, and I could use some help."

"An Tèarmann?"

"It's Gaelic for 'the Sanctuary.' "

"An Tèarmann," she repeated, trying it out. "I like that. What kind of working farm? As in chickens and pigs and cows, or timber cutting?"

His eyes started gleaming again. "As in horses. And I'll probably get some chickens and a milk cow. Can ye make butter?"

"Nope, I can't say that I can." Eve slipped off the stool and walked around the counter. "Maybe Camry could teach me, when she pops in to check on you."

He chuckled at that. "I doubt Camry has ever seen a butter churn. She's a scientist for NASA. So will you accept my offer?"

"To be your housekeeper? I need some time to think about it, Mr. Gregor."

"Are ye going to call me Mr. Gregor on our date tomorrow evening?" he asked, his eyes crinkled with amusement.

"I suppose that would depend on whether or not you're my boss tomorrow evening."

He touched her arm, all traces of amusement gone. "I just want to be your date tomorrow night, Eve," he said softly. "It seems like a hundred years since I've enjoyed the company of a beautiful woman."

Oh God, she hated it when men said things like that. She always got weak in the knees and was tempted to throw herself at them. Instead of foisting this handsome giant on unsuspecting women, Camry MacKeage should have plastered a warning label on his chest.

"Okay, Kenzie, a simple date it is."

She wasn't sure, but she thought he let out a sigh of relief as he looked around the store. "Where's Mabel?"

"She's at the library. I was just going to call over there and check on her. She's been gone three hours, although that's not unusual for her. Get Mom anywhere near books, and she loses all track of time."

"I have the same problem," he said, heading toward the door. "Point me to the library, and I'll go check on her. If Mabel is game, I'll take her to lunch before I bring her back here. Which way?" he asked, looking down the sidewalk.

Eve stepped onto the sidewalk beside him and

pointed toward the center of town. “See that gray granite building? That’s the library.”

“And a good place for lunch?”

“The Port of Call has great seafood,” she said, pointing to the restaurant next to the bank. “Mom loves their clams.”

“Then that’s where I’ll take her. Can we bring ye back something?”

“No, I packed us each a sandwich. I’ll just eat both.” She touched his arm. “Thank you for taking Mom to lunch. It’s been months since she’s eaten out.”

His gaze dropped to her hand on his arm, then back at her. “I believe that’s what friends do for each other, and Mabel and I became friends the day I arrived in Midnight Bay.”

Eve watched him walk away, not moving until he scaled the library steps two at a time and disappeared inside. She finally walked back into her store, trying to decide if agreeing to go out with him had been wise, or if she had just added one more item to her list of problems.

At least Maddy would have to stop bugging her about having an affair with him. Because if she took him up on his job offer, she couldn’t very well sleep with her *boss*, now could she?

Chapter Seven

"Are teachers *required* to be prudes?" Maddy asked, rocketing her compact SUV around a sharp curve. "Hell-o? This is the twenty-first century. Of course you can sleep with your boss. Women have been doing it since we lived in caves." She guided them through an S-turn, then accelerated out of it at what seemed like Mach One. "I thought the whole point of woman's lib was to make sleeping with the boss a sociably acceptable form of courtship."

"I am not a prude."

Maddy glanced over at Eve, her expression downright scary. "So help me God, if you come home tomorrow night and you're still wearing your panties, I swear I'll never speak to you again."

Eve braced herself as another curve raced toward

them. "When was the last time *you* got laid, anyway? You're showing signs of excessive estrogen buildup."

"Excessive estrogen buildup?" Maddy repeated with a throaty chuckle. "Is that what they call it in Boston?"

"That's the technical term for 'the hornies.' So when was *your* last date?"

Maddy brought them to an abrupt halt at an intersection, turned left, and shot off again. "We're not discussing my love life; we're discussing yours, and that sexy man you just bought that push-up bra for. If it really has been years for the poor guy, then it's your duty to jump his sex-starved bones."

"There's that wonderful word again. Should I perform this particular *duty* before or after dinner?"

"After, of course," Maddy said with another laugh. "You'll need the fuel. Kenzie Gregor is definitely an all-nighter kind of guy. Maybe Sarah and I should bring our pajamas when we babysit Mabel."

"God, you're scary. Look out!" Eve shouted, bracing her hands on the dash when she spotted something huge in the road.

Maddy slammed on the brakes and all four wheels locked, causing the SUV to go into a tire-screeching skid. They hit the soft shoulder of the road and the truck bounced into the ditch, the front bumper plowing into the gravel bank and plunging them into darkness. The engine clanked to a stop, enveloping them in eerie black silence.

"Shit! Shit! Shit!" Maddy shouted, beating the steering wheel with her fist.

"The ABS brakes didn't work." Eve rubbed her forehead. "And why in hell didn't the air bags go off?"

"Because this piece of shit is ten years old, and half the idiot lights on the dash have been blinking for the last six months."

"Why didn't you get it serviced?"

"Do you have any idea what it costs to even *talk* to a mechanic? I've been trying to save up enough money to get new brakes. Are you okay?"

"I'm not bleeding and everything works, so I must be. You?"

Maddy gave a humorless laugh that ended in a sniffle. "I hurt my hand when I beat on the steering wheel. What *was* that in the road? A bear?"

"Too big. It must have been a moose."

"Um, did it seem to you like it . . . flew off?" Maddy whispered into the darkness.

"Moose can't fly."

"It had wings."

"Those had to be antlers."

"Moose don't have antlers this time of year. So, what do we do now? That thing might still be out there. What if *it's* what ate that bear?"

"It was a moose," Eve insisted.

"Okay then, *you* get out and walk to the nearest house."

"Where's your cell phone?"

"They cut off my service yesterday. I can't get it back until I cough up a hundred and forty bucks. Where's yours?"

"In storage in Ellsworth. I canceled my Boston service and didn't replace it. We could just sit here until someone comes along, though that might not be until the fishermen head out in the morning. Why did you take the back way from Oak Harbor?"

Maddy blew out a sigh. "Because I wanted to stay off the main road. My inspection sticker ran out and I can't get a new one until I get new brakes."

"Well, we can't sit here all night. How about if on the count of three, we both open our doors and get out?"

"We can't see a damn thing when the moon goes behind the clouds. One minute we're surrounded by creepy shadows, and the next minute it's pitch black."

"Maybe the truck will start and we can back out. Or is the four-wheel drive broken, too?"

Maddy turned the key and the starter whined. The engine coughed and clanked but didn't sputter to life.

She continued trying until Eve reached over and grabbed her hand. "We're going to have to walk."

"But what if that beast is still out there?" Maddy whispered. "It ate a bear, Eve."

"We saw a *moose*. It had giant *antlers*, and it *leap*t into the woods. That's what you're going to tell the sheriff when you report the accident, and that's what you're going to tell the insurance company when you file your claim."

"I can't report this to anyone. My insurance ran out two months ago, which means if the sheriff gets involved, I'll get a huge fine for not having an inspection sticker or insurance." Maddy buried her face in her hands. "God, I'm screwed. I am *so* damn tired of holding everything together. Between Rick and Mom always butting heads, and Sarah needing attention, and work, sometimes I just want to walk into the woods where no one can hear me and *scream*."

Eve unfastened her seat belt and hugged her friend. "I know what you mean. I tell you what. We'll get out, scream as loud as we can, and we'll keep screaming the whole way to the nearest house. It'll be cathartic, and also scare the bejeezus out of whatever that animal was. On the count of three, okay?"

"Okay. One, two, three."

Eve opened her door and scrambled up the ditch to the back of the truck to meet Maddy—who wasn't there. She stumbled to the driver's side and banged on the window. "Get out!"

"I can't. My door won't open."

Eve kept her glare firmly locked on Maddy, afraid of what she might see in the shadows if she looked around. "Then get out my side."

As Maddy crawled across to the other door, Eve scrambled back up the ditch and around to the other side. "Do you have a flashlight?" she asked as Maddy got out.

"My dad always said that you shouldn't walk the woods at night with a light. It *attracts* animals."

"I am *so* going to kill you."

Maddy gave a somewhat hysterical laugh. "Then you'd be out here all alone. Okay, let's scream, so that thing will be more afraid of us than we are of it. One, two, three!"

Eve screamed at the top of her lungs, only to be rendered deaf when Maddy screamed even louder.

"God, that felt good," Maddy said when they both stopped screaming. "Let's do it again. Wait!" She crawled back in the truck to rummage around in the backseat. "Yes!" she cried as she backed out. "I couldn't remember if I still had this or not." She shoved a tall bottle at Eve. "It's spiced rum. Take a drink."

"Straight? You don't have any soda we can mix with it?"

"Just take a swallow. It'll calm your nerves for our walk."

Eve twisted off the cap, took a large swig, and immediately started coughing.

Maddy grabbed the bottle from her and did the same. "Holy shit, that's strong," she said with a gasp. She took another swig and shoved the bottle back at Eve. "If we drink enough, we won't care if that was a *lion* we almost hit."

"Lions don't fly, either," Eve said, taking another gulp, which actually went down a bit smoother this time.

"So you're admitting it flew away?"

Eve stepped onto the road and took another swallow before handing the bottle to Maddy. "We're not telling anyone what we saw. Not that anyone would believe us, anyway. It *had* to have been a hairless moose that forgot to shed its antlers last winter."

Maddy linked her arm through Eve's. "Okay. That's our story, and we're sticking to it. Which way do we walk?"

"That way," Eve said, pointing toward the way they'd been heading. "I don't remember seeing any houses for the last couple of miles. But let's get our purses first—I have a canister of Mace in mine."

"You carry Mace?" Maddy said in surprise, following Eve down to the truck.

"People frown on schoolteachers carrying handguns," she said, reaching inside and grabbing both their purses, as well as the fancy shopping bag she'd gotten in Oak Harbor. She'd be damned if she was leaving her new bra behind after using the last of her cash to buy it. She handed Maddy's purse to her in exchange for the bottle. "In fact, Massachusetts frowns on anyone carrying a gun."

Maddy giggled. "I can't imagine why. Let's scream again."

"One, two, three," Eve blurted in a rush.

They both screamed loud enough to wake the dead, and long enough that their voices cracked.

"Okay, now I'm ready," Maddy said, looping her arm through Eve's again and heading down the road. "Are you going to hog that bottle all night, or— What's that!" she screamed, dragging Eve to the side of the road.

The faint outline of a small furry creature waddled

through the shadows a hundred yards up the road. It stepped into the moonlight, and Eve saw two distinctive white stripes running down its back and up its large fluffy tail.

"It's a skunk," she whispered. "Maybe screaming is like having a flashlight, and it attracts animals, too. Let's just walk quietly." She took a swig of the spiced rum and handed the bottle to Maddy. "I'm all screamed out, anyway. I think that last one broke a vocal cord."

"The rum will heal it."

They fell silent after that, walking together arm in arm, taking turns drinking from the bottle. Fifteen minutes later, Maddy started humming softly.

"Are you humming that song from the *Wizard of Oz*?"

"Lions, tigers, and bears, oh my," Maddy whispered with a giggle. "I can't help it. It seems appropriate."

Now the song was stuck in Eve's head. "When was your last date?" she asked to distract herself.

"Does going to a bar in Ellsworth last November and getting so drunk that I picked up a guy count?"

"Did you sleep with him?"

Maddy took another drink of the rum. "I am such a slut."

Eve hugged her to her side when she stumbled. "You're not a slut, you're just lonely. Did you ever see him again?"

"He called me the next day and I met him for dinner a few days after that, but the guy couldn't have been twenty! He must have used his brother's ID to get in the bar. I nearly died when he sat down across from me in the restaurant. That's when I swore I'd never, ever drink again," she declared, lifting the bottle to her lips.

Eve found that hilariously funny. They both started laughing so hard, Maddy stumbled and Eve nearly fell trying to grab her.

"The bottle!" Maddy shouted. "Don't let it fall!"

Eve saved the rum and her friend. "I am a hero!" she cried, lifting the bottle in victory. "I saved you both! See, we don't need a man to ride in and rescue us. We're rescuing ourselves!"

"But Kenzie is sooo cute. Won't you sleep with him anyway? Please? For me? I'll be in your debt for life!"

Eve started them weaving down the road again. "Why don't *you* sleep with him? You're beautiful and smart and horny, and you're gainfully employed. You should go after Kenzie yourself."

"But you're beautifuler and smarter and hornier than I am," Maddy proclaimed, waving the hand that held her purse and accidently smacking Eve. "And you're gamely employed now, too. Tomorrow night you're going to officially become Kenzie Gregor's housekeeper." She snickered. "And the job comes with a very *full* benefits package, I happened to notice the other day."

Eve doubled over in hysterics. "You looked at his *package*? Madeline Kimble, you're going to hell!"

Maddy began laughing so hard that she tripped and fell, dragging Eve with her. "Save the bottle!" she shouted.

"I got it!" Eve yelped, falling on top of Maddy as she

juggled the bottle, her shopping bag, and her own purse. They sat there leaning against each other, their laughter turning to giggles until they simply fell silent.

"Kenzie scares the bejeezus out of me," Maddy whispered. "He'd swallow me up." She slung her arm over Eve's shoulder. "But you could hold your own against him. In school, you had all the boys in a frenzy trying to figure you out. You could have had your choice of boyfriends, and you didn't pick any of them because you were holding out for a prince."

Eve snorted. "Some prince Parker turned out to be."

Maddy waved that away. "Parker doesn't count. I know you kissed a lot of frogs in college but never found your prince, so you settled for Parker because he offered you a way out of Midnight Bay. Tell me honest, did you even love him?"

"I thought I did."

"You know what I think? I think you got snookered by his good looks and his from-away appeal. Everyone from away seems mysterious and exciting to us."

"Kenzie Gregor is good-looking and from away," Eve reminded her. "I don't want to get snookered again."

Maddy shook her head. "Kenzie's different."

"You don't know a damn thing about him."

"I know he likes you, and I'd bet my truck that it's the real deal."

"How can you possibly know that?"

"Because he's trying so hard *not* to like you," Maddy said with all the authority of a drunken friend.

"Asking me out doesn't sound like he's not trying."

"I didn't say he was winning the battle. Apparently he's got more testas . . . trone than . . . than . . ."

"Brains?" Eve finished for her.

"Getting you to go on a date with him took *major* brains." Maddy suddenly sat up straight. "Hey, do you think our moose had a couple of flashlights tied to its antlers, or is that a truck coming toward us?"

Kenzie drove slowly down the dark winding road, scanning the ditches for Maddy's truck. According to the directions William had given him, he should have come across the women by now, walking home from where they'd gone off the road.

That damned beast; he'd have an easier time keeping a three-year-old contained. Even though William had been hunting in a remote area, he'd still managed to cause trouble. If Eve or Maddy had been hurt in the accident, he was going to run William through with his sword.

Kenzie crested a knoll, and the beam of his headlights landed on the women sitting in the middle of the road. He didn't grow truly alarmed until he drove nearly up to them and they didn't even bother to get out of the way. He stopped the truck and shut it off, leaving just the running lights on so he wouldn't blind them.

"Kenzie, our hero!" Maddy cried, spreading her arms wide. She nudged Eve beside her, nearly knocking Eve over just as she was taking a drink from a bottle. "Is this guy amazing, or what? He keeps showing up right when you need rescuing. Now you definitely gotta screw him, just like in the romance novels. The hero always gets the girl!"

Kenzie stopped dead in his tracks.

Eve spat out whatever she was drinking and glared at her friend. "Will you shut up!" she hissed in a loud whisper. She waved the bottle in his direction. "He heard you, and now it won't be a surprise when I jump his bones tomorrow night."

Holy hell, they were falling-down drunk!

Maddy made a pout face. "I'm sorry." She snatched the bottle from Eve. "Damn, it's empty. Now what are we gonna do? The flying moose is gonna get us."

Kenzie had just started toward them, but stopped again.

Flying moose?

Eve started rummaging around in her purse. "We'll Mace the bastard," she said, her hand emerging with a tiny canister.

Kenzie immediately stepped forward and snatched it out of Eve's hand before she could accidently spray herself, and stuffed it in his pocket.

She glared up at him, tilting her head back so far that she toppled into Maddy. "That wasn't very nice."

"But necessary," he said, trying not to laugh. "Would you ladies like a ride home?"

"No, thank you," Maddy said, smoothing down the front of her jacket. "We're just out for an evening stroll. Nobody can know I ran my truck off the road, because the shitty thing isn't inspected or insured." She suddenly gasped and looked at Eve. "Omigod! We gotta go back and cover it up with branches so nobody will see it." She tried standing up, attempting to pull Eve with her, and they both fell back onto the road. "Come on! You have to help me because this is all your fault."

"*My* fault?" Eve said, rolling to her hands and knees. "How?"

"I had to take you to buy that stupid Wonderbra, that's how," Maddy said, also on all fours as she faced Eve. "And you should have done a better job watching for flying moose."

"*You* were driving."

"Hey, Kenzie," Maddy said, sitting back down so she could look up at him. "You got any spiced rum in your truck? We need it to keep away the flying moose."

"I'm sorry, I don't."

She looked at Eve. "He's so polite. I don't think you should wait until tomorrow night. Go on, jump him right now." She swiped a small bag out of Eve's hand, pulled out a tiny bit of cloth, and shoved it at her. "Here, put this on first, and maybe he won't notice you don't have any boobs."

Kenzie's shoulders shook as he fought to contain his laughter. He really should get them out of the road, but God help him, they were so oblivious.

He heard a whisper of sound in the trees and knew that William was also enjoying the entertainment. "Okay, ladies," Kenzie said, reaching down and scooping Eve up in his arms. "I think it's time I got you home."

"Oh! How romantic!" Maddy wailed, clutching the empty bag to her chest. "I swear I'm going to lose forty pounds so that, when my knight finally rides into town, he can carry me off like that. Forget the bra!" she shouted. "He might put an eye out trying to get it off you! Hey! Kenzie!"

He stopped beside the back door to look at Maddy. "What?"

"You make her forget all about Parker the prick head, okay? Wait! Kenzie!"

He sighed. "Yes?"

"Y-you won't take too long, will you?" she asked, looking around at the woods.

"I'm coming for you next, Maddy."

Eve gasped and started wiggling to get down. "You sleaze!" she cried, shoving at his chest. "I knew you were too good to be true."

"What the . . . Eve, I'm just putting you in the truck, going back for Maddy, and then taking ye both home." He opened the back door and set her inside. "Stay put," he said, smiling at the glare she gave him. "I have to go save Maddy from the flying moose."

Her eyes widened and she nodded violently, her soft curls bouncing around her face. "Yes, go rescue her before it gets her! It had antlers so big we thought they were wings, and its eyes glowed bright red when our headlights hit it. It ate a bear!" She suddenly slapped her finger to her lips. "But we're not telling anyone. Maddy's shitty truck isn't insured, so the sheriff will give her a big fine that she can't afford, and people will think we're crazy."

"Did you start drinking before or after ye saw the flying moose?"

"After!" she snapped. "We don't drink and drive. We only drink and walk."

"Kenzie! I heard a noise in the woods! Save me! Save me!"

He leaned down and flipped the child safety latch so Eve couldn't suddenly decide to get out and save her friend herself, and softly closed the door. He headed back to Maddy, smiling when he saw she was standing—though weaving—the empty bottle raised like a weapon.

"Are ye afraid of bogeymen, Maddy?"

She turned her dark eyes on him. "Bogeymen?" she squeaked.

"You know—the red-eyed, fire-breathing, foul-smelling beasts who like to scare beautiful young women? All ye have to do if ye see one is blow him a kiss, and he'll be so smitten, he'll turn as docile as a lamb."

The bottle lowered slightly. "That's it? I just have to blow the bogeyman a kiss?"

He nodded.

"Well, shit," she said, dropping her arm completely. "I wish I'd known that before we started walking."

Kenzie swept her up in his arms, smiling when she gasped and clutched his neck in a choke hold. "Go on," he said. "Blow a kiss in the direction ye heard the noise coming from. If there's a bogeyman out there and you listen carefully, ye might hear him fall in love with you."

Maddy frowned. "But I don't want the bogeyman to love me. I want a knight in shining leather just like you, only not so . . . intense. And he's got to be handsome and strong and polite. Oh, and I wouldn't mind if he was rich, too, because I gotta pay my insurance and get my brakes fixed so I can get my shitty truck inspected so I won't go to jail."

"You know what bogeymen really are, Maddy?"

"No. What?"

"They're most often strong, handsome men who've been cursed by a mean old witch, and all they need is to have a beautiful woman rescue them from their nightmare."

"Really?" she whispered, her eyes widening. She suddenly glared at him fiercely. "Are you funnen me?"

"Nay, Maddy. Bogeymen are really quite tragic creatures. Go on—blow this one a kiss and see if ye get a response."

She hesitated, then finally set the empty bottle and her purse on her lap against his chest, lifted her hand to her mouth, and blew William a loud noisy kiss. "Mmmwaa!" she said, tossing the kiss toward the woods. "Take that, Mr. Bogeyman!"

"Now listen."

A deep, lusty groan whispered through the night air.

Maddy squealed, "I heard it! I heard the bogeyman!"

"And now ye need never be afraid of noises in the

dark again, Maddy. Ye tamed him with your powerful kiss."

"My kisses are powerful?" she breathed.

He walked to the driver's side of his truck. "There's nothing more powerful in the world than the sweet kiss of a beautiful woman."

"Eve's beautiful."

"Yes, she is. And so are you."

"I'll be even prettier when I lose fort— A few pounds." She suddenly gasped. "You're carrying me! You're *so* strong."

"So is the bogeyman. And now that you've tamed him, he'll be your slave for life."

A snort came from the woods, and Maddy snapped her head toward it. "What was that?"

Kenzie opened the back door with his fingers. "Just an owl hooting."

She tapped him on the shoulder just as he was about to set her inside. "Do you have any brothers?" she asked.

"One. You'll meet him day after tomorrow. Matt and his wife are coming to visit."

"Oh. Do you have any *single* brothers?"

"Sorry."

"How about sisters?" She blew out a spiced sigh. "I'm getting so desperate, I'm open to just about anything."

He set her on the backseat next to Eve. "Sorry, you're out of luck on both counts," he said with a laugh, flipping the child lock and closing her door.

He walked to where they'd been sitting, picked up

Eve's purse and the empty store bag, then stood facing the forest. "You've had enough fun for tonight, William. Go pull Maddy's truck out of the ditch, fly it to the farm, and leave it behind the barn. But first erase the tracks where it went off the road."

"That truck has to weigh more than a warhorse."

"Ye have the strength to handle it. And William? That kiss was for Maddy's sake, not yours. Ye keep your distance, or I'll be forced to clip your wings."

Kenzie went back to his truck, opened his door, and smiled when the interior light came on to reveal the two women sound asleep in the backseat, cuddled against each other, Eve with her bra clutched to her chest, Maddy hugging her purse and the empty bottle.

He climbed in and headed home with his softly snoring cargo, wondering if Eve really had been planning to jump his bones tomorrow night, or if that had been the rum talking.

Not that he could let her. The storm he sensed heading his way could place her in danger, and he'd already proven he was incapable of protecting those he loved.

Chapter Eight

Eve opened her eyes and immediately shut them again when pain shot through her head. She was in her bed, and Maddy was lying beside her. Maddy's agonized moan told Eve that her friend was also awake.

"Do you know how we got here?" Eve asked softly, in deference to her splitting head.

"I remember something about a moose with wings. And strong arms carrying me. Oh, and I think I kissed the bogeyman," Maddy whispered. "And now he's in love with me, and is my slave for life."

"We really have to find you some new reading material—those paranormal romances are starting to mess with your brain. There's no such thing as bogeymen, Maddy. They're fictional monsters parents invented to keep kids in their beds."

"Kenzie said they're really handsome men who got cursed by a mean old witch, and that only the kiss of a beautiful woman can save them."

"He was teasing you because you were so drunk." Fragmented images of last night suddenly flashed through Eve's brain. She groaned, grabbed her head at the pain it caused, then groaned again because the act of grabbing her head hurt even worse. "I'm going to strangle you. Now I can't go on my date with Kenzie tonight."

"Why not?"

"Because I keep getting a horrifying image of you waving my bra at him."

"I'm sure the man has seen a bra before."

"You were screaming at me to have sex with him right there in the road!"

Oh, yelling hurt. Eve rolled onto her side and curled into a ball of agony.

"That's what you get for drinking an entire fifth of rum," her mother said, walking into the room.

"Please, Mrs. B, *whisper,*" Maddy pleaded. "Oh, God, I'm going to be sick." She bolted off the bed and ran down the hall to the bathroom.

"What time is it?" Eve asked, refusing to open her eyes.

"A quarter to ten."

"Damn, I'm late opening the store."

"It's Saturday. We close at noon, so it's not worth opening up for only an hour." Eve heard the curtains being drawn and the room darkened behind her eyelids.

She also heard the laughter in her mother's voice when Mabel said, "You girls sure had one heck of an adventure last night. I can't say I was real happy to see the shape you were in when Kenzie brought you home, but he assured me you didn't start drinking until after Maddy's truck broke down."

"Come to think of it," Eve said, slowly opening her eyes. "What was Kenzie doing out on that road last night?"

"Beats me." Mabel hunched down beside her and tucked a curl behind Eve's ear. "It's just lucky for you that he was. You want me to make you girls some dry toast?"

When Eve tried to sit up, her stomach revolted and she immediately lay back on the pillow. "Um, Mom?"

"Yes?"

"Tell me honestly, did I make an ass of myself last night?"

Mabel chuckled. "That depends if an ass wears a blue lace push-up bra like a necklace."

"Omigod," Eve groaned, covering her face with her hands. "I can never face Kenzie again."

"It's going to be hard to keep house for the man without ever seeing him."

Eve dropped her hands. "He told you about offering me a job as his housekeeper?"

"He offered it to me, too, since we come as a package."

"But I can't accept. You have no idea of all the crazy things Maddy and I said and did last night."

"Too late," Mabel chirped, heading toward the hall. "I accepted for us." She stopped at the door. "It's a perfect solution for us, Eve. We get to live here absolutely free, and he's going to buy all the food."

"I intended to look for a teaching position for this fall, and tutor kids this summer."

"But you can't teach school; you have to babysit me."

"Oh, so it's okay for me to watch you every minute if it suits *your* purpose?" Eve drawled.

"Who knows how bad I'll be by this fall?" Mabel said, adjusting one of the knitting needles in her hair.

Eve narrowed her eyes at her mother. "What a convenient illness you have."

"Are you accusing me of faking it?"

"No. I saw the CAT scan and talked to the doctors. I'm only accusing you of playing it up when it's to your advantage, and sending me on a guilt trip when it's not."

"I guess that must be one of the symptoms," Mabel said airily, disappearing down the hall.

Eve had managed to avoid Kenzie all day by taking a really long bath and then hiding in her room. But her mother and Maddy had joined ranks and were forcing her to go—on pain of never being talked to again—on her date.

"I feel like a sacrificial virgin, being dressed for a night with a sultan," she complained.

Maddy snorted. "*That* cow left the barn years ago."

Eve tried shoving her boobs deeper into her push-up

bra, and frowned when they popped right back up. She unsnapped the front closure on the bra and took it off. "I am not wearing this damn thing," she said, heading for her bureau. "I can't believe I let you talk me into buying it. My boobs are just fine the way God made them."

Maddy beat her to the bureau, dangling the cobalt blue Wonderbra in her hand. "You are, too, because you spent your last dime on it and because it makes you look irresistibly yummy. Don't force me to go get your mother."

"Why are you two so determined that I like Kenzie Gregor?" Eve asked with a glower, slipping the bra back on.

"Because you deserve him. And he deserves to end his dating drought. But mostly because you're going to make really beautiful babies."

Eve blinked at her. "How did we go from having an affair to having babies?"

Maddy walked to the bed, brought back the blouse she'd picked out, and handed it to Eve. "Affairs can lead to marriage."

"And then my neighbor can steal my *new* husband and run off with him and all our money."

"Pauline did you a favor. But Kenzie's different." Maddy finished buttoning the blouse, then handed Eve her coat. "He's waiting downstairs, and once you see him, you'll understand what I'm talking about. I swear he's more nervous than a canary at a cat convention. I don't think his 'not dating for years' was a come-on line at all. He got all spiffed up, and even brought you flowers."

"He did?"

Maddy nodded, looped her arm through Eve's, then guided her into the hall. "Promise me you'll be gentle with him."

"Are we talking about the same man?"

"We're talking about the nervous wreck in your kitchen waiting to take out the prettiest girl in the county," Maddy said, lowering her voice when they reached the bottom of the stairs. "I think you better keep your panties *on* tonight. If you try jumping his gorgeous bones, you're liable to give him a heart attack. Why do you think I buttoned your blouse all the way up to your neck?"

Eve felt beads of sweat collecting between her barely confined boobs. She pulled Maddy to a halt in the living room. "I can't face him. I made a complete ass of myself last night."

"So did I, but he acted like nothing happened when Sarah and I showed up this evening. He just explained that he had my truck towed here and hid it behind the barn."

"He did?"

"I really panicked when Rick drove me to where we'd left the truck and it was nowhere to be found. We couldn't even find where I'd gone off the road." She preceded Eve into the kitchen. "Here's your date, completely sober and ready for dinner."

"These are for you," Kenzie said, thrusting a bouquet of roses toward her.

"Th-thank you," she stammered.

Maddy took the roses and handed them to Sarah. "Okay, then," she said into the awkward silence. "You two go out and have a good time. Sarah and Mrs. B are going to make a batch of fudge, and I'm going to see how much of it Father Daar can eat before he turns green," she said with a laugh. "I expect you home no later than eleven, and you both had better be sober. Kenzie, did you fill up your gas tank today?" she asked as she ushered them onto the porch and down the stairs.

"Was I supposed to?"

She wagged a finger at him. "Running out of gas in the middle of nowhere is the oldest excuse in the book, and I won't buy it."

She opened the passenger door and looked at Eve. "Don't talk about Parker, politics, or your money problems. Oh, and don't have anything to drink. There's probably still enough rum in your system to make an elephant drunk. Get Kenzie to talk about himself."

She handed Eve her seat-belt buckle as she smiled at Kenzie. "Have fun, you two, and don't worry about anything here. I've got everyone covered," she said, closing the door and running back to the house.

"Is she always so bossy?" Kenzie asked with a chuckle.

"Sometimes she's worse." Eve took a deep breath, figuring she might as well get it out in the open so they could get past it. "Thank you for bringing us home last night."

He put the truck in gear and headed out the driveway. "You're welcome. I'm just glad neither of you were hurt when ye went off the road. I'm sorry I can't say the same for Maddy's truck. I had a mechanic come look at it today, and he said it probably isn't worth repairing. Maddy took the news . . . well, she asked for a large stick, so she could finish it off. Do ye have an idea what she'll do for transportation now? I offered to buy her a new truck, but she refused."

Eve's head snapped toward him. "You offered to buy her a truck?"

He shrugged. "It seemed like a simple solution to her problem." He glanced at her, his expression concerned. "She has a child, and she shouldn't be driving an unsafe truck. She borrowed her mother's car to come here tonight, and it doesn't appear to be any safer."

"What was her reaction when you offered to buy her a truck?"

He shot her a sudden grin. "She didn't say anything for several seconds, then got this really dark look on her face. And then she exploded."

"I'm not surprised. Maddy might be struggling to make ends meet, what with her ex-husband paying so little child support and her having to help out her mother financially, but she's very proud."

"I'm afraid I may have insulted her," he said, stopping when they reached the main road in Midnight Bay. "Which way?"

"Right. There's a nice restaurant in Oak Harbor. Don't

worry, I'm sure Maddy appreciates your unusually generous offer. She only exploded because she knew she couldn't accept it. I'll share my car with her until she can replace hers, since I have the delivery truck for going back and forth to work."

"You're a good friend." He glanced over, then back at the road. "And you'll be a good housekeeper for Daar and me, I hope?"

"Mom said she already accepted your offer for both of us."

"I'd still like to hear it from you."

Eve finally felt her muscles loosening up. Maybe tonight wouldn't be a disaster after all. In fact, she might even have a bit of fun.

"Tell me again what my duties will be," she asked, "besides cooking and cleaning, washing your clothes, and churning butter? Will I have to milk the cow, feed the chickens, and weed the garden?"

He glanced at her sharply, and Eve thought she caught the glimpse of a smile as he looked back at the road. "I have some shirts that need mending."

"Mom can do that, since I can't thread a needle without pricking myself. What else? Maybe I can wash your truck once a week? Heck, while I'm at it, I can vacuum it out."

"I wouldn't expect ye to clean my truck," he said, sounding way too serious. "It's mostly woman's work that I'm needing. I will milk the cow."

"Please don't take this the wrong way, but have you been living in a cave all your life?"

He stiffened again. “Excuse me?”

“Nobody says stuff like *woman’s work* anymore. And even if we are still quite traditional around here, you shouldn’t talk like that if you want to fit in.”

“That’s something else I wish you to do. I need you to help me learn the way of the locals so I don’t stand out.”

She laughed at that. “Then you better get yourself a different truck. This one practically shouts ‘person from away.’ ”

“It does? Why?”

“Because it costs more money than most people around here earn in two years, and it’s way too clean. How long have you owned it?”

“A little over a month. I bought it when I got my driver’s license. I just got used to how everything works on it; I don’t want a different truck.”

He’d just gotten his license? Maybe that was why he was driving like an old woman. “How long have you been in America?”

“Almost three years.”

“And you just started driving?”

He shrugged. “I had no need to before. So where is this restaurant?” he asked as they drove into Oak Harbor.

“Right there,” she said, pointing to a building sitting on the edge of the harbor. “You can park on the public pier.”

He pulled into an open slot, shut off the engine, and

smiled at her. "I hope you're hungry. Are ye ready to go in, or would you like to walk the pier first?"

"Actually, I'm starved. Let's walk the pier after."

Kenzie didn't know if this date was going well or not, because he didn't have anything to compare it to. He still couldn't understand what all the excitement was about. In his old time, when a man found a woman he wanted, he simply stole her out from under her papa's nose.

Kenzie smiled as he walked beside Eve to the restaurant. It was a great compliment to the woman for her future husband to follow her around for months, learning her routine so he could capture her unawares.

But Camry had told him that form of courtship was called *stalking* today, and would get him arrested.

Kenzie stepped around Eve and opened the restaurant door. She walked inside, slipped off her coat, and handed it to him. Having practiced this with Camry, he hung the coat on a hanger in the foyer, then walked over to the man at the tiny desk. "I would like a table for two, please."

"Yes, this way," the man said, picking up two menus and leading them to a nice table in front of a wall of windows, in the middle of several other diners.

"Could we have a table over there?" Kenzie asked. "Against the wall?"

The gentleman looked at him strangely, then led them to the back wall. "Your waiter will be right along," he said, leaving.

Kenzie pulled out a chair for Eve.

"You didn't want to enjoy the view of the harbor? I thought you liked being out in the open."

He took his own seat facing the entrance, and gave a shrug. "Not as much as I dislike being exposed. I'm sorry you'll be missing the view, but I prefer having a wall at my back."

She looked around, then returned her gaze to his. "Are you ex-military? Like Special Ops or something?"

"Yes, I was in the military." Camry had told him that would be the easiest way to explain his strange habits.

"What branch? Air force, army, marines, or navy?"

Camry hadn't said anything about branches, but those seemed self-explanatory. "Army." He picked up his menu. "Ye said you were starved. Do you feel like seafood?"

"You can't come to Rhapsody and not have seafood," she said, folding her hands on her unopened menu. "I'll have lobster."

Kenzie set down his menu. "Me, too."

"So, back to this housekeeping thing," she said, taking a roll out of the basket the waiter set in front of her. "How's the pay work?"

"We'll each have two of your largest lobsters," Kenzie told the waiter. "But first bring us each a glass of single malt Scotch, one with ice and one plain."

"Maddy said no drinking," Eve reminded him the moment the waiter left.

"Do you always do what Maddy says?"

She sighed, breaking apart her roll. "It does seem to be a new habit of mine."

"You look lovely tonight, Eve. That blouse brings out the blue in your eyes."

She narrowed those brilliant blue eyes at him. "Don't bother trying to butter me up," she said, slathering butter onto her roll. "My panties are staying on."

"Panties?"

She waved her knife in the air. "I don't know what you *think* you heard us talking about last evening, but my clothing is staying on tonight. So, does the job pay anything besides room and board?" she asked, taking a large bite of her roll.

"I'm not sure what it should pay. I'll ask Winter when she and Matt arrive."

"You have company coming?"

"My brother and sister-in-law are bringing down my horses tomorrow. I'd hoped they could stay for several days, but Winter is heavy with child, so they're only spending the night. She told me women want to be home when they're nearing childbirth."

"Where do they live?"

"In Pine Creek."

"That's in western Maine, isn't it?"

"Yes, up in the mountains."

"How come you didn't buy a farm near them?" she asked, taking another bite of her roll.

"Because I prefer to live by the ocean."

She was too busy chewing to comment. He hoped he'd ordered enough food. The waiter brought their drinks, and Kenzie took a large sip of his.

Eve stared at hers.

"Do ye not like good whisky?" he asked.

"Straight? Without mixing something with it?"

"It would be sacrilegious to put anything but ice in whisky. Go on, give it a try."

She tentatively took a sip, made a face that made him chuckle, and immediately put the rest of her roll in her mouth.

He took her glass, poured the Scotch into his, and waved the waiter back over. "What would you prefer to drink?" Kenzie asked her.

"Pepsi with no ice," she told the waiter. "Are you going to eat your roll?"

"No, you eat it."

So . . . here he was finally, out on an actual date with a woman he wasn't sort of related to, and he still couldn't figure out why men voluntarily put themselves through such a trial. He tried to remember the subjects Camry had said were safe.

"There's a storm coming," he said.

She stopped chewing. "Tonight?"

"No, in a couple of days," he told her, tugging the collar of his shirt. Damn, it was hot in here.

She suddenly set down her roll, folded her hands on the table, and smiled sheepishly. "I'm sorry. I get a little cranky when I'm hungry, and I can see you'd rather be anywhere else but here with me. How about if I stop being such a witch, and you just try to relax?"

"I don't care to be anywhere else. And you're a long way from being a witch," he said in complete honesty, picturing some of the old hags he knew. "I've especially never met one with your smile."

She looked at him strangely, opened her mouth to say something, then popped a piece of roll in it instead.

Kenzie sighed. Maybe he *would* rather be taking a swim in the ocean right now. The evening seemed to go on for eternity, the only high point coming when the waiter set two five-pound lobsters down in front of Eve, and her eyes actually crossed.

Yet she managed to eat nearly all of both of them, which kept their conversation to a minimum. Kenzie ate his two five-pound lobsters and some of hers—except for the tail she carried in a takeout container as they walked out of the restaurant.

"Would you like to stroll on the pier?" he asked, unlocking the doors as they approached the truck.

"Yes, it's a beautiful night," she agreed, setting her package inside.

At the pier rail, Kenzie pointed at one of the larger boats tied to a floating dock. "What does that boat fish for?"

"They don't have scallop draggers in Scotland?"

"None that look like that, exactly."

"Do you sail, Kenzie?"

"No," he said, eyeing the sleek sailing yachts moored

out in the harbor. "I did travel to the Outer Hebrides once, and quickly learned that I was born in the highlands for a reason. It was not a voyage I ever wished to repeat."

"Then how come you chose to live by the ocean, instead of in the mountains near your brother?"

"I can appreciate the sea without going on it. Are ye cold, Eve?" he asked, noticing she was holding her coat closed at her throat.

She moved closer, looking up at him, her lips curved into a beautiful smile. "I am getting a bit chilly."

Now that her belly was full, Eve was focused solely on him—and obviously expecting him to warm her up, and maybe give her a kiss.

He was fiercely tempted to oblige her, his palms itching to touch the soft skin of her face, his fingers twitching with his need to run them through her soft blond curls.

But if he kissed her, he feared he might not stop.

"Then we'll go to the truck and I'll turn on the heater. It's probably time we started home, anyway."

Her lips parted in surprise; her eyes widened in shock. A blush rose into her cheeks and she suddenly spun away and marched off to his truck.

Kenzie gave a heartfelt sigh of regret, not sure if he was an idiot, or if he might have just saved her life.

Eve stomped up the porch stairs *alone,* refusing to look back as Kenzie drove out the driveway toward his ocean campsite. She hoped that the storm he'd talked about came in tonight, and that his tent blew away—with him in it!

Maddy opened the door just as Eve reached for the knob, and stepped outside. "So, how did it go?" she asked, her expression expectant.

Eve pointed at her face. "Do these lips looked kissed?"

Maddy squinted at her mouth. "No, they don't. So what happened?"

"Exactly nothing," Eve snapped. "He didn't touch me—no body contact, not even his hand brushing against mine. And when we went for a walk on the pier after dinner and he asked if I was cold, I gave him the perfect opening to kiss me. And when he pulled up here and put the truck in gear, I just sat there like an idiot, waiting for him to make his move *then*. When I finally realized it wasn't going to happen, I got out and slammed the door on his polite 'Thank you and good night' without saying a word."

Maddy was laughing behind her hand. "Oh, God. This has never happened to you before, has it?"

"Will you quit laughing!"

"Either it really has been years for him, or . . ." Maddy's expression turned thoughtful.

"Or what?"

"Or he was playing you."

"How?" Eve said in surprise.

"He knew you intended to jump his bones tonight,

and that's why he didn't kiss you. Guys know that the best way to reel in a woman is to ignore her." Maddy shook her head. "How do you think I got pregnant with Sarah? Billy Kimble ignored me nearly our entire senior year, so I jumped him one night when he was coming out of the locker room after hockey practice."

"Madeline Kimble, you didn't!"

She shrugged. "I was seventeen and had the hots for the school hockey hero. I didn't know jock was spelled J-E-R-K."

"Well, I am *never* jumping Kenzie Gregor's bones. I don't even like him."

Maddy wrapped her arm around Eve's shoulders and led her through the door. "Really? Then why are you so pissed off?"

Chapter Nine

Blatantly ignoring Kenzie as he and Father Daar scurried in and out of the barn getting ready for the horses to arrive, Eve kept herself busy by cleaning out the accumulation of junk in her car while she waited impatiently for her mother to get back from her morning walk.

She may have promised to stop treating Mabel like a child, but it was damn hard. Her mom was all she had left, and if anything happened to her, Eve didn't know how she'd survive.

She tossed several empty soda cans in the bin sitting on the ground, then grabbed a bunch of clothes and tossed them in, planning to sort everything later. She looked at her watch, realized her mom had been gone almost two hours, and scowled at the path that led down to the ocean.

Two hours was too long for a morning walk.

Unable to wait any longer, Eve tossed a lone shoe in the bin and headed across the yard. But just as she reached the path, Kenzie stepped in front of her.

"Where are ye going?"

She tilted her head back to squint up at him. "For a walk," she said, trying to step around him.

He moved to block her path again. "Don't coddle her, Eve."

"She's been gone *two* hours."

"The tide's out. She's likely sitting on her bench in the morning sun, welcoming the first day of May."

"Or she might be floating facedown in the ocean."

He shook his head. "She's not."

"You can't know that."

"If something was amiss, the animals would tell us."

"What are you talking about?"

"Listen," he said, canting his head toward the trees. "What do ye hear?"

She was growing more frantic by the minute, and he was telling her to listen to . . . "I hear birds chirping."

He nodded. "Exactly. If there's trouble of any sort in the area, be it human or animal, the birds will go silent—except for the crows. They would be broadcasting the news that something is wrong."

"I just heard a crow caw!"

He shook his head again. "The sound they make when something is wrong is quite distinct. That one is calling its mate."

She tried stepping around him again. "Okay then, maybe *I'll* go sit in the sun and welcome the first day of May."

He took hold of her wrist. "No, you'll keep your promise to your mother," he said, walking back toward the barn with her in tow.

Of all the nerve! "Hey, you can't just grab me like that," she yelped, using her other hand to try to free herself. "Let me go!"

The air brakes on a large truck suddenly released, and a massive tractor trailer pulled into the dooryard. Kenzie changed direction, picking up his pace, his grip still unbreakable.

"My horses are here."

Eve stopped struggling, figuring he'd have to let her go to unload his horses.

A Suburban, identical to Kenzie's except it was pearl white, pulled into the driveway behind the semi. How many horses were they delivering?

Kenzie stopped when the Suburban pulled up beside him. The passenger door opened and a very pregnant, absolutely beautiful woman jumped out. "Kenzie!" she cried, running up to hug him.

Kenzie hugged her back, still holding Eve's wrist. "Sister," he said with a laugh. "I can see your condition hasn't slowed ye down."

"Your farm is beautiful! I love the house, and the way it sits on a bluff looking out at the ocean."

The woman continued extolling the virtues of Kenzie's

new home—that he didn't actually *live* in—but Eve stopped listening to study the man getting out of the Suburban. He had an amused look on his face as he studied her as well, his gaze dropping to Kenzie's grip on her wrist before returning to her face.

He was definitely a Gregor, his eyes the same gold as Kenzie's but more . . . downright intense. And there must be something in the water in the Scottish highlands that produced drop-dead handsome giants.

"Winter, this is Eve Anderson," Kenzie said, giving Eve a slight tug to get her attention. "Eve, this is my sister-in-law, Winter, and my brother, Matt." He thrust her arm toward Matt. "Could you hold on to her for me, please, while I go see to my horses?"

Eve couldn't believe it! She was handed from one shackling grip to another so smoothly, she didn't even have time to pull free. Kenzie and Winter headed for the tractor trailer, leaving Eve to glare up at Matt Gregor—who was looking far too amused for her liking.

"What exactly am I stopping you from doing?" he asked.

"From going to save my sick, elderly mother from drowning."

"That mother?" he asked, nodding toward the path.

Eve turned to see Mabel walking in the dooryard and sighed in relief. Matt Gregor let her go and she reached her mother just as Mabel stopped beside the tractor trailer. They both watched as the driver opened the side door and Kenzie vaulted up the ramp and disappeared inside.

"Oh my," Mabel gasped. "Will you look at that."

Eve gawked in awe. Kenzie's horses were the size of elephants.

"Whatever you do, don't call them plow horses or ask why they never get put in a harness," Winter told Eve and Mabel as she came to stand with them. "The men get very defensive."

"What are they?" Eve asked.

"Drafts. The stallion is Percheron. One mare is a Clydesdale, the other two are Percherons." She held her hand out to Mabel. "Hi, I'm Winter Gregor, Kenzie's sister-in-law."

"This is my mother, Mabel Bishop," Eve said.

"Kenzie has told us all about the two of you," Winter continued. "It's very nice of you to stay and help him and Father Daar." She made a comical face. "Daar can be a bit of handful sometimes."

"He's been a perfect houseguest," Mabel said with a laugh, "as long as we keep him well fed."

Winter pulled them back several paces, out of the way. "The stallion can be a handful sometimes, too. It took Matt over an hour to load him, before he finally persuaded Curaidh that we were bringing him to Kenzie."

"Curaidh?" Eve said.

"It's Gaelic for *champion*."

All three women turned at the sound of large hooves stomping down the ramp. Eve pulled her mother back even farther when Curaidh reached solid ground, immediately arched his neck, and whinnied so loud it felt like the air shook. The stallion then shoved his nose into Kenzie, nearly lifting him off his feet, and gave a soft fluttering sound that ended in what Eve could only describe as a horse sigh.

The mares in the trailer grew restless, whinnying and fidgeting in place. With a laugh, Kenzie ran toward the barn, Curaidh prancing beside him with his tail and nose raised in the air. Matt led one of the mares down the ramp.

"If they don't work in harness, what do they do?" Mabel asked Winter, her face lit with excitement as Kenzie released Curaidh into the sturdy paddock he'd been working on for two days.

"We ride them," Winter said.

Mabel grew even more excited. "Just like the ancient highland warriors used to do! They rode magnificent animals just like these into battle."

Winter nodded. "That's what they were originally bred for."

"There are highland games down on the coast every summer," Mabel told her.

"I've been to them. Various members of my family go each year. They're true festivals, just like in the old days."

Kenzie indicated that Matt should release his mare into the pasture on the opposite side of the barn, and came jogging back to the trailer. This time when he emerged, a baby horse followed his mother down the ramp.

"That's Curaidh's firstborn," Winter said. "Kenzie hasn't named him yet."

Eve held out her hand when the colt skittered by. "He's beautiful."

Kenzie brought the mare over. "Ye like the little one?" he asked, taking hold of Eve's wrist to offer her hand to the colt. "Move slowly so ye don't spook him, and let him smell ye."

"Will his mother mind if I touch him?"

"No. She trusts me, so she'll trust you." He looked at Mabel, nodding her over also to meet the colt. "I will ask that you ladies not go near the stallion, though, unless I'm with you. He's not a pet, and he can get very aggressive."

"William already warned me about Curaidh," Mabel said.

Kenzie stiffened. "William?"

Mabel shot her gaze to his, then suddenly laughed. "Oh, don't mind me. I get names mixed up all the time. It must have been in Quebec, when I was a little girl, that a friend of my father told me never to turn my back on a stallion. Don't worry, Kenzie, I won't go *near* the barn if you're not around. And neither will Eve, will you?" she said.

"Nope," Eve assured him, her attention on the colt, who nuzzled her sleeve. She tried to pat him, but he flitted away, running behind his mother.

"I *so* need to use the bathroom," Winter whispered, holding her protruding belly. "My darling daughter has been dancing on my bladder for the last twenty miles."

"How exciting that you're having a girl," Mabel said. "Come on, Eve. Let's go make breakfast for everyone." She looped her arm through Winter's and led her toward the house. "You probably left Pine Creek quite early, and you must be starved."

Eve started to follow, but Kenzie caught her by the arm. "I noticed blueberries in the freezer when I stocked it the other day," he said. "Could ye make us some blueberry pancakes?"

She deliberately looked down at his hand on her arm, then smiled up at him sweetly. "The next time you manhandle me like you did earlier, I will break every finger in your hand."

He let her go, his eyes crinkling with amusement. "That's right, I forgot you took lessons on how to defend yourself." He rubbed the mare's nose. "I'll try to remember in the future."

"My mother is my responsibility, not yours."

He nodded. "I shall attempt to remember that, too. I believe there's also some maple syrup in the pantry. Could ye heat it up for the pancakes?"

Eve casually walked to the ramp, looked inside the trailer, then shrugged her shoulders. "Oops, it appears your brother forgot to bring you a cow—so I can't churn up a quick batch of butter while I'm at it." She gave him a cheeky grin and headed to the house.

Kenzie watched Eve flounce off, looking quite proud of herself, and he couldn't help but smile.

Matt came over to stand beside him. "Did I just hear her threaten to break your fingers?" he asked, his voice laced with disbelief.

"I can't decide if her papa did her a favor or not by having her take self-defense lessons when she was growing up," Kenzie said, absently scratching the mare's forehead. "I fear they've given her a false sense of security."

"Fiona said you're attracted to her."

Kenzie looked at his brother. "I can't be. There's danger heading this way, and I can't risk Eve getting caught in the middle of the storm."

"I've sensed the growing energy, too," Matt said, confirming Kenzie's gut feeling. "But I can't quite get my own energy wrapped around it."

"That's because it's coming for me. The old hag's not happy that I'm helping William."

"Speaking of William, Fiona also told me that he might be getting out of hand."

Kenzie chuckled. "Our little sister always was one for carrying tales. She used to tattle on us to Mama and Papa every chance she got. William is hardheaded, but it's nothing I can't handle." He looked at the house, then back at Matt. "The older woman, Mabel. Is there anything you can do for her? She's slowly losing her mind."

Matt touched Kenzie's arm. "I'm sorry, but no. Mabel's illness is part of a much larger picture, and it's not my or Winter's place to interfere." He also looked toward the house. "I suspect Mabel still has something to teach, most likely to her daughter."

Kenzie chuckled again. "It's proving to be a hard lesson for Eve." He had a sudden thought, and looked toward the woods. "Or maybe the lesson is for William. Mabel mentioned him by name earlier. I fear that beast has introduced himself to her, thinking it's safe to befriend her because she's touched in the head."

Matt settled an arm over Kenzie's shoulder and started walking to the barn, the mare following quietly and the colt playfully trotting around them. "You need only say the word, and I will have William Killkenny back in his natural time before he can snap his big ugly tail."

"Nay. I gave my word to help him, and I will. So how is everything back home? Baby Walker must be growing like a weed."

Matt shot Kenzie a loaded grin. "Jack Stone sends you his wishes, and hopes you're settling in well—way down here in Midnight Bay."

Kenzie gave a snort as he released the mare into her stall. "I hope his new son whizzes on his shirt every time he holds him."

Matt chuckled. "So what are you going to do about Eve Anderson?"

Kenzie got hold of the exploring colt, guided him into the stall, then gave his brother a questioning look. "What do ye mean?"

"Even if Fiona hadn't said anything, it's obvious that you're attracted to her. And Camry told Winter that you two were going on a date last night. I'm only trying to find out if you're going to act on that attraction or not."

"I told you, I can't. Getting involved with Eve could put her in danger."

"And *not* getting involved with her will put *you* in danger."

Kenzie crossed his arms over his chest. "How?"

Matt sighed. "You've been denied the life you deserve for hundreds of years, Kenzie. If you continue to deny yourself happiness, you're going to turn into a cranky old man like Daar. You can't be giving to everyone else and not take something for yourself. You're in the prime of your life; it's unnatural for you to remain single."

"But necessary," Kenzie growled. "I have no right to ask a woman to share my calling, when I don't even know all that it involves yet. Every soul that seeks me out will be bringing more storms my way—and it's already been proven that I can't protect what's mine."

Matt's eyes hardened. "You are not responsible for what happened to our family. If that were true, it would mean that *I'm* more guilty than you are. I was the eldest son, and I wasn't there, either. At least you killed the bastard who raped Fiona, and were there to bury her babe beside her."

"And then I walked away from Papa, when I was all he had left."

"To protect him!" Matt snapped. "You weren't a little boy standing at the edge of the woods anymore, watching the other children play. You'd grown into a powerful warrior, which made you a threat. The villagers would have come up the mountain as a mob, forced you to watch as they hanged Papa, and then hanged you with the same rope." Matt took hold of Kenzie's shoulders. "What could you have done? Fought every man in the village? By leaving again, you gave Papa a chance to live out his last days in peace."

"And if the same thing happens here?" Kenzie asked softly. "Suppose the people of Midnight Bay connect me to the strange things that will happen here in the coming years? How can I protect Eve and my children from becoming outcasts like we were?"

"Society has evolved in the last thousand years. People are more tolerant today, and being different doesn't make you a threat—it makes you interesting." Matt gave him a bear hug. "And I am Cùram de Gairn now, brother," he said softly next to his ear. "I have the power to intervene." He stepped away. "If you want Eve, then go after her with all you've got. From what I've seen so far, she's exactly the sort of woman you need by your side."

Kenzie blew out a heavy breath, saying nothing.

"Promise me you'll at least think about it."

"If you promise you'll name your daughter Fiona," Kenzie said, attempting to lighten the conversation.

Matt rolled his eyes. "I know our sister has put you up to that, because every morning for the last month, a red-tailed hawk has been sitting outside our kitchen window, suggesting that *your* future son should be named Kyle, after *her* son."

"Apparently being a powerful wizard carries no more weight with Fiona than being her big brother does," Kenzie said, tossing hay in to the mare.

Suddenly he looked back at Matt. "A son? She said I should name my *son* Kyle?" he asked softly, his gaze moving to the colt suckling from his mother.

Matt wrapped his arm over Kenzie's shoulder with a laugh and started out of the barn. "You even *think* about naming a horse after her babe, and the coming storm will seem like a spring shower compared to what Fiona will do to you. So tell me what Eve meant when she said I forgot to bring the cow."

"De Gairn," Father Daar said, out in the yard.

Matt gave Daar a slight bow. "Pendaär. You're looking well. The salt air seems to be agreeing with you."

Daar scowled so fiercely, it should have hurt his face. "Why haven't ye done something about the evil tempest headed our way?"

"I've tried."

The old priest thumped his cane on the ground. "Try harder, de Gairn."

"I have. Nothing works. The energy is on a completely different vibration than mine *or* Winter's. We've both tried."

Daar snorted. "If you'd make yourself a proper drùidh's staff from that fancy new tree of life Tom gave ye, maybe you'd have enough power to do more than just bubble water out of the ground and make babies." He pointed his gnarled finger at Matt. "The bones of your forefathers are rattling in their graves, moaning their disappointment of ye. If I still had my powers, *I'd* find a way to stop the tempest."

Kenzie sighed. Matt wasn't here an hour, and Daar was already baiting his old rival. Their two-thousand-year-old feud wasn't going to settle itself anytime soon. It probably didn't help that Matt had stolen Daar's protégé by marrying her and getting her pregnant.

"It isn't Matt's fight, old man, but mine," Kenzie said. "The tempest is coming because of William, and I'm the only one who can stop it. Come, let's go see what the women have cooked for us. I believe Eve is making blueberry pancakes."

Father Daar gave Matt one final glare, then headed toward the path leading down to the ocean. "I prefer William's company right now. At least *he* can appreciate that today is May Day. Ye didn't even think to put up a Maypole."

"Don't worry that he'll go hungry," Matt said with a laugh. "His pockets were bulging with pancakes. Come on, let's see if your housekeepers have taught Winter anything about cooking. I've been in a state of semi-starvation since I married her." Matt headed for the house. "That's the one thing I still can't get used to in this modern time. It seems that as society evolved, women started cooking less, in favor of sticking their noses in men's affairs."

"Speaking of which," Kenzie said, "do ye remember how Mama used to churn butter?"

"I never paid much attention. Why?"

"I've got to find a churn once I buy a milk cow, and teach Eve to make butter. I believe she's quite interested in the process and can't wait to try it."

Chapter Ten

Over the next week life settled into a routine for the human inhabitants of An Tèarmann, while its animal population started growing out of control. Kenzie bought a milk cow from a dairy farm over in Oak Harbor, and everyone in town was still talking about how he'd led the cow right down Route One and through the center of Midnight Bay to bring it home. When Eve had asked why he hadn't had the farmer trailer the poor thing, Kenzie had looked at her strangely and said it was a mere ten-mile walk.

Two piglets had appeared a couple of days later, along with four goats—one of which had the cutest little kid Eve had ever seen, while the other three were about to give birth any second. The day after that, two dozen laying hens and a pair of monstrous geese were exploring the dooryard when she and Mabel had arrived home from work.

The geese had immediately claimed the area surrounding the rusted old hay baler next to the driveway, and the first time Eve walked to the road to check the mail, she'd been chased back to the house by the honking monsters. When she'd complained to Kenzie, he'd placed a stick by the door and told her and Mabel that it was only a matter of establishing a pecking order—preferably with the humans on the upper end of the scale. Then he'd given Eve a wink, and suggested she try some of her fancy self-defense moves on them.

Two puppies of indiscernible lineage had arrived the day after the geese. Eve fell instantly in love with them, but she quickly learned they were outside dogs. They rarely even came near the house, too busy shadowing Kenzie's every step. Eve had assumed they'd be camping out with him, but they slept in the barn. Father Daar had explained that Kenzie was training them to guard the livestock.

An Tèarmann was fast becoming old MacDonald's farm.

And Eve started to see a golden opportunity in the animals, with all the milk and eggs accumulating in their fridge.

But the four dozen baby chicks she found in a box under the kitchen woodstove were a bit much. For such little balls of fluff, their constant collective peeping was loud enough to drive a person to drink!

"Kenzie claims they have to stay in the house," Father Daar said, sitting at the table and watching Mabel fix supper. "They're only two days old, and we have to keep them warm." He shook his head. "In the old days we left that chore up to the hens, but it seems everyone has to do things the hard way now. I went with Kenzie to the post office to pick them up this morning. Can you imagine, flying chickens halfway across the country? What is this world coming to?"

"Armageddon is just around the corner, Father," Mabel said with a laugh, dumping several cans of corn into a pot.

Eve set the chick she was holding back in the box with the others, then slid the box back under the woodstove. "I'm going to talk to Kenzie," she said, rinsing her hands at the sink. She grabbed the stick by the door. "He can set up a heat lamp for them in the barn."

"Good luck," Daar cackled as she walked outside.

Eve stood on the porch and looked around for Kenzie. She noticed that Curaidh wasn't in his paddock, which meant the stallion must be in his stall, which meant that *she* wasn't going in the barn.

She looked toward the road, the quickest way to Kenzie's campsite, and decided she wasn't up to battling the demon geese, either. So she sat down on the top step and waited for Kenzie to come to her.

It had been almost a week since their date, and he hadn't asked her out again. In fact, he acted as if their date hadn't even happened.

The night Winter had stayed with them—Matt choosing to sleep under the stars with his brother—Eve had subtly tried to get her to talk about Kenzie. That had turned out to be an exercise in futility, as Winter was as tight-lipped as Father Daar when it came to talking about their families.

Eve had a whole new appreciation for the word *clan*, having decided that Scotts were a close-knit, close-mouthed, mysterious people.

Kenzie came out of the barn carrying a large plank of wood under one arm and a thick post and long tool over the opposite shoulder, the puppies energetically dogging his heels. Eve propped her chin in her hands with a sigh, and watched him stride toward the road. Contrary to Maddy's claim that she acted like a prude, Eve liked sex very much. And during her four years in college, more than one frog had told her that she was very good at it.

Too bad Kenzie would never know what he was missing.

Eve straightened when he suddenly stopped and looked at her. "I want to talk to you," she said, standing up.

"Then come along," he said, heading for the road again. "You can help me and talk at the same time."

Eve ran down the stairs and quickly fell into step behind him, figuring he was a better goose deterrent than her stick. The puppies started going after her heels instead of his, sending her stumbling into Kenzie's back.

Without even breaking stride, he said something in a

language she didn't recognize, and the two pups immediately fell into step beside him.

"What did you say to them?"

"I told them to heel, in Gaelic."

She rushed to catch up, eyeing the geese standing beside the baler as quiet as church mice, not even daring to honk their disapproval at the small parade marching by them. Apparently Kenzie had established *his* place in the farm's pecking order.

Eve wondered which slot she occupied.

"You're teaching the dogs Gaelic? I thought it was a dead language."

"It's still spoken in parts of Scotland and Ireland."

He set down the board, the post, and the posthole digger beside the mailbox, then apparently commanded the pups to have a nap, because they flopped down on the grass and immediately closed their eyes.

Kenzie walked across the road. "Come tell me where ye think I should set the sign," he said, turning to face the driveway.

Eve walked over and stood beside him, seeing now that the board—painted a rich, dark green—had the words AN TÈARMANN carved into it, the gold leaf lettering glistening in the late afternoon sun.

"Maybe there?" she suggested, pointing to the opposite side of the driveway entrance. "That way it will stand out coming down the road. Did you make the sign?" she asked, walking over to lean it up against a tree to study it.

The name was set to the left, and there was a branch of a strange-looking tree carved into it, running across the bottom. A carved and painted bird was perched on the end of the branch, taking up the entire right side of the sign.

"A man named Talking Tom made it." He picked up the double-handled posthole digger. "He's . . . a relative of mine and Matt's."

"*Talking* Tom?"

"Tom used to live in an old cabin on Pine Lake, and he was in the habit of talking to himself when he walked the woods so that the bears would know he was coming."

"Why would he want the bears to know? Wouldn't that *attract* them?"

"Surprising a bear can have unpleasant consequences."

"The detail is amazing," she said, fingering the bird. "Is this a hawk?"

He drove the posthole digger into the earth on the opposite side of the driveway. "It's a red-tailed hawk."

"Why a hawk for An Tèarmann?" She picked up the long post and carried it over to him. "Why not a draft horse?"

"Because Tom knew I'm partial to red-tailed hawks. Set down the post; this will take me a few minutes. The hole has to be deep enough that the frost doesn't lift it. So what is it you wish to talk to me about?" he asked, dumping the dirt, then driving the two-bladed shovel into the ground again.

"To begin with, the chicks can't stay in the house, especially in the kitchen. It's unsanitary. And they never shut up. Why not set up a heat lamp for them in the barn?"

He drove the hinged shovels into the ground again. "I'll move them to one of the sheds once the nights grow warmer."

"Why not put them in the barn until then?"

He stopped digging. "Because between their dander and what they kick up from scratching their bedding, they make a dust that's not good for the horses to breathe."

Eve raised an eyebrow. "But it's okay for *us* to breathe?"

He started digging again. "I'll get you a heat lamp, and you can move them into the room behind the kitchen."

The back room was better than the kitchen, but still unacceptable. "The shelves don't have doors, and our pots and pans will get dusty."

"Give them a quick wash before ye use them, then."

Eve took a deep breath, reminding herself that she had to pick her battles. "The fridge is so full of jugs of milk, there's hardly any room for food. What am I supposed to do with ten gallons of raw milk?"

He stopped again and frowned at her. "Ye drink it and cook with it."

"Four people can't possibly drink that much milk. And it's unpasteurized, and unsafe to drink."

He stopped digging. "Unsafe how?"

"Bacteria grows in milk that isn't heated to a hundred and something degrees."

"I grew up on what you're calling raw milk," he said, shoving the blades into the ground a bit more forcefully. "Why don't you go to the library and find a book that explains how to make butter, and tomorrow I will buy a churn. What ye don't use, we'll feed to the piglets."

Eve inched closer. "I have a better idea. How about if, in exchange for my helping you tend the animals, you give me the surplus milk and eggs?"

He stopped digging again. "For what?"

"I've already researched making butter and goat's cheese, and I want to expand our business by selling baked goods. Mom makes wonderful bread and pastries, and I've been experimenting making herbal cheeses. We can also sell the eggs we don't eat. Mom's actually excited about the idea. She even suggested that Maddy's mom could bake pies for us to sell, too."

Kenzie eyed her for several seconds, then drove the spades into the ground again. "You may have what we don't need for our own use, but I'll continue taking care of the animals. I don't want ye working near Curaidh if I'm not around." He stopped again. "Is there anything else?"

Eve could barely restrain herself from jumping with joy. She had just gotten a new business off the ground without investing a penny! And she didn't even have to milk the cow and goats! Was she brilliant, or what?

"Eve? Is there anything else?" Kenzie repeated, looking at her strangely.

Eve realized she was grinning like the village idiot. But the *something else* she wanted to talk to him about wiped her grin away.

"What is it, Eve?"

"It's about Mom." She glanced toward the house. "You know how she's started taking walks every morning? Well, I don't know if her mind's getting worse, but she . . . she's been . . ."

"Just spit it out, lass."

"She's invented an imaginary friend," Eve blurted. "Either there's a vagrant camping on your property, or Mom goes for walks every morning and talks to someone who doesn't exist."

He started digging again.

Eve balled her hands into fists. "Don't you dare dismiss this as my overreacting. She's referred to a guy named William several times in the past week, saying he said this or that about something. Then she suddenly catches herself and tries to laugh it off, saying it must be something she read or that an old childhood friend had told her."

Kenzie drove the blades into the ground beside the hole and walked over to her. "I'm not dismissing your concern. I know it's hard to watch someone ye love leave ye bit by bit every day. But wish as you might that it isn't so, you can't stop Mabel's illness from progressing. There's great peace in accepting what is, Eve—and when ye quit fighting it, ye just might discover it's not nearly as tragic as you thought. Ye can be thankful this illness isn't physically painful for her; Mabel is bursting with life."

"She talks to someone who doesn't exist!" Eve fought the tears welling up. "She ordered some book, and I think it's for *him*. She truly believes William is real!"

"Okay, then," he said gently. "Tell me what you would like me to do."

"I want you to look around your property, and make sure William isn't some real man who she's meeting."

"I will do that. But if he isn't, then ye have to consider that he might simply be someone Mabel can confide her worries to every morning." He cocked his head. "Did ye not have imaginary friends growing up?"

"When I was *four,* not seventy-four."

"Aye," he said with a crooked grin. "I remember how Matt and I made ourselves wooden swords, because we had a whole army of invading trees to battle. We still have the scars from where they fought back."

Eve took a calming breath. Put that way, William didn't sound so bad. "One of Mom's doctors told me she might regress into her childhood, since those memories are so ingrained. Maybe as a child she had a make-believe friend she called William." She wiped her eyes, feeling foolish. "But you'll still check your property?"

"I will do it tonight." He picked up the post and dropped it in the hole, pushed some dirt around it, then stopped to look at her again. "And maybe you could try playing along whenever Mabel mentions William? If he's that important to her, wouldn't you prefer she share her friendship rather than feel she has to keep it a secret?"

A lump the size of her heart suddenly rose in Eve's throat. He was right, of course. All week—heck, for the last two months—she'd been so determined to keep her mother sane, she had actually been driving a wedge between them. Tears spilled down her cheeks, and Eve spun away and ran toward the yard.

Within seconds Kenzie's arms came around her, stopping her in her tracks. He held her facing away from him, and bent to whisper in her ear. "Go to the ocean, Eve. Sit at the water's edge and feel its strength. Your world is not coming to an end, though it may seem like it is. It's merely changing, and you must find the strength to change with it."

"And if I can't? She's all I have."

"Nay, that's not true. Whether ye want us or not, you have me and Daar. And ye have your good friend Maddy to see you through this. You also have the power of the entire universe at your command, if you would just open yourself to it. Go sit with the waves, and let their powerful energy wash through you. Stay as long as ye need," he said, opening his arms. "We'll keep your supper warming on the stove."

Eve ran toward the path leading to the ocean, barely able to see the ground because of her tears. Dammit, she didn't want anyone to help her through this—because she didn't want it to be true!

* * *

"Land sakes, the wind has picked up!" Ruthie rushed into Bishop's Hearth and Home, wrestling the door closed behind her. "The weatherman said it was going to be sunny for the next three days, but those dark clouds blowing in say differently. Oh, what are you reading?"

Eve closed her book so Ruthie could see the cover. "A romance novel that Maddy gave me."

"Oh, I love historicals," Ruthie said. She set the package she was carrying on the counter so she could pick up the book. "Especially Scottish romances." She flipped it over to see the picture on the back, and sighed. "I think I was born in the wrong time. What I wouldn't give to meet a real live highland warrior." She looked at Eve, her eyes twinkling. "And you're living with one, aren't you? Kenzie Gregor came in my store two days ago, and he could have stepped right out of these pages. That man is *hot*."

"Ruthie Graham, he's young enough to be your son!"

"I'm old, Evangeline, not dead. And I'll have you know that most of my romance customers are over sixty."

"That's because *everyone* in Midnight Bay is over sixty."

"So tell me," Ruthie whispered, leaning on the counter. "Is he as good as the hero in that romance novel?"

"Good?"

"In bed," Ruthie clarified. "Did you go weak in the knees the first time he kissed you? It's a wonder you can even stay awake here all day; I bet he keeps you up all night making love!"

Eve nearly fell off her stool. Ruthie was always saying outrageous things, but this was a whole new side to the woman.

"We're not a couple, Ruthie."

"Your mother can't stop talking about how wonderful he is. And after Alma Fogg said she saw the two of you having dinner at Rhapsody last Saturday night, the pool the grange women have going sent your odds soaring eight-to-one over Susan Wakely."

"They're placing *bets*? But we're not *living* together! Kenzie is camping out down by the ocean. Mom and I are just keeping house for him and the old priest. Trust me, there is nothing romantic going on between us."

"Are you crazy, Evangeline, or just plain dumb?" Ruthie asked, her eyebrows rising into her hairline. She slapped her hand on the counter. "Then get something going! And you better be quick about it, before Susan gets her claws into him and *she* moves into that house and kicks you and Mabel out on your duffs. So start batting those beautiful blue eyes of yours, woman, before you lose him!"

"My God, you're serious."

"Damn right, I am," Ruthie said with an authoritative nod. "You catch yourself a rich husband, and all your problems will disappear."

Eve wondered what planet she was from. Or was that what *century*? "And I suppose his being handsome and charming is just an added bonus," she drawled. "So I won't have to close my eyes and think of God and country when we make love."

"Now you're getting it," Ruthie said. "But you need to strike while the iron is hot."

Eve stood up and walked around the counter, figuring she better get Ruthie out of there before she strangled the clueless woman. "If you're looking for Mom, she's at the library searching for books on making butter."

"Oh! That's why I came over," Ruthie said, picking up her package. "Mabel's book finally came in."

Eve took the paper bag from her, surprised by how heavy it was, and continued walking toward the door. "Thanks for bringing it over. I'll give it to her as soon as she gets back."

Ruthie didn't follow. "Um . . . Mabel hasn't paid for it yet."

Eve spun around with a forced smile and headed back. "How much do we owe you?" she asked, reaching under the counter for her purse.

"With tax, it's fifty-eight dollars and thirty-five cents."

Eve straightened. "Sixty bucks? What is it, a dictionary or something?"

"I had to call six different distributors before I found one that had it," Ruthie said. "It's a special edition."

Eve opened her wallet, saw only a ten and two ones inside. She snatched a credit card out of her wallet with a sigh of defeat, and headed for the door again.

"I'll walk you back, so you can run my card through."

"I have to charge another four percent if you use a card," Ruthie warned her, pulling up her hood as she finally followed. "That's what the processing costs me, and the price I gave Mabel was for cash."

Eve stepped into a blast of wind so strong, it nearly yanked the door from her hand. "Holy cow, that's quite a gale!" she said, tugging the door closed once Ruthie made it outside. "And it's gotten dark all of a sudden."

"I told you it was starting to storm," Ruthie said over the howl of the wind.

Eve glanced up and down Main Street, noticing that very few people were out and about, and that vehicles passing through town had their headlights on. She held on to Ruthie as they rushed to her book and gift shop.

Ruthie went over to the ancient television behind the counter and turned it on. "Let's see what the weatherman is saying," she said, switching channels to the noon news out of Portland.

The weather forecaster stood in front of a map of New England. Perfect mid-May weather was visiting them for the next three days, he claimed; sunny days topping out in the fifties and clear nights in the high thirties. No frost predicted for the coast, though some mountain valleys might touch the high twenties. A storm was forming off the Carolinas, but was predicted to turn out to sea long before it reached the Gulf of Maine.

"Is that guy on drugs?" Eve asked. "We have gale force winds!"

Ruthie switched to a Bangor station. "Enjoy this stretch of fine weather, people," the forecaster said cheerily. "This is Maine, after all, and we know it won't last long."

"They're both on drugs," Ruthie said, just as her store's plate-glass windows shuddered with a strong gust of wind.

"Ring me up," Eve said, handing Ruthie her credit card. "I have to get back and make sure my awnings are secure. The last thing I need is for them to get ripped off my storefront."

Eve fought the wind back to her own store, took down her open flag, and made sure her awnings were cranked tightly closed. She finally went inside, shoved her card and the sales slip in her purse, then pulled Mabel's book out of the bag.

Her mother had paid sixty dollars for a book about *dragons*?

"My heavens!" Mabel said, stumbling through the door. "It was sunny when I went to the library, and when I came out, the wind was blowing so hard I took two steps back for every one forward. And it's so cold, it feels like it's going to snow."

Okay . . . time to try out Kenzie's suggestion that she play along with her mother's little delusion. "The book you ordered finally came in," Eve said, lifting it for Mabel to see the cover. "The artwork is beautiful, and the binding feels like real leather. I didn't know you were interested in dragons."

Mabel set her library books on a stove by the door and slowly walked over as she unbuttoned her coat, her gray eyes apprehensive. "I've just recently become interested in them."

Eve turned the book toward her, took a calming breath, and said, "Did you buy this for William?"

Her mother grew even more guarded. "William?"

"The friend you meet on your morning walks. Did he get you interested in dragons?"

Mabel clutched her coat to her chest. "You've *seen* William?" she whispered.

"No, but I'd like to. Maybe I could go with you one of these mornings, and you could introduce me to him."

"Oh, but I can't. I promised William I'd keep his existence a secret." Mabel stepped closer. "He thinks he's ugly, and doesn't want anybody to see him."

"Except you?"

She frowned. "He seems to be comfortable with me, for some reason. I think it's because I didn't scream the first time I saw him. He was sitting on a rock by the ocean, sunning himself." Her eyes brightened. "It was a glorious sight when he spread his huge wings and flew off. He's really a magnificent creature."

Eve's heart thumped painfully. "William has wings?"

Mabel started leafing through the pages of the book, then stopped and pointed to one of the drawings. "There, that's him. William looks almost exactly like this painting of an ancient Celtic dragon."

Eve stared down at the large, fierce-looking dragon. "If William looks like this," she said, picking her words carefully, "then he certainly is a magnificent creature." She looked at her mother. "Does he . . . talk to you?"

"Oh, yes. He has a wicked accent, though, and

sometimes I can't understand what he's saying because he uses words I've never heard." Mabel slipped off her coat, set it on the counter, and started leafing through the book again. "He wasn't born a dragon, you know. He can talk because he's really a man. His full name is William Killkenny, and he's a ninth-century nobleman from Ireland." She made a disgusted face. "An old witch turned him into a dragon when he asked her to move off his land because she was scaring the villagers."

"How terrible," was all Eve could think to say.

"You know why she turned him into a *dragon*?"

Eve slowly shook her head.

"Because in ninth-century Ireland, dragons were everyone's idea of the big, bad bogeyman, and the witch claimed she wanted William to experience what it was like for people to shun him." She tapped the book with her finger. "That's why I bought him this book. I want him to see that dragons are really beautiful beasts, and how in most societies they're revered as symbols of powerful magic." She closed the book and ran her hand over the padded cover. "I know it cost a lot of money, but I wanted to give William a sense of his worth. He has very low self-esteem."

Eve was totally, utterly speechless.

"I have to read this thoroughly before I give it to him, so I can figure out which element he is: fire, water, air, or earth."

Eve couldn't stop fixating on the word *bogeyman*. Why did it ring a bell?

She suddenly sucked in a silent breath. Maddy had said she thought she'd kissed a bogeyman the night they'd crashed the truck and gotten drunk.

"Um . . . exactly how big is William?" she asked.

"Around the size of a large horse." Mabel looked up and shrugged. "Maybe a little bigger than Curaidh."

"And you say he has wings, and can actually fly?"

"Oh, yes. He has huge, powerful-looking wings." Her mother giggled. "I think he actually blushed when I said they were like gossamer. They're silky and delicate-looking, but when he let me touch them, I realized they're quite tough."

"Y-you touched him?"

Mabel nodded. "Once he got really comfortable with me, he even started showing off a bit." She leaned closer and whispered, "He lit a twig on fire with just his breath because I asked if he could breathe fire."

Eve didn't know whether to burst into tears or scream. Either her mother was further gone than she thought, or *she* was the one who needed a reality check. Because honest to God, the dragon Mabel had pointed out in the book looked exactly like the animal Maddy had ditched the truck to avoid hitting.

She plopped down on her stool. "But dragons aren't real; they're mythological creatures," she said softly.

"I thought so, too," Mabel said, picking up the book and heading for the back office. "Until I met William." She stopped in the doorway. "Eve?"

"Yes?"

"You believe me, don't you, that William is real? I mean, you don't think that I'm just imagining him, do you?"

How in hell was she supposed to answer that? If she said yes, then she would be encouraging her mother's delusion. But if she said no, she could drive a wedge between them so deeply, it would split *both* their hearts in two.

"Never mind," Mabel said sadly, turning away. "I'll just ask William if you can meet him. Then you'll be able to tell me if I've lost all my marbles."

"Wait. You mean you're not sure yourself?"

Her mother rolled her eyes. "I've just spent the last ten minutes telling you I talk to a dragon, Evangeline. How can I *not* question my sanity?"

Chapter Eleven

"We have to go tend the animals," Daar said, turning from the window, his eyes dark with concern. "I doubt Kenzie will be back for a long time, so ye have to help me feed the livestock."

"Is Curaidh in the barn?" Eve asked.

"No, Kenzie rode out on him."

"In this weather?" She stood up from the table, where she'd been trying to skim the cream off several gallons of milk. "I'm sure he'll be back soon, Father. It's getting dangerous out there."

"He won't be back tonight." Daar grabbed his coat off one of the pegs. "And we need to milk the cow before she becomes uncomfortable."

Oh, goody. She couldn't wait to try that. "What makes you think he won't be back? Where did he go?"

"I don't know where he went, girl," he said, thumping his cane on the floor. "I'm not his keeper."

"Yeah, well, milking cows wasn't in my job description, either," she grumbled, grabbing her rain slicker off the peg. She walked to the living room as she slipped it on. "Mom? Daar and I are going to the barn to feed the animals. We might be gone awhile, because we also have to milk the cow."

Mabel looked up from her dragon book. "You want me to come help you?"

"No, you just sit tight. You have a flashlight handy, in case the power goes out?"

"Right here," Mabel said, nodding at the table beside her. "And you better take one with you."

"Don't worry, I will. If you get tired of reading, you can always skim cream."

Mabel laughed, waving her away. "I never tire of reading. Go milk your cow, Evangeline. You just might discover that farming suits you."

Eve walked back through the kitchen. "Okay, Father, brace yourself," she said, pulling up her hood and opening the door.

The wind ripped the screen door out of her hands. It was no longer blowing a gale; it felt like a hurricane! When Daar stepped out beside her, she looped her arm through his. "Hang on, we'll keep each other from blowing away."

They made it to the barn, and Eve pulled open the door and looked around. All the inhabitants seemed warm and cozy, and totally oblivious to the storm raging outside. They also appeared quite happy to see her and Daar, probably because, to them, humans meant supper. The goats started bleating, the mares stuck their heads out of their stalls and softly whinnied, and the piglets started squealing. The puppies jumped up from their bed of straw and started wagging their entire back ends.

Daar said something to them in what she assumed was Gaelic as he scurried away, only to return and shove a bucket of grain at her. "Go out to the coop and feed the chickens, and gather the eggs," he instructed. "And make sure ye latch the coop door behind ye. We don't want any fox in the henhouse tonight."

"No fox worth his pelt would go out in this weather," Eve replied, stepping into the storm.

By the time she fed the hens and started back to the barn, the cold rain was coming down so hard it stung her face. She'd have to warm her hands before getting up close and personal with the cow's udder. Goats she could handle, but cows could kick.

"What's next, Father?" she asked as she started to take off her slicker.

Daar tossed an armful of hay into one of the mare's feeding bin. "We need to water the animals. Kenzie ran a hose from the house until he can install a water line. Ye'll have to go turn it on at the house."

"Lovely," she growled, rezipping her slicker and heading back out into the storm. She ran to the house and tried to twist the spigot, only to discover the water was already turned on. She spun around with a curse, and nearly made it back to the barn before she slipped in the mud and fell flat on her back. The rain pelted her face, and she cursed again.

"What took ye so long?" Daar asked when she stumbled back into the barn, winded, wet, and wanting to strangle someone. "Here, this is for the goats," he said, handing her a small sack of grain. "We don't have to milk the nannies tonight; their babes can take care of that chore for us. When you're done feeding them, start filling all the water buckets."

It took them another twenty minutes to get everyone fed, watered, and bedded down for the night. And then Eve found herself sitting on a stool, her face about ten inches from a cow's belly, wondering if priests had divine permission to lie. She was damn sure Father Daar could milk the cow; she'd been watching him toss hay and spread straw with a pitchfork for the last half hour. His claim that he couldn't do this was an outright lie.

He just wanted to watch her make an *udder* fool of herself.

"Ye just give them a tender squeeze at the top, then urge the milk out with a gentle tug," he instructed, standing bent over behind her.

She took hold of the two closest teats, the cow jumped in surprise and kicked over the bucket, and Eve scrambled backward off the stool.

Daar cackled and set the bucket back into place. "Ye might want to warm up your hands first."

Damn. She'd forgotten. She sat down on the stool again, blew on her cupped hands, and eyed the cow—who was eyeing her back. "Does she have a name?"

"The farmer told Kenzie she was number six forty-three, just like that tag in her ear says. But I call her Gretchen, after Kenzie's mother."

"Why?"

"To annoy Kenzie."

"But he's your friend. Why would you antagonize him like that?"

"Because it's the only power I have left. You intend to talk all night, girl, or give poor Gretchen some relief? At the rate you're going, it'll be time to milk her again before you're done."

Eve slowly took hold of the teats again. Gretchen didn't flinch this time, and after a couple of false starts, Eve was able to get milk to come out.

It took her twenty minutes of tender squeezing and gentle tugging before Daar told her she could stop. Then she had to strain the milk through a cloth into a metal pail, and then carry the milk to the house while trying to keep Father Daar from blowing away.

And if her initiation into farming hadn't been adventurous enough, when Eve finally drifted off to sleep that night, her curiosity about where Kenzie was somehow transformed into them being together, in a spine-tingling, toe-curling, passion-charged embrace.

Then, *finally,* he kissed her.

And damn if she didn't go weak in the knees like a proper romance heroine!

"Eve. Wake up," her mother said, shaking her shoulder. "Wake up!"

Eve bolted upright into absolute darkness, broken only by the sharp beam of a flashlight. "What's wrong?"

"You have to go save Kenzie," Mabel said, pulling back the covers.

Eve shook off the last vestige of sleep as her feet touched the floor. "What happened? Did his horse throw him? How bad is he hurt?"

"I don't know how badly he's hurt. Just hurry." Mabel said, handing Eve a pair of pants, then going to her bureau and pulling out some jerseys. "You need to dress warmly."

"Where is he?"

"Somewhere on the cliffs on the west side of the point."

"Did you call 911?" Eve asked, pulling a turtleneck over her head, then pulling a sweater down over it. "Who found him? Is the person downstairs?"

"The electricity's out and so are the phones. There's no one to help us. Here's some heavy wool socks."

"If there's no one, then who found Kenzie?" Eve repeated.

"William dragged him onto a sheltered ledge well above the tide, then immediately came here to tell us."

Eve froze in the middle of zipping her pants. "William?"

"He had to run here, because the wind was blowing too hard for him to fly."

"Mom! You can't expect me to go out in this storm because an *imaginary friend* told you Kenzie is hurt."

Mabel pulled her into the hall. "We don't have time to debate my sanity, Evangeline. Kenzie could be dying! Come on, your boots are downstairs."

She was damned if she went, and damned if she didn't. A *dragon* had told her mother Kenzie needed help . . . but what if he really was hurt? She couldn't take the chance of not going to look for him.

Lightning flashed through the windows as they made their way to the kitchen, where a kerosene lamp was already lit. Eve sat down at the table to put on her boots while Mabel started filling a backpack with emergency supplies. Father Daar walked into the kitchen, and as soon as Eve straightened from tying her laces, he slid something over her head.

Eve looked down at her chest to see what appeared to be a gnarled ball of wood dangling from a leather cord.

"As loathe as I am to trust this to ye, I don't have much choice tonight," he said, pulling it out of her hand and letting it fall back against her sweater. "The less ye touch it the better. When ye find Kenzie he'll know what to do with it."

Eve stood up. "Did *William* also tell *you* that Kenzie is hurt?"

"Aye. The beast said he dragged him to the cliffs." Daar pointed a finger at her chest. "If Kenzie isn't awake when ye find him, just put that burl around his neck so that it's touching his skin."

Wonderful. She was dealing with *two* delusional people.

Mabel shoved Eve's rain slicker at her, then started pushing her toward the door. "You be careful on the rocks. They'll be slippery."

"I should drive into town and get help," Eve protested. "I can't possibly get Kenzie back here all by myself, if he's hurt."

"He'll get himself here, once ye get that burl on him." Daar grabbed her sleeve. "Give this to him, too," he instructed, handing her an unusually heavy pen that also appeared to be made of wood.

He was sending her to save Kenzie with a ballpoint pen and a knot of wood?

She had to be dreaming.

Eve zipped the pen into her pocket as Daar gave her sleeve another tug. "Ye might hear and see some frightening things out there tonight, girl, but ye just ignore them. Ye should be safe as long as ye keep that pen on you."

"And once I give it to Kenzie?" she asked, alarmed by how serious he was, hoping this was only a dream.

"Kenzie will keep ye safe, then."

If Kenzie was hurt, how was he going to save her from . . . frightening things?

"I still think I should drive into town and get help."

"William told me there are trees down all over the place." Mabel settled the backpack over Eve's shoulders, then handed her a powerful spotlight. "You can do this, Evangeline. Remember how strong you are."

Eve stopped with her hand on the doorknob. "Um . . . where exactly *is* William right now?" she asked, remembering the creature she and Maddy had seen.

"He went back to guard Kenzie." Mabel gave Eve a quick kiss on the cheek. "You be careful, Evangeline," she whispered. "And be brave. I love you."

"I love you, too, Mom."

Eve finally stepped onto the porch, where the wind-driven rain nearly knocked her off her feet. She grabbed the porch post for support and panned the spotlight beam around the yard. Sure enough, one of the large trees at the end of the driveway was down, tangled in a mess of power lines. She turned the beam on the barn. Everything there seemed normal but for all the branches littering the ground.

What in hell was she doing out here?

Oh, right. She was rescuing an idiot who went horseback riding in a raging storm.

Eve made her way down the stairs and ran across the yard, dodging debris and getting battered by the wind as she aimed for the path that led to the ocean. Once she reached the bushes, they gave enough shelter that she could at least walk without feeling like a drunkard.

She froze when she suddenly realized something wasn't right, and she shut off her spotlight. The lightning was all wrong. It didn't flash like normal, but slowly throbbed, making the turbulent sky appear as if it were *breathing*. And there was an eerie brown tinge to it, instead of the clean, brilliant white of normal lightning.

There also wasn't any thunder. All she could hear was the wind growling like an angry animal as it whipped the bushes around her.

Eve reached into her pocket and touched the pen Daar had given her, which *should* keep her safe. What kind of storm had lightning but no thunder, and didn't show up on weather radars?

Eve tilted her head back to let the rain wash over her face. "I promise I'll never utter another cuss word if you just let me wake up now."

She was suddenly shoved from behind. She stumbled forward with a scream, then spun around with her spotlight raised, ready to strike back.

Only there was no one there.

She snapped on the light and scanned the bushes. The branches next to where she'd been standing were spread wide, and there was . . .

Oh shit, what had made that deep gouge in the mud!

She spun around and ran toward the ocean. Too terrified to glance back to see if she was being pursued, Eve finally broke into the open and came to a sliding stop.

"Oh my God," she whispered. In all of her thirty-one years, she'd never seen the ocean so angry or the waves so high. They were cresting halfway up the trees on the island! The lightning, still strobing in a breathing rhythm, made the frothy spray dingy as the wind whipped it toward her.

"Damn," she muttered, snapping her gaze west. If Kenzie really was on those cliffs, he was in danger of being swept into the sea.

She started along the grassy lip of the shoreline, but walking soon grew treacherous as the path gained altitude when she neared the cliffs. More than one plume of seawater knocked her to the ground, and she was forced to move slightly inland to avoid getting swept into the sea.

She scaled a protruding ledge and had to climb over several broken trees, then was forced to work her way down to within feet of the turbulent waves when she came to a wide fissure in the granite. She stopped and cupped her hand to her mouth. "Kenzie!" she shouted. "Kenzie!

She listened for an answer, aiming her spotlight along the jagged cliffs. Hadn't her mother said something about a sheltered ledge?

"Kenzie!"

Only the eerie growl of the wind and the roar of crashing waves answered her. Eve gritted her teeth. What if she found Kenzie floating facedown in the surf, his lifeless body being battered against the rocks? That image was almost as bad as the one she'd had of finding her mother like that, and Eve started shaking uncontrollably.

She lifted her hand to her racing heart. Kenzie's calm certainty that day, that she would have pulled herself together eventually, was all that kept her from panicking now.

"I can do this. I can do—"

Something crashed down the cliff behind her. Eve spun around with a scream, the beam of her spotlight illuminating several rocks the size of basketballs tumbling into the sea. She pressed into the cliff, aimed her light at the ledge above her, and caught a glimpse of . . .

Holy shit, that looked like an alligator tail!

She snapped off the light. If someone—or some-*thing*—was up there, she didn't need to advertise her location. She started making her way toward where she hoped the ledge was, determined to find Kenzie. Even being with an unconscious body was better than being out here alone.

She felt her way toward the tallest part of the cliff, the pulses of lightning the only thing allowing her to see that she wasn't stepping into nothingness. But what really sent a chill up her spine was that the closer she got to where she thought the ledge was, the stronger the wind seemed to blow, the louder and angrier it growled, and the higher the waves reached.

A rogue wave slammed her up against the rocks and she was nearly sucked into the sea, the water pulling at her like a hundred grasping hands.

Eve swore as it stole her spotlight, cursing herself for being here, and cursing Kenzie for being an idiot.

Then her hand suddenly touched something soft—and warm!

"Please be Kenzie. *Please* let it be him," she prayed.

She touched cloth, then flesh again—definitely warm.

"Yes!" she cried, heaving herself onto the ledge just as another wave reached up and snatched at her legs. She kicked frantically, scrambling over Kenzie's body to the sound of a shrill, bloodcurdling scream.

Eve flopped back against the ledge and stared out at the ocean, panting to catch her breath, her quivering legs lying over Kenzie's thighs. The lightning strobed wildly in deep angry reds now, the ocean spray looking like tongues of fire lashing up into the sky.

But the rain wasn't pelting her anymore, and Eve realized she was under a rocky outcropping just deep enough to keep out the wind and rain. She undid her hood and pushed it back, then wiggled around to slide off her backpack. She jumped when something cold and sharp pricked the back of her thigh.

"What the . . ." She reached down beside Kenzie's body and touched metal, snatching her hand back and sticking her finger in her mouth, tasting blood. "Let's not do that again, shall we?" she muttered, shrugging out of her slicker more carefully.

Then she scrambled to her knees and knelt beside him, careful not to cut herself on whatever was lying beside him. "Okay, big guy, let's see if we can't wake you up." Eve cupped his face. "Nap time's over, Kenzie. Come on, open your eyes."

He appeared dead but for his shallow breathing, and she worriedly gave his cheeks a gentle slap. "Come on, Kenzie—wake up."

Still nothing.

Eve unzipped the pack and felt around inside it, and touched something she instantly recognized. "Thank you, Mama!" she cried, pulling out a headlamp.

She clicked it on, then settled it on her head and looked down at Kenzie again. "My God," she whispered on an indrawn breath. "Just look at what you've done to yourself."

He was bruised and battered and a bloody mess. He was also naked but for the length of plaid wool wrapped around his hips, across his chest, and over one shoulder.

He was wearing a kilt?

His legs were bare but for the blood oozing out of multiple scratches and cuts, some of them deep enough to need stitches. The beam of her headlamp flashed off something metal running along his left leg, and she panned up the length of what looked like a sword, which was heavily speckled with dried blood.

His? Or someone else's?

Or some*thing* else's?

Her hands shook as she held open her pack. She pulled out a blanket, and . . . a jar of white liquid and a bag of cookies?

Her mother had sent her after Kenzie with milk and cookies?

Eve shone the light in the pack again. "Where in hell is the first-aid stuff? Bandages? Gauze? *Something* to stop his bleeding?"

She turned back to Kenzie, carefully slid her hand behind his neck, and lifted his face up to her chest while she placed the empty pack under his head.

The cave suddenly filled with blinding green light, and Eve straightened in shock.

The green light just as suddenly disappeared.

She glanced out at the ocean and saw the lightning was now pulsing between angry red and its original dingy brown.

She grabbed her slicker and laid it along Kenzie's right side, then carefully took hold of his right shoulder and hip and pulled him toward her. Holding one hand on his back to keep him against her, she tucked the slicker under him as far as she could.

The cave filled with brilliant green light again.

She straightened, and the green light disappeared as she carefully rolled him onto the slicker. "There—that'll keep the ground from stealing your body heat." She then took hold of the wool plaid and started to spread it over his torso, but suddenly stopped.

The cuts on his right side were gone!

She trailed her fingers over the perfectly healthy skin, blinking in disbelief. She'd swear his ribs had been covered in cuts.

He groaned, and Eve snapped her gaze to his face, the beam of her light obediently following. "Oh my God," she whispered, touching his cheek. His face didn't have a scratch on it!

She bent over to cup his head in her hands, and as the wood dangling from her neck touched his chest, the cave filled with blinding green light again.

She bolted upright and the green light disappeared.

"That's it!" she cried, grasping the burl—and instantly releasing it when she felt it softly vibrating, emitting a heat that made her whole arm tingle. "The light is coming from the wood," she whispered in bewildered amazement.

Was that why Daar had told her to put the burl around Kenzie's neck? To heal him?

But it was a piece of *wood.*

Being careful not to let it touch her face as she lifted it over her head, she held it in the beam of her headlamp, untied the leather cord, then placed it on Kenzie's chest.

But just as she started to tie it around his neck, another angry, bloodcurdling scream pierced the night, mixing with her own scream of terror as a towering wave rose up and curled toward them.

In a blur of movement, Kenzie's hand closed over the burl and he rolled toward her, pinning her against the back of the ledge just as the giant wave crashed over them.

"Christ, woman, would ye quit your screaming," he muttered, his lips brushing her cheek as the wave receded. "You're making my head pound."

"You ungrateful jerk," she cried, trying to wiggle free. "Ow! Your sword is digging into my leg—get off me!"

He rolled onto his back with a groan, still clutching

the wooden burl to his chest. "Tie it around my neck," he said in a pained growl. "And shut off that light. You're blinding me."

"You are so bossy," she grumbled, shutting off her headlamp and reaching around his neck to tie the cord.

"Get off my sword," he said, rolling toward the ocean. Apparently satisfied that nothing was climbing up the cliff, he sat up and laid his sword across his lap, the pointed end safely pointing away from her.

"How did ye get here?" he asked.

"I ran, crawled, and climbed through this freaky storm."

"How did ye know where to find me?"

"William came to the house and told Mom that he'd left you on this ledge."

He stiffened and stared at her.

"You remember William, don't you? Mom's imaginary friend? Well, you can quit looking for a vagrant hanging around your farm, because it turns out he's not a guy at all, but a dragon."

Kenzie still said nothing.

"Mom said he's about the size of your horse, and that he has huge gossamer wings and can fly. He can talk, too, because he's really a ninth-century nobleman that some witch turned into a dragon. And you might be interested to know that Father Daar also talks to him." Eve suddenly remember the pen. "Oh, Daar gave me something else to give to you," she said, groping on the floor for her slicker.

She found the pen and handed it to him with a snort. "He sent me after you with a knot of wood and a pen. Mom sent you milk and cookies. Personally, I think a first-aid kit would have been a lot more helpful—because after what I've been through tonight, I could *really* use some aspirin!"

"What have ye been through, exactly?"

Eve finally began to shake with reaction. "You mean beside spending the last hour in a violent storm that has lightning but no thunder and doesn't show up on radar?" Her laugh was close to hysterical. "Well, I also got chased by Maddy's bogeyman; then he threw a bunch of huge rocks down at me. And I swear to God the ocean was trying to kill me. First by trying to drown me with several well-aimed waves, then by grabbing my legs and trying to suck me off the cliff."

Kenzie gently put his hand over hers. "Yet ye kept searching for me."

She sniffed. "Only so I could tell you in person that I'm not working for you anymore. Dealing with a delusional mother is quite enough." Then she pulled herself upright and pointed at his pen, which had started glowing softly when he'd closed his fist around it. "So please wave your magical little wand and zap me back home."

He stiffened again. "Ye know about the magic?"

Eve sighed. "You were on death's door five minutes ago, and now you don't have a scratch. That seems pretty darn magical to me."

He looked down at the pen and pressed the clicker.

A beam of intense white light shot out the end, exploding into the ledge floor and sending up a spray of tiny pebbles.

Eve scrambled back with a squeak. "Watch where you point that thing!"

"I'm sorry; I'm still quite groggy." He wedged the pen into a crack so that its beam shone across the lip of the ledge. Then he laid his sword between himself and the beam, unfastened the thick leather belt at his waist, and started unwinding his wool plaid. "Take off your clothes, Eve."

"In your dreams," she said, her eyes wide.

"I need to lie down before I pass out, and you're soaked to the skin," he explained.

She still didn't move, and he sighed. "You can either undress yourself, or I will," he said, his patience obviously waning. "Your choice."

The pen was giving enough light for Eve to see he was deadly serious. Okay, she *was* soaking wet and half frozen, so hypothermia was a real risk, but she was damn tired of his bossing her around.

"Is the word *please* even in your vocabulary?" she muttered, unlacing her boots and taking them off. She pulled the hems of her sweater and shirt out of her pants but then stopped, remembering she hadn't put on a bra. "Turn around," she commanded.

"Finish undressing, Eve. I want to see if you're hurt."

"I'm not hurt."

Before she could even scream again, he pulled her

sweater and shirt off over her head. And before she could retaliate for that indignity, he spun her around, pinned her arms to her sides, and unzipped her jeans.

"You can rail at me tomorrow, once I've gotten you home safe and sound. But tonight ye must do exactly as I tell you, when I tell ye," he said, pulling her pants off.

Eve closed her eyes and went utterly still as he ran his hand up her legs, over her belly and ribs, then along her arm and shoulder to her face. It wasn't being naked that bothered her so much as being so helpless to stop him.

He brushed a tear off her cheek. "Don't cry, Eve. I'm sorry, but I had to assure myself ye weren't hurt before I pass out. Come on," he said, turning her to face him. He covered her first with the blanket she'd brought, then with part of his wool plaid, cocooning her against him.

"I want to get dressed," she muttered into his chest.

"Your clothes are wet, and we need to share our body heat. Try to get some sleep. You're safe now."

She wanted to argue, but she knew he was right. And since she was cold and he was putting out more heat than a woodstove at full roar, it wouldn't kill her to lie in his arms for a while.

And maybe, if she was really lucky, she would wake up back in her bed.

Chapter Twelve

Despite being utterly exhausted and feeling almost drunk from the burl medicine, Kenzie couldn't seem to fall sleep. He knew the pen Matt had made for him would keep them safe from the wickedness embedded in the storm. And his wounds were healing and his strength would return soon, thanks to the burl made from the Tree of Life that Daar had been hoarding since losing his powers.

But, Eve was keeping him awake. Just thinking of her battling the storm to find him made his blood run cold. She had to have been terrified, yet she hadn't turned tail and run like a lot of supposedly brave men he'd seen on the battlefield.

Her fearlessness both humbled and terrified him.

He wanted her more than ever. She felt so delicate and vulnerable in his arms, yet she trusted him enough to fall asleep despite all she had seen and heard tonight. What he wouldn't give to make love to her, to be able to claim her as his.

Kenzie sighed as he felt the burl mending his wounds, his muscles slowly relaxing and his eyelids growing heavy. There was no more powerful drug than the magic, and he could think of nothing more right than sharing it with Eve tonight. He'd been granted his wish of dying one last time as a man, but he'd been so many different animals for so many hundreds of years, he'd forgotten how deeply a woman could stir his senses.

And so it was with the yearning of a man too long alone, Kenzie finally fell sleep holding Eve securely against his heart.

When Eve opened her eyes, the first thing she saw was an impressively solid chest just inches from her nose. Right—she wasn't in her bed; she was on the ledge in a raging storm, plastered against a man whose gorgeous body should be outlawed in all fifty states.

Acting on impulse, Eve pressed her lips to Kenzie's chest.

His arms around her tightened.

Encouraged, she touched her tongue to his nipple.

His chest expanded on an indrawn breath.

So far, so good—he wasn't pushing her away or protesting. There was something rather provocative about pestering a man in his sleep—especially one whose body made her fingers itch to touch it. But since he was holding her so tightly, the only thing she could reach was his . . . his . . .

The moment she wrapped her hand intimately around him, Kenzie rolled on top of her and covered her mouth with his.

And Eve lost all control of the situation.

Her dream man pinned her hands over her head and spread her thighs to nestle intimately against her as she rubbed her naked body provocatively against his.

Sliding her legs up the length of his, she kissed him back. When he finally lifted his mouth, she opened her eyes to find him staring at her so intensely, an alarm bell went off in her head. Maybe this wasn't such a good idea after all—he appeared downright . . . *focused.*

With one hand holding both of hers, he gently trailed his other hand over her cheek and down her neck, his gaze following its sensuous journey.

Eve shivered in delight, the alarm bell turning to a crescendo of anticipation as to where that hand was headed. When he gently closed it over her breast she gave a soft cry of approval, then cried out again when his thumb brushed her nipple. She arched into his touch, using her legs to pull him more intimately against her.

He took her nipple in his mouth and suckled, and Eve freed her hands to knead his powerful shoulders. He made a raw sound, moved on to her other breast as he poised himself against her entrance, and flexed his hips.

His maddeningly slow invasion started the alarm bell faintly ringing again. But seeing how his tongue was doing such wonderful things to her nipple, Eve stroked her hands down his back to cup his buttocks, and pulled him deeper with a moan of pleasure.

He wove his fingers through her hair to position her head for another assault on her mouth, and swallowed her gasp when he seated himself fully inside her. He drew back and she gave a moan of protest, but he returned to thrust even deeper.

Suddenly overwhelmed with emotion, Eve nearly wept at how hot and solid and amazingly good he felt so deep inside her. She must have sounded more distressed than joyous though, because he brushed his fingers through her hair, kissed her forehead, and soothingly whispered something in Gaelic.

Eve sucked in ragged breaths as he returned to his slow, deliberate thrusts, which turned her boneless as she opened to him, then gently wound her into a coil of sexual tension.

He lifted himself up, every muscle in his body humming with barely controlled restraint. And with his gaze locked on hers, he reached down between them and stroked her intimately, at the same time increasing the tempo and depth of his surges.

Eve suddenly shattered into a hundred million pieces. Her fingers dug into his shoulders and she bucked into his thrusts, shouting his name as waves of molten pleasure shot through her.

He went utterly still, threw back his head with a masculine groan, and pulsed deep inside her.

Though he was careful not to crush her when he collapsed, she still had to take shallow breaths because of his weight.

After he finally stirred and slipped out of her, he settled behind her and spooned them together. Then he growled something that sounded like "mine" as he cupped her breast and pulled her tightly against him.

Mine? Was that Gaelic for *good lay,* or maybe *thank you*? Or had he been speaking English?

Should *she* say something?

Eve reached down and patted his thigh he'd thrown over hers. "Mine," she repeated, imitating his burr.

He gave a grunt as he tightened his hand on her breast, then started gently snoring.

Eve's mouth curved in a grin, which turned into a gasp. They hadn't used any protection!

How could she have been so dumb? It was Human Nature 101: when a naked man wakes up to find a naked woman fondling him, hot, passionate lovemaking *will* ensue!

Her body still tingling with lingering pleasure, Eve stared at the shadow of their entwined bodies on the rock wall. Talk about facing an awkward morning after—what should she say to Kenzie when he woke up?

Should she point out that they hadn't used protection? Or should she say nothing at all, and hope he thought it was just an erotic dream?

Ha—what were the chances he wouldn't remember having delicious, mind-blowing sex?

And when he realized they hadn't used protection, would he blame her? She *had* started it, after all. He'd merely gotten her out of her wet clothes, wrapped her snugly up in his wool plaid and warm body, and very chivalrously gone to sleep. It certainly wasn't his fault she couldn't seem to keep her hands off him.

Please let this be a dream, she silently pleaded, listening to the storm slowly retreat as mysteriously as it had arrived.

But as the first hint of daybreak finally crept over the horizon, Eve knew nothing about last night had been a dream. She had definitely made love to Kenzie Gregor. And his strange wood burl and glowing pen and sword were all very, very real.

Kenzie woke up to find a very naked Eve spooned against him, his hand cupping her breast. For the first time in more years than he could remember, he flushed like a young boy caught touching something he had absolutely no business being near.

Thank God she couldn't know what he was thinking, because the remnants of his drug-induced dream lingered so strongly, he could practically taste the sweetness of her lips on his. His need to feel her surrounding him had been so great, he felt as if the dream image of their lovemaking was *real*.

"Are you awake?" he asked softly.

"Mm-hmm." She remained as still as a statue.

He knew she wasn't moving because she was mortified. In fact, he'd bet his best dagger she was blushing all the way to her toes.

He removed his hand from her breast. "Eve, I'm sorry about last night, but we needed to stay warm." He hesitated, but she didn't respond. "I was exhausted, and it was like I was drunk or something. I'm sorry I manhandled ye to undress you."

She still said nothing.

He sighed. "I imagine Mabel and Daar are worried about us. I'll turn around so you can get dressed, and then I'll help ye up the cliff and get you safely headed home."

"You're not coming?"

"I have to find Curaidh first."

He gently hugged her to him. "Thank you for coming after me last night, Eve," he whispered against her ear. "It was amazingly brave of you. You likely saved my life."

She seemed to be holding her breath.

It was quite possible she was still in shock about all that happened last night. It wasn't every day that a modern witnessed the magic firsthand, and rarely both sides of it at once. Dark magic could be terrifying to the hardiest of souls, and people often preferred to deny what they couldn't explain. As for what she might be wondering about the burl and his pen . . . at least she knew there was a powerful counterbalance to the darkness, and on which side he and Daar stood.

She shifted as if testing his grip. He released her and

rolled away, sitting up to face the gently swelling ocean. As she scrambled to put on her clothes, Kenzie wrapped himself in his plaid while trying to decide how to explain the magic to her.

Or if he should at all.

Maybe it would be wiser to wait until *she* broached the subject. Or maybe he should ask Greylen and Grace MacKeage to come for a visit, and let them talk to her. They'd had plenty of experience explaining the magic to several modern sons-in-law.

"I'm ready," Eve said.

Kenzie grabbed his sword and stood up, biting back a curse when he saw how dirty and torn her clothes were. He picked up the scabbard to his sword, slid the blade into the leather, then settled the harness over his shoulders to ride on his back.

He wanted to roar. He had come to care for Eve far more than was wise, but they were from two different worlds. And though he was trying to adapt to this one, he knew Eve might never be able to adapt to his.

He bent down to pick up the jar of milk and bag of cookies, and saw the thick cream floating on the top—a grim reminder that if he ever did ask Eve to love him, she would try *too* hard to adapt. She was one of those all-or-nothing women, and if she loved a man, she would give him everything or die trying.

And in his line of work, that was a very real possibility.

Kenzie tucked the cookies in his plaid, then opened the jar and drank the milk.

Eve's eyes widened.

He held the jar out to her with a smile. "Want some?"

She quickly shook her head.

He finished off the milk, then held the jar out to her. "Put this in your pack. Wrap the blanket around it so it won't break, and don't forget your little flashlight."

He turned toward the ocean as she scrambled to obey him, whatever courage she'd had last night seeming to have deserted her this morning. He didn't like seeing her this way, but considering what horrors she must have witnessed trying to find him, he did understand. And he knew she'd eventually find her courage again, because when push came to shove, Eve Anderson didn't know the meaning of cowardice.

Kenzie studied the ledge they were on, his blood running cold when he saw the sheer drop to the ocean. How in hell had she made it up here in the dark, in the middle of a storm?

"That was quite a climb you made last night," he said.

She leaned forward enough to look over the ledge, then immediately pressed back against the granite, her skin turning white.

It was a good thing she hadn't been able to see where she was going last night. He scanned the granite on both sides of the ledge, then decided they'd be better off climbing up than down. He pulled his pen out of the crack where he'd wedged it, clicked it off, and tucked it in his belt.

He moved to the left, found a promising route, and held out his hand. "I want you to go up ahead of me."

When she hesitated, he took the backpack out of her hands and lobbed it up over the top of the ledge. Then he pulled her in front of him, grabbed her waist, and lifted her up. "Start climbing," he told her, letting go as soon as she got a toehold. "I won't let you fall."

She scrambled up the ledge like a billy goat, and by the time he reached the top she was slipping the backpack over her shoulders as she studied the destruction around them. Branches littered the ground, and whole trees had been uprooted. The heavy rains had created deep gouges in the soil, even displacing rocks.

"I don't remember much of what happened last night after you found me and put the burl around my neck. But did you say someone threw rocks at you?"

She glanced at him in surprise, then looked away. "It must have been a landslide," she said, heading inland to avoid the deep fissures the rain had carved into the bank.

He followed, looking around for Curaidh, occasionally giving a whistle and calling out in hopes the horse was near. There was a good chance the stallion was standing outside the barn, waiting to be let in his stall.

Or lying dead under some tree, or floating in the ocean.

When they reached the path leading into the bushes, Eve suddenly stopped, apparently hesitant to go any farther.

Kenzie vaguely remembered her saying something last night about a bogeyman trying to kill her. He moved past her into the low-growing spruce and alders. "I'll walk ye back," he said. "With luck, maybe Curaidh is home."

He heard her sigh of relief as she fell into step behind him, and he cursed under his breath when he saw how she kept scanning the bushes, as if she expected something to jump out and grab her.

Dammit, he wanted his smart-mouthed Eve back!

When they reached the dooryard, she ran ahead of him and disappeared into the house.

Daar came outside and made his way toward him.

"Thank God she found ye in time," the old priest said, falling into step as Kenzie headed to the barn. "Curaidh came back about an hour ago. I let him in his stall. He's got a gash on his right flank, but other than that he seems fine. Did ye send that old hag back to hell where she belongs?"

Kenzie stopped with his hand on the door handle. "She's a lot more powerful than either of us anticipated, and she's very angry that I'm helping William. I'm afraid we haven't seen the last of her or her minions. Unless Killkenny can lift the curse himself, this won't be over until either he's dead or I am."

"Why won't he just listen to you?"

"Because he's hardheaded and too goddamned proud to lower himself to do what he must. He considers opening his heart to anyone to be a sign of weakness, and he'd rather remain cursed than appear weak."

"Then have your brother send him back," Daar growled. "And let us finally be rid of the blackguard. Ye can't help someone who isn't willing to help himself, and he's putting us all in danger. The old hag nearly killed ye last night!"

"And Eve," Kenzie said, looking toward the house. He lifted the pine burl off and handed it back to Daar. "Thank ye for sending this to me, and for the pen. I only wish you hadn't gotten Eve involved."

"I had no choice." Daar gave Kenzie a rare smile. "She obviously met the challenge."

"Aye, but at what cost?"

Chapter Thirteen

Eve nearly ran over Father Daar as she rushed to get inside. Her mother spun around from the counter with a cry of relief and hugged her fiercely.

"Oh, Evangeline, I've been so worried. This has been the longest night of my life." She stepped away, wiping her eyes with her apron. "I knew you probably wouldn't be back until morning, but I kept picturing all sorts of terrible things. Daar kept telling me to quit fretting, but he was just as nervous." She took hold of Eve's shoulders to inspect her. "Are you okay?"

"I'm fine, Mom. I don't think I have a scratch on me."

"And you obviously found Kenzie in time." Mabel squeezed her shoulders. "I'm so proud of you, Evangeline, for going out in that storm like that. Did you see William? Did he lead you to Kenzie?"

"No, I can't say that I saw him," Eve said, stepping away to shrug out of the backpack. "Thanks for thinking of the headlamp, by the way. It came in quite handy," she said, turning to hang her slicker—which had more than one tear in it—on the peg.

She turned back to her mother. "I think I'm going to take a long hot bath and go to bed. As you can imagine, I'm a bit tired," she added with a forced smile.

"Sorry, you can't take a bath yet. The electricity's still out." She waved at the counter. "I kept busy last night by turning all that cream into butter, but now I need water to rinse out the buttermilk before I mold it into blocks. Daar said if I don't, it will turn rancid."

Relieved that her mother wasn't asking questions about last night, Eve looked in the three large bowls. "Good Lord, how much butter did you make?"

"There must be eight or ten pounds there," Mabel said, coming up beside her. "Daar also explained how to cook the buttermilk I don't use with oats to feed to the piglets. That man is a veritable fount of information."

"I'm sure he is," Eve said, covering a yawn with her hand. "I'll just go straight to bed, then. You should try and get some sleep, too, Mom. The power will come back on soon."

"Where's Kenzie?" Mabel asked, glancing toward the door.

Eve stopped in the living room doorway. "He's out looking for Curaidh."

"But the horse showed up here over an hour ago. Daar

just opened the barn door and he ran straight into his stall."

"Then I'm sure Kenzie is checking him for injuries."

"Was Kenzie very badly hurt when you found him?"

"Um . . . I didn't see a scratch on him this morning."

"Thank goodness," Mabel said, taking off her apron with a sigh, suddenly looking very tired. "Everything turned out well."

"I'm only going to sleep for a few hours," Eve said, leading the way upstairs. "Then I'll drive into town and see if there was any damage to the store, and then go see how Maddy made out in the storm."

"But the roads are impassable."

"Now that it's daylight and I can see what I'm doing, the delivery truck should make it through. It has plenty of clearance, and what I can't drive over, I should be able to push out of the way with the bumper."

"It was a really strange storm, wasn't it?" Mabel asked, stopping at her bedroom. "The wind blew so hard, I thought the roof was going to come off. And the lightning was sort of brown and then red. And we never heard any thunder."

Eve nodded. "It will be interesting to see what the meteorologists have to say about it. Will you be okay here while I go into town?"

Mabel waved away her concern. "Now that I know everyone's safe and sound, I'm more than fine. And Kenzie will be around; it's going to take a month of Sundays for him to clean up the mess in the yard."

"Right." Eve walked into her room, closed the door, and leaned against it with a sigh. Oh, yes, Kenzie would definitely be around—but *they* would be moving just as soon as she could arrange it.

Eve sped toward town, feeling only a little guilty for pretending she hadn't seen Kenzie waving when she'd driven the delivery truck over the branches blocking the driveway. She was in no mood to talk to anyone—except maybe Maddy—after tossing and turning in bed for two hours. Every time she closed her eyes, she kept seeing an alligator's tail snapping in a pulsing red light, and she kept feeling grasping hands trying to pull her into the ocean.

That is, when she wasn't reliving her lovemaking debacle.

Eve eased back on the gas pedal when she realized she was picking up speed. She really had to get her emotions under control, or Maddy was going to have her committed. Eve laughed out loud, the sound startling her. At the rate she was going, she would be sharing a room at the looney bin with her mother.

"As soon as the power comes back on," she said, "I'm getting our well tested. There *has* to be something in the water that's making us all delusional."

Last month she'd read in the newspaper that a family's well, not fifty miles from here, had been contaminated from chemicals buried at an old mill site, making them all sick. Maybe there was a toxic dump somewhere on this farm, and chemicals had leached into the well over the years, and that's what was making her and her mother delusional. How else could she explain deep wounds that healed in minutes, pens that glowed, and dragons with wings? Heck, Maddy spent plenty of time at their house and drank their well water, too, and she'd seen a flying moose and kissed a bogeyman!

Her mother had been living there for six years, which could easily explain her illness. She was sending in a water sample first thing, and until the results came back, they were drinking bottled water. Eve finally started to relax, now that she had a plausible explanation and a plan of action.

Oddly, the closer she got to town, the less wind damage there seemed to be. By the time she reached Main Street, everything looked quite normal. Everyone had power, and it was business as usual for all the shops.

Maddy stood in front of Bishop's Hearth and Home, a perturbed look on her face. Eve pulled the truck to a stop and got out.

"Where have you been?" Maddy asked as Eve stepped onto the sidewalk. "I've been calling your house, but your phone isn't working." She tapped her watch, then glanced at the truck. "You're three hours late opening the store, and you look like hell. And where's Mabel? Is she okay?"

"She's fine. She was sleeping like a baby when I left," Eve assured her, unlocking the door and walking inside. She went to the back office and snapped on the lights, then tossed her purse on the desk. "And I look like hell because we don't have power out at the farm, so I couldn't take a shower. Did you guys lose your electricity last night, too?"

Maddy shook her head. "Nope. It rained all night and the wind blew, but not hard enough to knock down any trees."

"It felt like we got a hurricane right along the coast," Eve told her. "But I didn't see any damage a mile or two inland."

"That's weird," Maddy said. "You want to come to my house and take a shower? I'll even lend you some clothes."

Eve looked down at herself. "These clothes are clean."

"But you're not. You actually have grass in your hair. What'd you do all night, sit in the hayloft with Kenzie and make sure the animals were safe?"

Eve collapsed in the desk chair with a sigh. "If I tell you something, do you promise not to tell a soul?"

Maddy pulled up a chair and sat, nodding.

"Kenzie rode out on his horse just as the storm started, and when he didn't come back by midnight, I went out looking for him."

"In the storm, in the dark? All by yourself? Why didn't you call 911?"

"Because the phones were out and there were trees down all over the place. It was me or nobody. Father Daar certainly couldn't go, and neither could Mom. So I took a spotlight and went looking for him. I found him on a ledge on the cliffs about a half mile from the house, and since I couldn't very well carry him back, I stayed with him. The ledge was sort of like a cave, and we were out of the rain and wind."

Maddy plucked a piece of grass out of Eve's hair. "So you took off all his clothes to dry him out, and then you took off all *your* clothes to warm him up, and then you . . ." She slapped her hand to her chest. "Omigod, you jumped his bones!"

Eve said nothing, her cheeks filling with heat.

Maddy shook her head. "I wouldn't have had the courage."

"He was unconscious at first. Then he woke up, undressed us because we were soaking wet, and *he's* the one who insisted we use our body heat to warm each other up. It wasn't until we'd been asleep for a while that I got the idea to . . . to start something." She pointed at her. "This is all your fault, Madeline Kimble. If you hadn't put the crazy notion in my head of having an affair with him, I wouldn't be in this mess."

"What mess? Did he wake up, shout, 'Jezebel!' and toss you off the ledge?" She laughed.

"Will you be serious for a minute? I didn't exactly have a condom in my pocket; we didn't use any protection! I could be pregnant. Or what if he's got herpes or something? I had unprotected sex with a virtual stranger!"

"No germ would dare invade that gorgeous body," Maddy said. "So what happened this morning when you woke up?"

"He apologized for undressing me, and then we walked home."

Eve wasn't about to mention all the other weird stuff that had gone on; having unprotected sex was bad enough. "So, what do I do?"

"About what? The VD part, or the getting-pregnant part?"

"What do I say to him? This morning, he acted as if nothing had happened between us."

Maddy frowned. "Maybe he thinks he had an erotic dream." She shrugged. "If that's the case, you simply don't tell him. We'll just cross our fingers about your getting pregnant."

"It really annoys the heck out of me that he doesn't even remember," Eve groused.

"There, there," Maddy said, patting her back. "You'll get another chance. He'll probably be so grateful you went looking for him in the storm, he'll take you out to dinner again. And with His 'erotic dream' lingering in his mind, he'll finally kiss you, and you can take it from there."

"I'm not going out with him again." Eve started fussing with some papers on the desk. "And I'm going to quit being his housekeeper, and move us into the store until we can find a rental."

"Because of last night? Eve, you really didn't do anything wrong. And you and I are the only two people on earth who know about it. Get over it and go about your business as usual."

"It's not just the sex that's bothering me." She sighed. "I think there might be something in our water that's making Mom sick. I'm getting it tested, and buying bottled water from now on. I haven't been feeling like myself lately, either."

"I know you don't want it to be true, but Mabel had a CAT scan, Eve," Maddy said gently. "They actually found where her brain is leaking. Water doesn't cause that. And I haven't seen you sick since you've been home."

"But I get as confused as Mom does sometimes, and I actually imagine things."

"Like what?"

"Like last night, when I was looking for Kenzie. I swear there was something in the bushes, following me."

Her friend gave her a crooked smile. "Eve, you don't like the dark any more than I do. I still can't believe you went looking for Kenzie all by yourself last night. Either you're far more attracted to him than you're willing to admit, or you should be given a medal for bravery."

Eve sighed again. She couldn't make Maddy understand without explaining about William—and she'd rather have a lobotomy than tell her friend she'd gone out in the storm on the say-so of a dragon.

"Come on," Maddy said, dragging her out front. "Let's go to my house and get you showered. You'll feel like a brand-new woman."

Chapter Fourteen

Eve sat on her stool behind the counter, her chin resting in the palms of her hands, and contemplated her life as of late. It had been three weeks since the freak storm, and she had acquired several new skills in that time—some she was pleased with, and some she wasn't so proud of.

On the pleased side of things, she could boast that she made the best herbed goat cheese in the county, and eight-ounce containers of it were zooming out of her store faster than the nanny goats could produce milk. Mabel's hand-churned butter was an equally big hit with the locals, as well as the few tourists who came through town.

The sign she'd put on the sidewalk, with a bunch of balloons, advertising that the farm-fresh eggs from her natural-diet-fed hens made lighter, moister cakes might be a bit over the top, though. Because when asked what that diet was, Eve had to claim it was an old family secret rather than admit that the hens ate bugs, grubs, and worms they scavenged around the yard, and leftovers from her dinner table.

But the pastries and artisan breads her mother baked, as well as the blueberry pies Maddy's mom made, were their biggest hits. Eve had already ordered a new sign and renamed their store Bishop's Hearth and Home Bakery.

She'd also discovered that she really enjoyed tending the goats, which she insisted on milking herself while their adorable kids danced around her. At the rate sales were going, the store would be in the black by the end of the summer.

Which ultimately meant that she hadn't been able to move—because if she and her mom quit housekeeping for Kenzie and Daar, they would lose access to their profit source.

Which eventually brought Eve to her not-so-proud-of skills: she had become a master skulker when it came to avoiding Kenzie, as well as an expert at redirecting the conversation whenever her mother mentioned William.

Skulking, Eve had come to realize, was an art. She had to know where Kenzie was at any given moment and where he was going next, in order to avoid him. In the last three weeks, she could count on one hand the conversations they'd had.

Although to be fair, he didn't seem all that interested in talking to her, either.

The ungrateful jerk. Sex aside, she *had* saved his life.

She hadn't developed any unexplainable rashes or other symptoms, so she figured she was safe in the STD department. As for getting pregnant—well, she was only five days late, which was still within her margin of error. She wasn't giving herself permission to worry about the price of diapers for another week.

Since the storm, which seemed to have hit only An Tèarmann, things had been fairly uneventful—except for the rumors that Midnight Bay had its own—and better—version of the Loch Ness monster. A couple of kayakers claimed they saw something the size of a large horse swimming off Birch Point early one morning last week, and that it had a long neck and tail and wings.

The lobstermen were complaining that the monster had ripped apart their traps right in the water, eaten their lobsters, and shredded their lines. Some of them had started carrying rifles on their boats, hoping to get a shot at whatever was stealing their income.

Eve had been tempted to warn Kenzie that her mother's imaginary friend was getting the locals riled, but that would mean she not only would have to talk to him, but that she'd have to admit she believed there was a dragon living in their woods.

And she *didn't*.

They could dangle her by her heels off Mount Katahdin, and she wouldn't admit she'd seen anything out of the ordinary the night of the storm. All of it—every damn, unexplainable thing—had only been adrenaline-laced fear conjuring up bogeymen, ocean waves full of grasping hands, magical burls of wood, and pens that glowed.

The shop's front door opened, and her mother and Kenzie walked in, their arms laden with bread. Eve jumped up to catch one of the loaves falling out of Mabel's arms.

"Just set them down right here, Mom," she said, relieving her of several more loaves. "People have been coming in all morning, asking if I had any of your olive or rosemary bread. They're our best sellers."

"Can you imagine people are *paying* for my bread?" Mabel said with a giggle of delight. She took off her coat and started arranging the loaves in the baskets on a table. "I think I'll start making Mem's old recipe for banana bread." She winked at Eve. "She always soured the milk with a dash of vinegar, which gives the bread its unique flavor. But we'll keep that little secret between us, okay?"

Eve pretended to lock her lips and throw away the key. "I loved when you baked Mem's banana bread when I was little. We could even fix up a gift pack of banana bread with a quarter pound of butter. It'll become our best seller, I'm sure," she said, relieving Kenzie of his loaves. "Thank you for bringing her to town," she told him, sorting their loaves into the proper baskets.

"Would ye walk with me to the truck?" he asked. "I believe Mabel also brought some butter."

Eve looked up, sensing an odd note in his voice, and realized he wanted to talk to her in private. Damn.

"I'll be right back, Mom. Why don't you design a new sign for the banana-bread gift pack," she suggested, following Kenzie.

When she reached the sidewalk, she saw him standing by the curb two stores down. "What's up?" she asked apprehensively.

He glanced behind her, as if making sure her mother hadn't followed, then took her arm and led her even farther away. "I'm afraid Mabel might be getting worse. She had a rather bad spell this morning and came very close to starting a kitchen fire."

"What? Other than talking about her imaginary friend, she's seemed perfectly fine lately."

Kenzie frowned at her, started to say something, then apparently thought better of it. "I noticed smoke in the yard this morning, and saw Mabel holding open the porch door, waving a towel in the air. I ran inside and smoke was billowing out of the range."

"She forgot to set the timer again," Eve said. "Heck, I've done it myself. It doesn't mean she's getting worse."

"When I got the oven shut off—which I noticed was on broil—and opened the door, I found a loaf of bread in a roasting pan. I carried it out to the yard and saw the bread was still in its plastic wrapper. The plastic had melted and caught fire. Then, when I went back in to open the windows, I found a chicken in the sink with the cavity stuffed with plastic bags."

Eve hugged herself against the sudden chill of the breeze. She'd thought her mother was actually getting better, now that they were drinking bottled water.

The water test had come back negative for anything out of the ordinary, but she'd sent in another test, just in case.

"She also got lost on her walk this morning, Eve, and I found her on the road to town. She'd walked half a mile past the driveway before I realized anything was wrong and went looking for her. I'm sorry. I know ye don't want it to be so, but ye can no longer deny that she's getting worse."

"But I was sure she was getting better," Eve insisted, balling her hands into fists.

"Eve, you have to accept that she never will. In fact, Mabel seems to be dealing with her illness far better than you are. She's devised little tricks to keep herself on track, like stacking little piles of rocks to mark her way on her walks. And Daar told me she always carries a pad and pencil in her pocket, and writes notes to herself about things she doesn't wish to forget. She's accepted her illness for what it is, Eve, whereas you have chosen to pretend she's perfectly fine."

"Haven't we had this discussion before?" she growled.

"Yes, we have. But apparently you were too busy telling me this is none of my business to hear what I was saying."

"And it's *still* none of your business. If Mom is becoming such a bother to you, we'll move out."

"You are missing the point."

"No, I'm not. You told me that she nearly burned down your house this morning, and that you had to leave whatever you were doing to go hunt for her. I can solve your problem by simply moving."

Kenzie ran his hand through his hair, obviously as frustrated as she was. "The point I'm trying to make is that you *can't* do this all by yourself. I wasn't complaining when I told ye what happened this morning; I was trying to open your eyes. Moving Mabel to a new home would only confuse her even more, and she would likely withdraw from life. She's thrown herself completely into her baking business, and taking her away from An Tèarmann would be the worst thing you could do to her right now."

Eve stared down at the sidewalk, knowing he was right but not liking it one damn bit. She looked up, feeling defeated and defensive. "Then what do you suggest I do?"

"Accept her just the way she is."

"I do."

"No, ye don't. Ye shut her out. Whenever she tries to talk to you about William, you change the subject. Do ye not think she realizes what you're doing, and that it doesn't hurt her?"

"I see she doesn't have any problem talking to *you*."

"Because it doesn't matter to me if William is real or not: all that matters is what Mabel believes. If she tells ye the sun was green when it rose this morning, then maybe you could go sit on the island with her this evening, and see if it's still green when it sets."

"How will feeding her delusions help anything?"

"Maybe the question you should ask is, what could it hurt? If Mabel isn't in this world, why not join her in the world she is in?" He reached out and touched her cheek, catching her so completely off guard that she didn't step back. "Think about it, would ye? What harm could possibly come from sharing something special with your mother, even if it *is* a delusion?"

Eve stared at him, unable to utter a word, then turned and quietly walked back to the store.

"You have to tell him," Maddy said, coming to sit beside Eve on the bed.

Eve stared at the pregnancy test in her hand. "I can't."

Maddy flopped back on the bed with a sigh, pulling Eve with her. "Will you keep it?" she asked softly.

"Yes," Eve said, blinking back tears, as she stared up at the bedroom ceiling.

"Then you're going to have to tell him. He has the right to know he fathered a child, whether you two are together or not."

"But you've seen how old-fashioned he is. What if he asks me to marry him?"

"Then you start dating him seriously, and maybe it *will* lead to marriage."

Eve turned her head. "Only to have it work out the way it did for you and Billy?" She looked back at Maddy's ceiling. "I'd rather stay friends with Kenzie and share the baby, than get married and have him start resenting me."

"There's a world of difference between Billy and Kenzie, and you know it." Maddy rolled onto her side to face Eve, and brushed away a tear running down Eve's cheek. "You have to tell him."

"But not today. Or tomorrow. I have to decide what *I* want to do before dealing with what *he* thinks I should do. And I have to consider Mom, and how this is going to affect her."

"Mabel will be thrilled to have a grandchild."

"But how am I going to take care of her *and* a baby? At some point, they're going to be acting the same age."

"You're going to do it with Kenzie's help." Maddy sat up and pulled Eve with her. "Even if you don't marry him, he's still going to be part of your life. Sarah still spends a great deal of time with Billy and his family. You're not just having a baby, you're having a toddler, a nine-year-old brat, and a teenager. Kenzie has an entire family in the mountains who are going to love this child, too. You can't steal that from them—or from him."

"Oh, God, this is so complicated," Eve sobbed, burying her face in her hands. "I hadn't even thought about his family."

"The sooner you tell him, the better. You can hide your pregnancy for five or six months, but three months isn't long enough for a man to get used to the idea he's going to be a father. Why do you think God gives us nine months to plan for the big arrival?"

"How did you get so wise?" Eve sighed.

Maddy snorted and stood up. "I came by it the hard way." She took the pregnancy test out of Eve's hand, then handed her another one made by a different company. "Take it again, just to make sure." She pointed at the drugstore shopping bag on the bureau. "I bought six. We'll do two more in a few days, and two more next week."

Eve threw herself at Maddy and hugged her fiercely. "You are such a good friend. Where would I be without you?"

"On a train heading for a washed-out bridge," Maddy said with a chuckle, hugging her back. "But don't worry, I won't let you crash. Go on," she said, pushing her toward the bathroom.

When Eve finally came back, she silently sat on the bed next to Maddy. Maddy looked at her watch, and Eve looked anyplace but down at the frightening future in her hand.

Three weeks and several positive pregnancy tests later, Eve was discovering there was more to the art of deception than she had realized. Keeping her condition from her mother made hiding Mabel's illness from everyone in town seem easy in comparison.

Eve was sick to her stomach morning, noon, and night, and the lilac bush behind the house was flourishing. Whenever she walked in the kitchen to find her mother had set another bouquet of those amazingly vibrant lilacs on the table, Eve would run out back and give that poor bush another dose of whatever was in her stomach.

Maddy, bless her heart, was keeping Eve supplied with thermoses of ginger tea, saltine crackers, and plenty of reassurance that the urge to throw up every time she smelled coffee brewing would eventually pass.

Eve had *accidentally* broken the coffee carafe. She was going to hell for sure, because Kenzie probably wouldn't say anything, thinking Mabel was the likely culprit. But Eve was just desperate enough to let her mother take the blame.

But when she'd arrived home that evening, there was a brand-new carafe sitting on the counter—along with a month's supply of coffee!

Eve waited until her mother was washing potatoes in the sink and Father Daar was collecting the eggs before she carried the bags of coffee into the back room. She opened the freezer, dumped in the bags, then covered them with packages of frozen meat and vegetables.

"Where would ye like me to put these?"

Eve jumped, slamming the freezer closed with a gasp.

"I'm sorry, I didn't mean to startle you," Kenzie said, looking amused. "Mabel left these books in my truck. I thought she might want them before she went on her walk this evening, but it seems I've missed her."

Eve took a calming breath. "She's right in the kitchen."

"Nay, I believe she's already left for her walk." He held

the books toward her. "If ye hurry, you could catch up and give them to her."

"But she was just washing potatoes," Eve said, scooting past him into the empty kitchen. She went over to the sink and found the potatoes sitting in . . . good Lord, in *soapy* water. Eve immediately pulled the plug to let the water drain. "She left right in the middle of preparing supper," she said in disbelief. "Why don't you take them to her? I have to cook supper."

"Supper can wait until ye get back."

Eve sighed and took them. "These are school books," she said, snapping her gaze back to Kenzie. "What would she want these for?"

"She asked me to take her to her old school this morning when I brought her to town, so she could pick them up. I believe she's teaching William to read."

Eve stared down at the books, and without the least bit of warning, she suddenly burst into loud, uncontrollable sobs. "My mother is teaching a dragon to read!"

Kenzie patted her shoulder. When that didn't slow her down, he tossed the books on the counter, led her over to the table, and sat her in one of the chairs.

Eve buried her face in her hands, trying to get control of herself. She didn't even know why she was crying, only that she couldn't stop.

Kenzie started patting her again. "I need ye to stop now, Eve," he demanded.

"I can't!"

He pulled out a chair and sat down in front of her,

then pulled her hands down and held them in his. "You've been dealing so well with Mabel talking about William lately. Why is this so upsetting all of a sudden?"

"H-have *you* seen William?" she asked on a sniffle.

"I told ye, it doesn't matter if I have or not. Mabel's all that matters."

"*Have* you?"

"Okay. Yes, I have."

That surprised her enough to stop her crying. "And is William a dragon?" she asked, eyeing him suspiciously.

He hesitated, then quietly said, "William thinks he's a dragon."

"That's not an answer! Is he or is he not a dragon?"

"William is a man who *thinks* he's a dragon," Kenzie softly repeated.

Eve stood up, walked over to the counter, grabbed the books, and marched to the door.

Kenzie stepped in front of her. "He's not going to let you see him. He doesn't trust you."

"Then we have something in common," she snapped.

He set his hands on her shoulders, the warmth of his palms radiating all the way down to her toes. "If ye go after Mabel angry, it'll undo weeks of your getting close to her."

Dammit, why was it that whenever he touched her, she always felt calmer? Eve took a deep breath. "I'm not angry anymore."

He dropped his hands and she nearly started crying again, but at least this time she knew why. She really,

really liked it when he touched her. She just didn't like it when he *talked* to her, because he made too much sense.

And sometimes she didn't want sense, she wanted *sensation*.

Oh, God. Growing a baby was an emotional roller coaster!

She shoved the books at him, grabbed her stomach, and spun around and ran upstairs, making it to the bathroom just in the nick of time. As soon as she finished, she washed her face, sat on the edge of the tub, and stared out the window.

Why on earth would a man who thought he was a dragon want to learn how to read?

Chapter Fifteen

Every time the wind blew or it started to rain, Eve grew nervous. Part of the reason was because Father Daar would get out his prayer beads, sit in the rocking chair by the kitchen window, and murmur under his breath. But she suspected it was mostly because she was afraid Kenzie would mysteriously take off again.

The evening after her unexplained crying, they had just sat down to dinner when it started to rain. Eve jumped when lightning flashed in the windows, but relaxed when she heard the rumble of thunder.

Until Kenzie suddenly pushed back his chair and stood up.

"Where are you going?" she blurted out. Without even thinking, she rushed to block the door.

He looked at her curiously, then his expression

suddenly changed and his eyes filled with concern. "I was just going to put Curaidh in his stall, but never mind," he said, going back to the table. "The rain will do him good. He needs a bath, anyway."

"You're not afraid he'll get struck by lightning?" Mabel asked.

"He's in no more danger than a deer or moose is." Kenzie sat down and picked up his fork. "Come eat, Eve. It's just a summer cold front sweeping through. The weatherman said to expect thunderstorms this evening."

Knowing she was wearing her chagrin on her cheeks, Eve sat down and pushed her food around her plate.

"Daar and I are going to Pine Creek the day after tomorrow, to visit Matt and Winter and their new daughter for a couple of days," Kenzie said into the silence. "Would you ladies like to come with us?"

"Oh!" Mabel said. "Winter had her baby girl!" She canted her head in thought. "That's right, the summer solstice was last Sunday. You said she was having it on the solstice."

"She had a cesarean?" Eve asked.

Kenzie looked over at her. "No, what makes ye think that?"

"The only way to know when a baby will be born is to schedule a cesarean."

He smiled at her. "It's a tradition for the MacKeage women to have their babies on the solstices. Winter and her six sisters were all born on the winter solstice."

"All seven?" Eve asked in amazement. "Wow, what are the odds of that happening?"

"Very high, if you're related to Grace MacKeage. She and her sister, and their six brothers, were all born on the *summer* solstice." He looked at Mabel. "So, would you like to visit the mountains for a couple of days?"

"I would love to," Mabel said.

"But who will take care of the animals?" Eve asked.

"Winter's cousin, Robbie MacBain, has offered to come watch over An Tèarmann for me."

"Does he know he has to milk a cow and the goats?" she asked with a crooked grin.

Kenzie smiled back. "He knows. Can ye close your store for three days? Or if ye want, I can ask Camry to come with Robbie, and she could watch the store for you."

"I thought Camry was a rocket scientist for NASA, and lived in Florida."

"She's taken some time off to visit with Winter."

"Let's go, Eve," Mabel said excitedly. "I want to see Winter's baby. You know how much I love newborns."

Well, why not? She wouldn't mind seeing a newborn herself, if only to find out what *she* was in for. And Maddy would kill her if she didn't take the opportunity to meet Kenzie's extended family.

"I don't see any reason why not." Eve looked at Kenzie. "And since Camry has taken time off to visit her sister, I'll just close the store. Maybe it'll make our customers crave our products even more, if they have to do without them for three days." She shot her mom a wink. "Especially Johnnie Dempster. I think he's addicted to your banana bread."

"I know, he bought three loaves this afternoon, and ordered three more. Oh, how exciting," Mabel said, spearing a carrot with her fork. "It seems like forever since I've gone anywhere and met new people." She suddenly stopped with the fork halfway to her mouth, and looked at Kenzie. "What about William? He's gotten used to my bringing him treats."

"Robbie will look after him for ye," Kenzie assured her.

Eve also stopped eating. "Robbie knows about William?"

"Yes."

"But how? He's never been here." She frowned. "Unless that means William came here with you."

"Well, of course it does, Evangeline," Mabel said, her tone implying that was a given. "Why else do you think Kenzie would move to such a desolate place? Dragons need plenty of room to hunt and fish."

"There's plenty of room in the mountains," she said, determined to play along. "And there must be all sorts of places for him to hide up there."

"But he's from Ireland," Mabel reminded her. "He likes being near the ocean."

Eve looked at Kenzie. "So William is the reason you moved here?"

"Partly. And because I like the ocean, too."

"So where will we be staying?" Mabel asked, apparently

satisfied William would be looked after. "Do Winter and Matt have room for us all?"

"They're building a large home, but it won't be ready for at least another year. Grace and Greylen MacKeage have invited us to stay with them."

"They own the TarStone Mountain Ski Resort, and Gù Brath is their home right beside it. It was built just like the ancient castles in Scotland." He looked at Mabel. "I should probably warn you, the MacKeage family is quite large, and many of them have come back for the birth."

"Do they do that every time one of them has a baby?" Eve asked.

"Winter is Grace and Greylen's youngest daughter, and this particular child has been greatly anticipated."

Wow. Eve couldn't imagine living in a large family, or having everyone make such a fuss over a baby.

"But surely you'll stay with your brother?" Mabel asked.

"Nay. Matt and Winter and baby Fiona need time to bond before they let the world intrude. That's why I waited a week to go visit my new niece."

"They named her Fiona?" Mabel said. "How pretty."

"It was our sister's name."

"Was?" Eve asked.

"Fiona died years ago," Kenzie said, then filled his mouth with food.

"I'm not staying at Gù Brath," Daar declared, speaking up now that his plate was empty. "I'm going up to my old cabin."

"You'll probably be sharing it with raccoons," Kenzie warned.

"I don't care. I'm not staying in a house full of heathen children."

"Um . . . maybe Mom and I should find a place to stay in town," Eve said, suddenly having reservations about staying in a house full of strangers. Maybe they could find a motel nearby that wasn't too expensive. "If it's such a family affair, we don't want to intrude."

"Trust me, Grace MacKeage is happiest when her home is overflowing. You would hurt her feelings if ye didn't stay at Gù Brath. She's the one who suggested I bring you both with me."

Eve gave a quick glance toward Mabel, then looked back at Kenzie. "You don't think all those people might make things a little . . . confusing?"

"I could help with the cooking," Mabel interjected, obviously catching Eve's meaning. "And tomorrow I'll bake some bread to take up, and we'll bring some butter."

"I'm sure Grace would love your help, Mabel," Kenzie said. He looked at Eve. "And I would love to take you horseback riding in the mountains."

"Do the MacKeages' have normal-sized horses, or big ones like yours?"

"Two of my mares came from Grey's stable," he said with a gleam in his eyes. "All the MacKeage girls got a draft horse for their fifth birthday. You're not afraid to ride a horse, are ye?"

"Not at all. So why didn't you invite William to come with us?" she asked, wanting to change the subject because she had absolutely no intention of riding one of those elephants. "If there isn't enough room in your truck, he could just *fly* up."

That gleam intensified. "Because William isn't exactly welcome in Pine Creek anymore. The police chief, Jack Stone—who happens to be Winter's brother-in-law—more or less asked him to leave and not come back."

"Because he kept eating all the bears in the area?"

"No, because he kept eating all the doughnuts," Daar said with a snort, standing up. He walked to the fridge and came back with a strawberry-rhubarb pie in one hand and a bowl of whipped cream in the other. "And if Mabel is going to be helping with the cooking, maybe I *should* stay at Gù Brath," he said. "Just to keep her and Eve from getting lost, you understand. The place is a veritable fortress, with more crags and crannies than even the old castles."

Eve cut a large piece of pie and set it on Daar's plate—to which he added about a cup of whipped cream—and her stomach suddenly tightened. What in heaven's name had she gotten herself into?

The trip to Pine Creek took a while, especially since Eve had made Kenzie stop three times so she could throw up. She'd tried to cover up her motion sickness by claiming she must have drunk some raw milk, which was odd. She'd been drinking a lot of milk lately, but she always scalded it, then cooled it, then poured it into jugs that she labeled Eve's Milk in bold black letters.

After they arrived and she felt better, he would take her for a ride up the mountain. He couldn't wait to get her alone—away from Daar, Mabel, Maddy, and everyone else she used as a shield to avoid being alone with him.

He hadn't had a decent night's sleep since the storm, because he couldn't get Eve out of his head. Her taste still lingered on his lips, and the feel of her sweet body surrounding him still haunted his dreams.

He was through torturing himself. He wanted Eve so badly he was willing to risk everything to have her, including the new life he'd been granted—because he finally realized he'd rather be dead than alone. He could no longer live as only half a man, watching Eve flitter about every day and not claiming her as his.

Once he got her up on the mountain and away from her small army of shields, he would declare his intentions. She would probably balk at first, but she would come to love him—because he would settle for nothing less.

Kenzie finally pulled into Gù Brath and turned off the engine.

"Oh my God," Mabel exclaimed, her nose pressed up to the rear window. "It really is a castle."

"It's built of black stone. And look, Mom, there's even a moat!" Eve said with equal excitement, pointing at the stream gushing under the bridge that led to the large wooden doors.

"Is that Greylen and Grace MacKeage?" Mabel asked as two people walked across the bridge toward them.

"That would be them," Kenzie said, opening his door.

"What a handsome couple," Mabel said.

Kenzie opened Eve's door, then quickly walked around and opened Mabel's and Daar's.

As he turned, Grace threw herself into his arms. "Oh, Kenzie, I've missed you," she said, hugging him tightly. She stepped back, keeping her hands on his arms. "I've been so worried you would turn into an old hermit like Daar," she said with a laugh.

She then stepped over and hugged Daar. "I see the salt air agrees with you, my old friend," she said, giving him a kiss on the cheek. "I've missed you, too."

"No need for all this hugging and kissing," Daar said gruffly, smoothing down his cassock. "You women make such a fuss over everything. We've only been gone a few months."

"And Gù Brath has remained standing despite your not being here," Greylen said with a laugh.

"Grace, Greylen," Kenzie said, "this is Mabel Bishop and her daughter, Eve Anderson. They're the ones responsible for keeping me from turning into a hermit."

"It's so nice to meet you," Mabel said, shaking the hand Grace held out to her. "Kenzie's told me so much about you. And it was nice meeting your daughter, Winter, when she brought Kenzie's horses. What a beautiful home you have."

"Thank you." Grace took Eve's hand, cupping it

between both of hers. "I'm glad you decided to come with Kenzie. Grey and I have been wanting to meet you ever since Kenzie told us he'd bought the house you were living in." She glanced over at Mabel. "Your brother-in-law should be shot for what he did."

Mabel shrugged. "I've long since decided Alvin did us a favor. Things have worked out even better than we could have hoped for. Kenzie is a delight, and Father Daar is a joy to have around."

Grey started coughing, and Grace finally let go of Eve's hand to pat her husband on the back. She then looped her arm through Mabel's. "I'll show you and Eve to your room. I hope you don't mind doubling up. We're still celebrating the summer solstice, and are packed with people. Daar, you leave the desserts in the fridge alone!" she called out to the priest, who was already halfway across the bridge.

"Go on," Kenzie told Eve. "I'll get your bags." He turned to Grey as soon as she left, and shook his hand. "Thank ye for sending down those mares." He chuckled. "And the next time they come into heat, Curaidh will be thanking ye, too."

"You mean that stallion didn't tear down his stall trying to get to them last month?" Grey asked, taking the bag Kenzie handed him from the back of the truck.

"Nay, I kept the horny beast in the woods with William, upwind of the barn." He chuckled softly. "A warhorse and a dragon becoming friends, now that's a sight I never thought I'd see. I've a fear William will try to steal Curaidh, once he's a man again."

"Do you think that will happen?" Grey asked. "It's my understanding that Killkenny's head is harder than granite and twice as dense."

Kenzie glanced toward the house as the women disappeared inside, then looked back at Grey. "Mabel has befriended William, and I think she might actually be the key to this whole thing."

"Mabel?" Grey said in surprise. "How? I understand she suffers from some sort of aging disease, so Killkenny would be comfortable around her, but how can she possibly help him?"

"This is the first time I've seen William interested in anyone besides himself. Mabel is openly affectionate and so accepting of him just as he is, that he's grown quite fond of her. It's my hope that William will finally open his heart."

"From your lips to God's ears, Gregor. Come on. We better go save your pretty little housekeeper. Camry has been her usual impatient self all morning, waiting to meet 'your new girlfriend.' "

"Eve will be my wife by the fall equinox, if I have my way."

Grey stopped and stared at him, then roughly pounded his shoulder. "It's about damn time! Matt was worried you might never come to your senses. Congratulations."

"Don't congratulate me," Kenzie warned. "I haven't told Eve yet."

Grey waved that away and started across the bridge.

"If she gives ye any trouble, just steal her away and don't let her go until she agrees to marry ye. I happen to know where there's a secluded cabin up in the mountains you could use."

Kenzie chuckled. "I wonder if you'd be spouting the same wisdom if a man stole one of your daughters?"

Grey stopped and glared at him. "Your brother kept Winter up in that cave on Bear Mountain, then flew her to Nevada to get married without asking my permission." He shook his head. "As for Camry, I fall asleep every night praying some poor brave bastard will steal her out from under my nose. I even leave the front door unlocked when we go to bed."

"But I thought Camry's been at NASA all spring?"

Grey shook his head. "She goes back to work, but she's gone only a short time before she finds another excuse to come home."

Grey opened the door and Kenzie walked inside, only to nearly be run over by an ecstatic young dog being chased by a troop of children brandishing wooden swords and yelling war cries.

Kenzie was pleased to see that some things never changed.

Grace and Mabel were coming down the stairs, Grace holding on to her guest because Mabel was too busy gawking at everything to watch where she was going.

"Where's Eve?" Kenzie asked, worried Camry had already ambushed her.

"She's having a nap," Grace told him.

"Another one?" he asked in disbelief. "But she slept most the way here—when she wasn't throwing up on the side of the road."

"She's sick?" Grace asked in alarm.

"Nay, I believe she just doesn't travel well." He looked at Mabel. "She kept muttering that it was going to take forever for us to get here because I drive like a geezer. Would you know what she meant by that?"

"She meant you were driving like an old person."

"And do I?" he asked.

"You'll eventually get the hang of it," Mabel said, patting his arm. "Just don't start driving like you ride, okay? I've seen you on Curaidh."

"Come on, Mabel, I'll show you the kitchen," Grace said, leading her down the hall to the back of the house. "I hope Daar left us some cake to have with our tea."

"Kenzie!" Camry cried, running into the foyer.

Kenzie dropped the suitcase he was holding to catch her. "Camry, darling," he said, swinging her around. He gave a loud groan and set her down. "Have ye gained weight?" he asked, knowing it would rile her.

Instead of a scathing comeback, she dropped her gaze and turned pink.

He lifted her chin with his finger. "I was teasing, lass. You're as beautiful as ever." He made a show of looking behind her toward the living room. "So, where's your new boyfriend? Or was your Frenchman not brave enough to face his future in-laws?"

"He is *not* my boyfriend," she said, her blush

intensifying. "And he's not even French; he's from British Columbia. He's working in France for one of Mom's old race-into-space rivals." She gave him a fierce glare, which she also turned on her father. "And even if I did have a boyfriend, I certainly wouldn't bring him here." She made a production of looking behind Kenzie, then around the foyer. "Where's *your* new girlfriend?"

"She heard you intended to ambush her, and is hiding in her room." Kenzie picked up Eve's bag and handed it to Camry, knowing he couldn't stop the inevitable. Besides, he owed Eve for her geezer comment. "Since ye have every intention of harassing the poor woman as soon as I turn my back, why don't ye make yourself useful and bring up her bag?"

Camry snatched the bag out of his hand and bounded up the stairs.

"That wasn't wise," Grey said, watching his daughter race along the balcony.

Kenzie picked up the suitcase he'd dropped. "Any suggestions as to what I should have done, short of locking Camry in the lab downstairs for the next three days?"

"You could have talked William into coming with ye," Grey said. "That would have occupied her."

"As well as Jack Stone."

Grey waved that away. "Jack's too busy rescuing all the lost treasure hunters who have been mobbing Pine Creek lately."

"When did Pine Creek get a treasure?"

"A week ago, on the summer solstice, in fact. A UFO was sighted streaking across the northern sky in broad daylight. First only the local news stations mentioned it, then the national networks picked up the story. Since then, we've been overrun with treasure hunters."

"What's a UFO?"

"It's an unidentified flying object. Or as Grace would tell ye, it's probably just a meteor, an old satellite that's fallen out of orbit, or debris that fell to Earth. But many people believe it's a spaceship from some other planet, and they're flocking here to find it. But they're unprepared for the terrain and keep getting lost, and Jack has to keep going out to find them."

"That must not sit well with Megan, seeing how they have the baby now."

Grey shrugged. "Jack's never gone more than a day. He goes out by himself, and seems to know right where to find them."

Kenzie snorted. "Yet he continues to claim he doesn't possess any of his great-grandfather's shaman heritage."

"He'll have to acknowledge it eventually, when little Walker starts showing his own powers."

"The baby's a shaman?" Kenzie asked.

"He comes from a long line of magic makers on both sides of his family. I'm eager to see what comes from a mix of Celtic drùidhs and North American shamans."

Kenzie looked up the balcony to where Camry had disappeared, then back at Grey. "Speaking of the magic, could ye give me a clue as to how I'm supposed to explain it to Eve? Or do ye think Grace would be willing to talk to her for me?"

Grey took the suitcase out of Kenzie's hand and set it on the bottom step, then threw his arm over Kenzie's shoulder and headed toward the front door. "Come on out to the barn with me. I have a bottle of fine Scotch hidden in the hay, and since this might take a while, we might as well be comfortable."

Chapter Sixteen

There was a knock on her door, and Eve sat up just as it opened and a beautiful woman with short red hair peeked inside. She smiled when she saw Eve was awake, and walked in carrying Eve's overnight bag.

"Hi. I'm Camry," the woman said, dropping the bag by a chair as she came to sit on the foot of the bed. "I'm Winter's sister." She held up three fingers. "I'm daughter number three, and the only MacKeage girl smart enough to remain single."

Eve instantly liked Camry MacKeage. "Eve Anderson, and apparently I'm not very smart. But I do usually learn from my mistakes, so I'll probably stay single from here on out, too."

Camry laughed at that. "Are you really not feeling

well, or are you just allergic to chaos? Because either way, I can find an instant cure for you."

Eve wished. "I . . . my stomach's a bit queasy, is all. I'm an elementary-school teacher, so I'm immune to chaos."

"Then we'll go see my Aunt Libby," Camry said, standing up. "She's a doctor. Trauma's her specialty, but she's got this eerie way of knowing what's ailing a person and can usually fix them right up."

Eve hesitated. She didn't want to see a doctor who had an eerie way of knowing what was ailing her—especially one who was sort of related to Kenzie. Besides, she had an appointment with Maddy's ob-gyn next Tuesday in Ellsworth.

"I'm sure it's nothing," Eve said, getting up. "In fact, I'm feeling better now that I'm not riding in anything that Kenzie is driving."

"My God, you really are a pixie," Camry said, running her gaze up the length of Eve, now that she was standing.

"Pixie?"

Camry lightly touched one of Eve's curls. "Kenzie called you a pixie a couple of times during our phone conversations, and now I see why. You're so tiny and cute and delicate-looking, I bet you have to beat men off with a stick."

"Kenzie called me a *pixie*?"

"He was complimenting you," Camry assured her with a laugh. "Everyone thinks pixies are cute and cuddly, but they're really powerful little mischief makers.

Let's go down to the kitchen and get a cup of tea," she said, heading for the door. "I promise not to let the little heathens capture you, and we'll take our tea outside and go for a walk. I'm just dying to hear how Kenzie has *really* been getting by on his own," she said, leading Eve down the hall.

He'd called her a *pixie*? Eve didn't know which confounded her more: that he thought she was a mischief maker, or that he'd been talking to Camry about her.

Eve followed Camry in the opposite direction Grace had brought her upstairs, and she assumed this was the back way to the kitchen. She still couldn't believe there was an authentic castle up here in the western mountains of Maine. For all of its modern conveniences, it looked like it had been built a thousand years ago. And she'd swear some of the artifacts hanging on the walls were *not* reproductions.

"You grew up in a castle," Eve said. "What fun it must have been for you as a child."

Camry suddenly stopped. "See this section of floorboards?" she said, pointing at the oak. "They've got a creak in them that we girls spent countless hours trying to fix." She pointed at the tall door on their right. "That's our parents' room, and we suspect Daddy kept undoing our repairs so he could hear whenever we were trying to sneak out."

"Why didn't you just sneak out the way we're headed now?"

Camry started walking down the hall again. "Because

our uncles slept in the rooms on either side of the back stairway before they got married, and there's more creaky planks outside their bedrooms. They had us boxed in—or so they thought, until my twin sister Sarah tied all our bedsheets together, and we shimmied out Winter's bedroom window because it was over the kitchen roof."

"Did you get caught?"

"Oh, yeah. By the time we made it to the ground, Daddy was waiting for us."

"And?"

"And it took the seven of us two weeks and over a hundred gallons of paint to spruce up the barn and all the outbuildings. How about you? What sort of pranks did you and your siblings pull on your parents?"

"My mother was forty-two when she had me, and I'm an only child," Eve told her. "The worst trouble I got in was when I was fourteen and I snuck out one night to meet my friends." She made a face. "My parents never punished me, because a skunk did it for them. When it rains, I swear I still smell like a skunk."

Camry laughed, looping her arm through Eve's. "I can't imagine being an only child. But don't worry, once you marry Kenzie, *we'll* be your sisters if you want. In fact, I think we'll start our sisterly duties by taking you to the new bar in town. Everyone's been dying to go."

Eve barely heard the last of what Camry was saying, because she'd stopped in her tracks to gape at her.

"What?" Camry asked, walking back to her.

"I'm not marrying Kenzie."

"Sure you are. You just don't know it yet."

"We went on *one* date, and it had to have been the weirdest date in the history of dating. Besides, I swore off men when my husband ran off with my neighbor's wife five months ago."

"Kenzie would never run out on his wife. In fact, he'll probably smother you to death with his attention."

"Where did you get the notion that we're getting married?" Eve asked curiously.

"Oh, I don't know," Camry drawled, starting them walking again. "Maybe from the fact that Kenzie can't stop talking about you whenever I call him. Or that you're so curious about his family that you came up here with him."

"I came because my mother wanted to come."

"And then there's the little fact that you're keeping house for him," Camry continued. "And oh, yeah: he's rich and handsome and more man that one woman can handle, and you'd be an idiot not to fall in love with him." She shot Eve a smug smile. "And I doubt you're an idiot. So, about tonight. If you didn't bring anything to wear to a bar, after our walk we'll go raid some of my sisters' suitcases."

Chaos was putting it mildly. They couldn't even seat everyone at one table for dinner, although the table was thirty feet long and six feet wide. So Grace and Mabel had arranged a beautiful buffet on it instead, and people were eating anyplace they could find a seat out of the traffic zone.

Kenzie was conspicuously absent, and Eve learned from her mother that he'd gone to have a quiet dinner alone with Matt and Winter and baby Fiona.

Camry and five of her sisters had ganged up on Eve at the buffet table, and they'd brought her downstairs to a large room they called the lab. Eve had often taken her fourth-grade class to a real lab at MIT, but the one she was eating in this evening made it pale in comparison. She didn't know which impressed her more—the lab full of equipment or the women who had grown up using it.

They all had startling green eyes filled with intelligence, and personalities to match. They were also bubbling with energy, and had asked Eve more questions about herself than her kids did on the first day of school.

Now, though, they were talking about her as if she wasn't even there.

"I don't know if it's such a good idea," Elizabeth said. "I've heard Pete's Bar and Grill is a rather rough place. Kenzie will kill us if anything happens to Eve."

Elizabeth was the next to the youngest, an elementary-school teacher here in town, and the mother of . . . Eve couldn't remember how many of the adorable little heathens belonged to Elizabeth.

Heather, the oldest, who now lived in Scotland, waved Elizabeth's concern away. "We won't let anything happen to her," she said, stabbing a cherry tomato. "As a group, we could level the place if we wanted to."

"Jack said he's been called there at least six times since it opened," Megan said, holding two-month-old Walker to her breast with one hand and trying to eat with the other. "It's not like most of the lounges we have here in town. It's a *bar*."

"I've been there," Camry said. "It can get a bit rowdy, but it's not like it's dangerous. I like Pete's. It's about time we had a place to party hearty around here."

"The TarStone Lounge is pretty hip," Sarah—Camry's twin—said. "We could take Eve there. She's never seen it."

Chelsea—who was a lawyer in Bangor, and daughter number four—set down her water. "But *we* certainly have, ad nauseam. I vote we go to Pete's."

"Kenzie will kill us," Elizabeth repeated.

"That's why we're going to sneak Eve out," Camry told her. "We'll make sure nothing happens to her."

Eve wondered if they even cared if she wanted to go. "Hello?" she interjected, smiling when the women looked startled. "I've been living in Boston for six years. I'm pretty sure I can take care of myself."

"Oh! We weren't implying . . . I mean, we're sure you can." Heather smiled sheepishly. "It's just that you don't know Kenzie like we do."

"What I'm trying to figure out," Eve said, "is what possible say Kenzie has about my going to a bar."

Camry sighed. "All the men around here are very old-fashioned, which means they're annoyingly overprotective. Kenzie is the biggest atavist in the bunch, and since you came here with him, he'll feel responsible for you." She shrugged. "But because we love all our men so much, it's just easier for us to sneak out instead of trying to remind them—again—that we are perfectly capable of taking care of ourselves." She looked at Megan. "You can come, too, can't you? If Jack can't watch Walker tonight, I'm sure Mom would."

"But I can't drink. I'm nursing."

"So pump," Heather said. "Come on, Sis. How long has it been since we've all been out together?"

"Six months," Megan drawled. "On winter solstice eve? Remember? Winter and I had to pour you all in the truck and drive you home."

"I remember our husbands had to come down and carry us up to bed," Chelsea said, shaking her head. "And you and Winter were the only ones who could eat birthday cake the next day."

"We deserve to cut loose a couple times a year since we're all such angels the rest of the time." Sarah grinned at Eve. "So, are you brave enough to go out on the town with the MacKeage women?"

Finally, she was being asked! "I'm definitely game, as long as you don't expect me to get roaring drunk. I'm still trying to recover from a spiced-rum incident several weeks back."

Eve sat at the crowded table in Pete's Bar and Grill, and sipped her third soft drink. At first, she'd been so excited about sneaking out with the Mackeages that she'd completely forgotten her mom would be left alone in a house full of strangers. When Mabel had come up to the bedroom, utterly exhausted and the happiest Eve had seen her in months, Eve had told her what the women had planned, then explained that she'd decided not to go.

Mabel had gotten all huffy, claimed she didn't need babysitting, and insisted Eve go on her adventure with those sweet, charming, wonderful women. Heather, bless her intuitive heart, had shown up at their door with her ten-year-old daughter, introduced Mary to Mabel, and asked if the girl could sleep in Eve's bed since Mary didn't want to bunk with the smaller children tonight.

Mabel and Eve had both known it was a flat-out lie, but not only had Mabel eagerly agreed, she'd told her young roommate they'd sneak down to the kitchen and make hot cocoa and popcorn.

So sporting a plaid blouse Camry insisted she just *had* to wear, Eve left Gù Brath by way of the back stairs. Now, after three sodas and several turns on the dance floor with many of the sisters, she was quite pleased with her decision to join them.

Or she was, until she finally noticed that each of the women were also wearing either a scarf or blouse or belt made of plaid, and innocently asked, "How come the plaid you all are wearing is the same, but mine is different?"

Chelsea lifted an end of the scarf hanging loosely around her neck. "This is the clan MacKeage plaid. It's become a tradition for us to wear it when we go out together. You're wearing the clan Gregor colors."

Eve arched a brow at Camry. "Why am I wearing the clan Gregor colors?"

"Because you belong to Kenzie," Heather said before Camry could answer.

Eve turned the brow on Heather. "I don't belong to anyone."

"You're living in his house," Megan pointed out.

"Because I *work* for him, and the pay is room and board for my mother and me."

"I think it's much more than that," Sarah said. "Kenzie wouldn't have brought a mere employee home to meet the family."

Eve blinked at the women. Did they all have *couple syndrome,* or what?

Camry laughed. "Welcome to my world," she said. "They've been trying to get me married off for years. Why do you think I jumped at the NASA job and moved to Florida right after college?"

"You live in Florida?" Megan asked in surprise. "Then why are you always *here*?"

Camry stood up. "I need to go to the powder room." She looked at Eve. "Want to come with me?"

Oh, yes she did—if only to chew her out for making her wear the Gregor plaid. Eve followed Camry through the crowded bar, and just as they entered the narrow hallway leading to the restrooms, she pulled Camry to a stop.

"That was a dirty trick," she said, holding her sleeve two inches from Camry's nose. "You know how I feel about Kenzie."

"I'm sorry. I know it was a dirty trick, but I am really, really desperate. If everyone's busy matching you up with Kenzie, that takes the pressure off *me*."

"But what's wrong with our being single?"

"Oh, neither one of you lovely ladies should be single," a deep voice said from behind them.

Eve and Camry turned and came face-to-face with two men—both holding beers in their hands and swaying slightly, both looking rather lecherous.

"Come on," Camry said, taking her hand. "Let's go back to our *husbands*."

The men didn't move, blocking their exit. "But you just said you're both single," the dark-haired, unshaven man said. He waved his bottle between him and his friend. "And it just so happens we're both single, too." He winked at Eve. "And seeing how I got this thing for tiny little blondes, maybe you and I can hook up for the night. Maybe even *all* night, cutie-pie?"

Camry nudged Eve behind her. "My friend prefers her husband's bed."

Eve leaned into her. "That's it? All you've got is the threat of a nonexistent husband?" she whispered.

"You got a better idea?"

"Maybe the women's bathroom has a lock on the door."

"I tried that last week—it doesn't. I'll distract them, and you go find the bouncer."

"I'm not leaving you," Eve hissed softly, eyeing the guy who was eyeing Camry.

He looked more inebriated than his buddy, and no less horny.

"Hey, don't worry about choosing between us right now," the guy on the left said, stepping forward. "If you can't decide, we can all go back to my place." He grabbed Camry's arm.

The other guy lurched toward Eve, backing her up against the wall. He tried to kiss her on the mouth, but drunkenly missed when Eve cried out in disgust and turned her face away—which got her kissed on the ear as his overlarge body pressed into hers.

When his beefy paw grabbed her breast, Eve exploded. She grabbed his hand and bent his fingers back, then drove her palm against his nose to shove him off her, snapping his head back. He went flying into the crowd of people who had stopped to stare at his yelp of surprise.

"Shit!" Eve's guy cried, covering his face. "She broke my nose! And my fingers!"

Camry's assailant was sitting on the floor next to his buddy, holding his knee and groaning.

"I guess you *can* take care of yourself," Camry said, staring at Eve in awe. "Oh, please, you just have to marry Kenzie."

Eve grabbed her hand. "Let's get out of here."

They didn't make it three feet before a man in a Pete's Bar and Grill shirt stepped in front of them. "I believe you ladies need to stay right here. That was the owner's little brother you just assaulted."

"We were defending ourselves," Camry pointed out.

He just stood with his arms crossed and his feet planted.

"What's going on?" Heather asked from behind him, her sisters sliding to a stop beside her. "Dammit, Camry, now what did you do!"

"Step back, ladies," the bouncer said, holding his arms out to the side. "We're just waiting for the police to arrive."

"Well, shit." Camry looked at Eve. "How are you when it comes to enduring long-winded lectures on proper female behavior?"

"What?"

"Because once Daddy is done with us, Kenzie will likely take over. Then Heather's husband, then Chelsea's," Camry continued, waving her hand in the air. "And on down the line until we can only hope our ears will fall off."

"You're kidding, right?"

"Sorry, but you're about to see true highlanders in action—as well as a few modern wannabe highlander husbands." She suddenly shot Eve a broad smile. "Welcome to the family."

Eve couldn't believe how fancy the tiny Pine Creek's police station was, nor could she understand why these six intelligent, sophisticated women sat looking like naughty children about to be scolded.

Hell, the fourth-graders she sent to the principal's office weren't this somber.

Megan leaned across Camry to tell Eve, "Don't worry, Jack will talk them out of pressing charges. He's really good at getting people to see things his way."

Heather, sitting on Eve's other side, snorted. "Of course they're going to press charges. She broke the guy's nose and fingers. And Camry probably tore a cartilage in the other guy's knee."

Megan patted Eve's thigh. "When Kenzie gets here, don't say anything, okay? *Especially* don't say anything about the guy grabbing you. Just smile and nod, and agree with whatever he says."

"Excuse me?"

Chelsea pulled her chair away from the wall to see better. "If you try to reason with Kenzie, it'll just prolong the lecture. Nodding will cut it in half."

Eve blinked at them. "Are you for real? This is the twenty-first century. We stopped letting men lecture us sometime in the last century."

Megan snorted. "Not in our family, we didn't. Even Mom still sits through a few of them from Daddy." She grinned and leaned closer. "She raised all us girls to realize that it's better just to let the men blow off steam once in a while, because it makes them feel better and gets everyone past the problem quicker."

"But that's archaic."

"Yup. But Mom explained it this way: testosterone can't be turned on and off like a faucet, and the things that we love about our men are often the very things that drive us crazy. Protectiveness is programmed into their genes."

"And if you want a peaceful household," Camry interjected, "then you have to learn when to keep your mouth shut and when to speak up."

"And you only speak up when their bellies are full," Heather said with an authoritative nod. "Never, ever when they're in the middle of a full-blown bluster."

"They're angry because they're actually scared," Sarah clarified, "and lecturing us is the only way they know how to deal with it."

"But what are they afraid of?" Eve asked, utterly intrigued.

"Of something terrible happening to us."

"So let me get this straight," Eve said. "Kenzie will walk in here as angry as a bear, because he's afraid something terrible could have happened to me?"

"Now you're getting it," Heather said. "He'll be upset because he wasn't there to protect you from that jerk tonight."

"And I'm supposed to quietly sit here and let him lecture me so that *he'll* feel better?" She shook her head. "I don't know if I can."

"If you can't do it for Kenzie, then please do it for us," Sarah pleaded. "When you're back in Midnight Bay, you can argue with him all you want."

"We are *not* a couple," Eve reminded them. Then she gasped. "Camry, quick! Change blouses with me before he gets here."

"Too late," Camry said, looking at the door.

Eve was starting to feel like she'd fallen down a rabbit

hole—or a time warp. Greylen MacKeage and Kenzie came striding into the police station, both men looking downright . . . lethal.

Maybe she *should* keep her mouth shut just this once.

For the women's sakes, of course.

Kenzie strode right up to Eve, grabbed her by her shoulders, and lifted her to her feet. He gave her a visual inspection from her toes to her nose, then pulled her against his chest in a crushing embrace that actually made her squeak.

By the time he loosened his grip enough that she could breathe, the lobby was full of people. Men mostly, except for Grace MacKeage. Eve assumed she'd come to protect her daughters from their husbands, because she'd positioned herself in front of her girls and stood facing the men.

Eve had a whole new appreciation of the meaning of clans.

And the definition of atavism.

"Are ye at all hurt?" Kenzie asked, holding her by the shoulders as he gave her another inspection. He must have answered his own question, because when his gaze locked on hers, she could see the hint of a grin. "They told me ye broke three of the bastard's fingers *and* his nose."

The nervousness that had been building in her suddenly vanished. "Now do you believe that I can take care of myself?"

"Against a drunken man," he pointed out. He pulled

her into his arms again with a sigh, and used his chin to tuck her head against his chest. "I should have realized something like this would happen if I brought ye anywhere near the MacKeage girls."

"Hey, this isn't *our* fault," Camry said, jumping up to glare at him. "Eve and I were merely going to use the powder room."

"Which just happened to be in a rough bar," Kenzie growled, hugging Eve so tightly that she squeaked again.

Camry tried to pull them apart. "You're smothering her!"

Her father took hold of Camry's shoulder and sat her down in the chair. "Stay out of this," he said, his voice unbelievably soft. He looked at Megan. "Where's your husband?"

"He's at home with Walker."

The door opened, and when Kenzie turned to look—still not releasing her—Eve saw what looked like a pregnant man walk in. Then he unzipped his police jacket as he took in the full lobby of people, and she realized he had a baby strapped to his chest. Megan immediately jumped up and went to him.

"Leave him," the man said when she reached out to take the baby. "He's sleeping. So, people," he said to the room at large. "Did the little heathens finally capture Gù Brath, and you've all taken refuge in my police station?"

"Camry and Kenzie's girlfriend got into a little scuffle at Pete's," Megan told him.

"Camry?" he said, his gaze shooting to her. "No. She

would never get into a little scuffle." He walked over and smiled down at her. "Now I might believe you got into a *big* scuffle." He shook his head. "Why aren't you in Florida?"

"It's the summer solstice."

"That came and went over a week ago, Cam," he said, smiling affectionately. "But you didn't." He turned to Kenzie and peered at Eve, his eyes widening in surprise. "Good Lord, man, be careful you don't crush her."

Eve tried to wiggle free, but Kenzie simply tightened his arms. "Make this mess go away, Stone."

"If I do, will you go away, too?"

"Day after tomorrow."

Chief Stone blew out a defeated sigh, then walked to the officer who was standing in the hallway, looking overwhelmed. "Okay, Pratt, fill me in. You said something about assault charges. So who assaulted whom?"

"Um . . . Miss Anderson"—Officer Pratt nodded toward Eve—"broke Ray Dowdy's nose and some of his fingers. And Camry MacKeage dislocated Jay Johnson's knee."

Jack Stone looked at Eve, again in surprise, then turned back to his deputy. "Are the men pressing charges?"

Officer Pratt nodded. "They just called from the clinic a few minutes ago. They should be here shortly."

"Any witnesses?"

"About fifty people."

"If they press charges, so will we," Eve declared.

"Absolutely—they assaulted us, and it was self-defense," Camry agreed.

"Okay, then," Jack said, patting his baby on the bottom when the infant made a noise. "I'll be in my office. Knock on the door to let me know when they get here. Megan, come feed your son," he told her, stepping around Pratt.

"I can't," Megan said. "I've been drinking."

He turned, glared at *Camry,* then looked back at his wife and sighed. "Okay, then come feed him the bottle I brought. He wouldn't take it for me."

"That's because you're not soft and squishy in all the right places," Megan said as she waltzed past him into the hallway.

Jack looked around the lobby. "Any of you who didn't throw any punches or break anyone's nose can leave. I only need Camry and Miss Anderson to stay." He nodded slightly. "And Greylen and Grace, if you want." He looked at Kenzie and sighed again. "I suppose you can stay, too, Gregor, since you can't seem to unglue yourself from Miss Anderson."

Kenzie finally released her, and Eve nearly fell down in surprise.

"I'm staying," Heather said, glancing at her husband.

"Me, too," all the other sisters said in unison.

Jack started unzipping his son out of his chest pack

as he headed down the hall after Megan, but then he returned to the lobby and walked over to Greylen. "Your word that you will be civilized when Dowdy and Johnson show up."

Greylen hesitated, then nodded.

Jack walked over to Kenzie. "You, too, Gregor. Your word."

Kenzie didn't so much as bat an eye.

The door opened and two men walked into the station. Well, one walked; the other one hobbled in on crutches. They immediately stopped when they saw everyone, and the people in the lobby collectively sucked in their breaths.

The guy Eve had defended herself against had two black eyes and a piece of padded tape over his nose. He was cradling his bandaged right hand against his chest. Camry's assailant was wearing a brace on his left knee.

Jack Stone handed his son to Grace. "Would you take him to Megan?" he asked, reaching in his pocket and handing her a small feeding bottle. "Gentlemen," he said, going over to the two men. "Let's go into the conference room, shall we?"

They quickly followed him through the utterly silent lobby.

As soon as the conference room door closed, Greylen MacKeage looked at Eve and started laughing. "Good Lord, woman, I don't ever want to get on your bad side."

He pounded Kenzie on the back. "And neither should you, my friend."

Kenzie was also looking at her in disbelief.

"So does this mean you'll finally stop going on about how I need a man to look after me?" Camry asked her father.

Greylen stopped laughing.

All the sisters groaned, and one by one they grabbed their husbands and filed out until only Kenzie, Eve, Camry, and Greylen remained in the lobby.

Camry started smiling and nodding at her father, and Eve burst into tears.

"What the . . . Eve, what's wrong?" Kenzie asked, hugging her again.

Eve muttered something into his shirt.

"What, lass?" he asked, lifting her chin.

"I said you didn't even notice I was wearing the Gregor plaid," she sniffled.

"Oh, I noticed," he said gruffly, hugging her again.

She muttered into his shirt again.

"Now what?" he asked, leaning back to look in her eyes.

"I need to use the powder room," she whispered.

He let her go, and Eve took Camry by the hand and led her up to Officer Pratt. "Could you take us to the bathroom, please?"

He hesitated, glancing toward the conference room, then led them down the hall.

"Thank you," Eve said, pulling Camry inside. Then she went over to the mirror. "Oh my God, I look like I've been in a barroom brawl!"

"You looked perfectly fine when we left Pete's. Kenzie messed up your hair and blouse."

Eve tried to smooth her blouse. "I think his body heat actually pressed in creases."

"Where did you learn to cry on demand like that?" Camry asked. "You actually made tears!"

"I had an overprotective father, too. He drove me to karate lessons for six years straight, and he made sure every boy who picked me up for a date knew I was a brown belt. But whenever I burst into tears he didn't know what to do, so he usually just caved in."

There was a knock on the door, and Grace walked into the restroom. "It's safe to come out," she said. "Your victims have left. They decided not to press charges, so we can go home."

"Why didn't they press charges?" Camry asked.

"Jack pointed out that if they did, the assault would become public knowledge. Then he asked if they wanted the whole county to know that two women who didn't even come up to their armpits had beaten them up. Come on," she said, motioning for them to follow. "Those adorable little heathens will be awake in five hours, and the chaos will start all over again."

Camry started to follow Grace out of the bathroom, but Eve held her back. "For one last time, Kenzie and I are *not* a couple."

"Whatever you say. As long as I get to be your maid of honor."

Without stopping to think, Eve said, "You can't. My friend Maddy is going to be."

Camry shot her a smug smile, then strode down the hall. Eve groaned and followed, wondering if there was a back staircase out of the rabbit hole she'd fallen into.

Chapter Seventeen

"She's fallen asleep again," Eve pointed out.

"She does that a lot." Kenzie explained. "Butterball is well over thirty years old."

"Maybe we shouldn't disturb her," Eve said hopefully.

"She really won't mind."

"She's awfully tall, isn't she?"

"Nay, you're just awfully short."

Eve eyed the elephant-sized horse standing next to the mounting block, saddled and bridled, with the reins thrown over her neck. Her eyes were closed.

"I think we should wait until you can find a normal-sized horse for me to ride."

"She won't hurt you, Eve."

"I'll make you blueberry pancakes every day for a month?"

Kenzie took Eve by the hand and led her up to the mounting block. The horse opened the big brown eye facing them, then lazily closed it again.

Kenzie then lifted Eve onto the block, since she wasn't in any hurry to climb the steps herself. He put her hand on the horse's neck, and ran it over the mare's glistening coat.

Butterball made a noise that sounded like a sigh.

"See, she likes ye."

Eve pulled her hand out from under his. "She's just pretending to be asleep. The minute I climb on her back, she's going to decide she doesn't want to lug me up the mountain today, and gallop back to the barn."

"Butterball is as docile as a lamb. In fact, she's safe enough that Megan was five months pregnant when she rode her up the mountain last winter, in two feet of snow."

Eve knew she was being ridiculous, but she didn't care. She kept picturing Curaidh galloping as fast as the wind whenever Kenzie rode him. And then there was the fact that if she did find the nerve to climb in the saddle, she would have to spend the entire afternoon on the mountain with Kenzie.

All alone.

Just the two of them.

"What exactly are ye afraid of, lass?"

That you're going to kiss me.

Even worse, Eve was afraid she would start kissing him back, because she couldn't seem to control herself when he touched her. Then one thing would lead to another, and she'd probably start undressing him, and then . . . Oh, God. Then she'd have to explain that they'd made love the night of the storm, and now she was pregnant.

And then he'd insist she marry him, because he was an old-fashioned *highlander*!

Kenzie sighed hard enough to move her hair, and reached out and undid the cinch holding the saddle on Butterball's back. Eve sighed in relief when he set the saddle on the mounting block, glad she didn't have to ride up the mountain and risk humiliating herself.

But just as she started to climb down off the block, Kenzie lifted her onto Butterball's bare back! And before she could finish gasping in surprise, he vaulted up behind her and started them toward the path leading into the woods.

"What are you *doing*?"

"Just enjoy the ride. I'll keep ye safe," he said, pulling her against his chest.

She was practically sitting in his lap! She could feel his heat where she was plastered against him. And because his arms were around her to guide Butterball she did feel safe, but she also felt excited and frightened.

"You are such a highlander," she muttered, grabbing Butterball's mane when the horse's hoof clinked on a rock.

"What's that supposed to mean?" he asked, sounding amused.

"I'm beginning to realize it means that if things aren't

going the way you want, you simply *make* them go your way."

He laughed. "Ye just described yourself, lass."

"What are you talking about?"

He lowered his head beside hers. "Ye burst into tears last night at the police station to save Camry, when she made that foolish remark to Greylen."

"You knew I was faking it?"

"Ye expect me to believe my not noticing you were wearing my plaid made ye cry?" He snorted. "After you'd just beaten a man to a bloody pulp?"

"Just for the record, I didn't know it was your plaid when Camry gave me the blouse to wear."

"Also for the record," he said, his lips sinfully close to her ear, making her shiver. "I hope ye noticed that I didn't give ye hell for being in that bar in the first place."

"Does that mean you wanted to?" She broke out in goose bumps, despite the fact he was radiating enough heat to start a forest fire.

"I won't ever smother ye, Eve. I'm trying very hard to be the kind of man a modern woman would want."

Well, hell. He just had to take off his clothes, if that was all he wanted.

He laughed, and Eve realized she'd spoken her thought out loud! She ducked her head with a groan, blushing to the roots of her hair, and he laughed harder.

"Ah, little one, ye do please me."

She snapped her head up, clipping his chin. "I am not

little, I'm petite. And that reminds me. You called me a *pixie* to Camry, and she told me they're tiny creatures who go around making mischief. I am *not* a mischief maker."

He actually laughed harder. "Did she also tell ye that pixies like to sprinkle their magical dust on sleeping men and give them wonderful dreams?"

Eve shivered again. Oh, God, he wasn't taking her up the mountain to kiss her—he simply wanted privacy to confront her!

"I—I'm going to be sick," she said, grabbing her belly.

"No, you're not." His arms tightened around her. "Just breathe through it."

Of all the arrogant . . . "You can't *command* someone not to be sick."

He placed his hand over hers on her belly. "You will not be sick," he said, his voice deep and commanding—and definitely amused again.

She should throw up all over him, the jerk.

"Look," he whispered, suddenly pulling Butterball to a halt.

Eve silently sucked in her breath at the sight of a mother doe and fawn standing less than thirty yards in front of them. The doe had her ears perked forward, her large fluid brown eyes fixed on Butterball. The tiny spotted fawn, oblivious to them, was dancing around its mother and butting its nose in her udder, then flittering off again.

"Babies are nature's promise to us of tomorrow," Kenzie whispered against her ear. "And when a fawn shows itself to ye, it's blessing your tomorrows. Would ye like to give it a kiss, to thank it for the wonderful gift it's giving ye, Eve?"

"The minute we move, the mother's going to bolt into the woods with her fawn," she whispered back.

"Nay, not if we ask her to trust us," he said, slowly sliding off Butterball. He reached up and slid Eve down, took her hand, and started walking toward the deer as he softly spoke to her in Gaelic.

She couldn't believe the deer didn't bolt. But Kenzie simply kept leading Eve closer, murmuring softly as he held out his hand. The doe twitched her ears, lifted her nose, and gave a soft snort, then actually walked toward them!

She touched Kenzie's fingers, her nostrils billowing to take in his scent, then nudged his hand. Unable to believe what she was seeing, Eve held herself as still as a statue, not even daring to breathe.

Kenzie slowly lifted his hand holding hers, and turned her palm upward as he whispered to the doe, his voice reassuring. The doe pressed its moist muzzle against Eve's hand, and every hair on Eve's body stood on end at the delicate touch.

Something bumped her leg.

"Get down on your knees," Kenzie said in the same soft voice. "Don't try to touch it; let the fawn do the touching."

As slowly and as silently as she could, Eve knelt on the moss-covered ground.

The fawn flittered away, then came back, this time butting its tiny wet nose against her cheek, its whisper of breath warmly fanning her skin. Eve shivered in absolute delight, and turned her head just enough that her lips touched the downy-soft fur of the fawn's face just above its pink little nose.

It immediately flittered away again, giving a squeaky bleat as it sprinted around its mother. It peeked under her belly at Eve, and bleated again.

Kenzie gave a soft chuckle, lifted the doe's head by her chin, and softly blew on her snout. He said something in Gaelic again and stepped back, and the doe turned and bounded into the woods, her fawn bounding after her.

Eve knelt in the middle of the path, staring after them in mesmerized awe. It wasn't until they disappeared that she finally looked up at Kenzie. "I . . . I just kissed a wild fawn," she whispered. "How is that possible?"

He pulled her up into his arms, then kissed the tip of her nose, his golden eyes gleaming in the filtered sunlight. "It's possible because the doe took one look at you and knew she wanted your blessing on her babe."

"But I thought *it* was blessing *me*," Eve said, still whispering out of reverence at what just happened.

"And that, my little one, is exactly how the magic works," he said. "To give a blessing is to receive one."

He lifted a hand to the back of her neck, and when his head lowered again, his lips settled on hers. He kissed her with the same gentle caution he'd used to handle the doe . . . until Eve began kissing him back.

His mouth began moving over hers more urgently, and she fisted her hands against his shoulders, determined to stay in control of herself. He wouldn't think he was dreaming this time, and she wanted to savor their first real kiss. She could feel the lust radiating from every pore in his body, but he seemed to be more interested in giving than taking.

Maybe even a bit hesitant.

That thought bolstered her as nothing else could have, and she wrapped her hands around his neck and leaned into him, even as she cautioned herself about not letting things escalate.

Still wreaking havoc on her mouth, his hand slipped down her back to cup her buttocks. He pulled her against him, and every muscle in Eve's body tightened at the feel of his erection on her belly. One part of the women's lecture from last night suddenly popped into her head: how the things they loved about their men were usually the very things that drove them crazy.

And Eve suddenly understood one of those things.

When Kenzie Gregor touched her, he made her crazy with need. She tightened her fingers on his neck, the feel of his strong pulse under her thumb sending her heartbeat into overdrive. She made a noise of frustration and tried to climb up his rock-hard body, wishing she could simply crawl inside him.

He lifted her off her feet, and she immediately wrapped her legs around his waist. He cradled her bottom to hold her against him and buried his face in her neck, his lips on her own pulse sending her reeling.

"We have to stop now, Eve," he growled against her skin, making her shiver.

She fought to rein in her growing passion even as she pressed more intimately against him. "But we're just getting to the good part." She leaned back enough to look in his eyes, and was surprised at the war she saw waging inside him. "And I really want you."

He suddenly stepped back and sat down so that she was sitting on his lap, straddling him.

Which was even better, since now she could use both hands on him.

He stopped her by gathering her hands in his. "I want our first time to be as husband and wife."

She blinked at him.

She couldn't have heard right. Not only had that sounded *sort of* like a marriage proposal, it had sounded way too old-fashioned even for him.

"I brought ye up here, Eve, to ask you to marry me."

He *was* proposing to her!

"Why?" she asked.

"Because I want ye," he said gruffly, color darkening his cheekbones. "And because I believe we'll do well together. I told you earlier, ye *please* me. And ye don't seem put off by my touch; in fact, ye seem to like it. And it's important in a marriage that two people are physically attracted to each other."

Her rabbit hole just kept getting deeper and deeper.

"What century were you born in?" she asked in

disbelief. "Because you sound ancient even by Scottish standards. Or anyone's standards," she muttered, trying to tug her hands free again.

He stiffened, not letting her go. "What does when I was born have to do with anything? I'm here now, we're a good match, and I'm asking ye to marry me."

"Do you love me?"

His cheeks darkened even more. "Love is different for men and women."

"How?"

He was definitely getting hot under the collar, and Eve was intrigued despite her growing frustration. Not only was her rabbit hole getting deeper, but her definition of a highlander was expanding exponentially.

He shifted uncomfortably. "Women are born needing to love their husband and children, whereas men are born just needing."

"Needing what?"

"Women," he snapped. "We need a woman's softness to . . . to keep us . . ."

"Civilized?" Eve hazarded a guess.

"Fine, yes, to keep us civilized!" he growled.

Boy, did the MacKeage women know their highlanders, or what?

"And we women need men to protect us from bad things like . . . oh, I don't know . . . bogeymen, maybe?"

His golden eyes—which had tiny flecks of green in them—narrowed. "Are ye trying to divert the conversation?" His features softened, and he let go of her hands to cup her face. "I see that I've shocked you and ye don't know what to say, so you're asking questions to distract me." He kissed the tip of her nose, then smiled. "You don't have to give me an answer right now, little one. You can sleep on it a few days. Just allow yourself enough time to plan our wedding on the fall equinox."

"When?"

"I believe it's September twenty-first."

That was less than three months away! "Oh, God," Eve said, grabbing her belly. "I think I'm going to be sick."

Eve scrambled back to stand up, but she wasn't fast enough.

"Shhh," Kenzie said, gently patting her back as she crouched on all fours and alternated between dry heaving and sobbing in utter humiliation. "Easy now. Fighting it just makes it worse. Try to relax and breathe through it."

If he continued patting her, she was going to smack him! "Go away," she groaned, hugging her belly.

He actually left!

She looked around and didn't see him; it was as if he'd vanished into thin air. Eve straightened to her knees and peered into the woods on either side of the path. Where had he gone?

She stood up and walked over to Butterball, took the horse's reins just in case she woke up and decided to leave, too, then sat down on a rock.

Sheesh, hurl on the man, and he vanishes!

Eve placed her hand on her belly. Suppose their baby

threw up on him? Would he hand the kid off to her and leave?

She tried to picture Kenzie with a chest pack like Jack Stone had worn last night, and couldn't help but smile. Baby Walker certainly had looked safe and cozy on his daddy's chest. Their baby would be safe and cozy on Kenzie's chest, wouldn't it?

Eve rubbed her chin with her sleeve, then buried her face in her hands as tears began to fall. What a mess she was in. Kenzie wouldn't make love to her until after they were married, so how could she tell him she was already pregnant?

She jumped when something suddenly touched her hair.

"It's just me," Kenzie said, crouching in front of her.

Eve barely had time to register that he was naked from the waist up before he pressed a wet cloth to her face and began wiping her teary eyes. She leaned into the cool cloth even as she tried to take it from him to do it herself.

Of course he wouldn't cooperate. "Maybe we should ride over to the MacBains and have Libby take a look at you. You seem to be sick a lot lately, and it's starting to worry me."

"Camry offered to take me to see her yesterday," Eve said, finally getting the cloth away from him. Oh—it was his shirt. "There's no need to bother her. I have a doctor's appointment in Ellsworth next week. I'll ask about my mor— My motion sickness then."

When her gaze strayed down to his lovely, bare chest, she forced her gaze back to his eyes. "Where did you go? You left me out here all alone."

He sat down beside her, then picked up a rock and rolled it back and forth between his hands. "Unlike your first husband, I will never abandon you. In fact, I have a fear I may be quite smothering."

He looked at her with a crooked grin that didn't quite reach his eyes, then back at the woods again. "I ran away from home when I was fifteen," he said softly, "abandoning my aging mother and father, and my younger sister Fiona, which left no strong male to defend them."

"Where was Matt?"

"He'd gone seeking a new life of his own the year before. I was all they had left, and I let them down." He started rolling the rock in his hands again. "Several years after I left, a man raped Fiona and got her with child, and she died giving birth. And because our mother had taken sick and died two years before that, Fiona's son only lived a couple of weeks."

Eve's skin prickled at his obvious pain, and she touched his arm. "You're talking as if you blame yourself, when it had nothing to do with you."

"Aye, but it did. I wasn't there when my sister needed me the most."

"Did she press charges against the man who raped her? Was he convicted?"

"He was punished for his crime."

"But you couldn't have stopped her from dying, if the doctors couldn't even save her. As for the baby . . . your father must have taken him to the hospital."

Kenzie looked out at the woods again. "Papa was quite insane by then."

Eve held his damp shirt on her lap, not knowing what to say but desperately wanting to say *something*. "It wasn't your fault," she whispered. "If you had known, you would have come back immediately. But you were in the army, weren't you? It's not like you could just up and leave."

He shifted to face her, and took one of her hands in his. "If you agree to marry me, Eve, ye have my word that I will never abandon you."

The top of that rabbit hole was way, way over her head now. Oh, God—the minute she told him she was pregnant, he would have her standing in front of a minister before she could finish explaining how it had happened.

And *love* would forever be beyond her reach, because *duty* would take its place, possibly even usurping his *need* for her.

At this point, even need sounded better than duty.

She patted his hand. "I have to think about your proposal," she said softly. "But I promise that if the answer is yes, we can be married on the fall equinox."

He stared at her, saying nothing, then stood up to lead her over to Butterball's side.

"Can we walk?" she asked. "We're not that far from Gù Brath."

"I was hoping to show ye the view from the ridge."

"Is it much farther?"

"It's just around the next corner and up a short rise."

She started walking up the path. "Then come on, Mr. Highlander. Let's see if you can walk faster than you drive," she said with a laugh, determined to chase away the somber mood.

He caught up with her, then took her hand in his as he matched her stride.

She glanced over her shoulder. "What about Butterball?"

"We might as well let her nap," he said, gently swinging their hands between them. "She'll be right there when we come back."

They walked in silence after that, and Eve felt her heart expanding with each step she took. It really had nothing to do with his wrenching story, but more with the very things about him that drove her crazy. There was something rather endearing about his ancient behavior—maybe even romantic.

What she saw was exactly what she got with Kenzie: no pretenses, no posturing to impress or suppress, and only a tad of arrogance. He always meant what he said, and wasn't afraid to say what he thought.

She could do worse. She *had* done worse. She'd been living in Boston less than a year when Parker had started making her feel like he'd done her a really huge favor by marrying her, a sentiment that was echoed by everyone in Midnight Bay whenever she came back for the summer. How smart she'd been to snag herself such a handsome and rich husband who had taken her off to the big city. She had to be the luckiest girl in the world!

But at the first mention of her mother's illness, instead of being concerned about Mabel, Parker had only seen the ensuing costs of her long-term care. Around the time Eve suggested moving her mom and Nathan closer to them, Parker had turned openly hostile. And when Nathan had died last winter and Eve had suggested her mother come live with them, the bastard had cut and run.

"You know that if we were to get married, I come with a sick mother," Eve said into the silence.

"I am aware of that."

"And the medical bills are going to pile up, and she's eventually going to have the mind of a child."

"I'm quite fond of children." He lifted the hand he was holding and kissed it. "And do you know that if we were to get married, that I come with a cranky old priest who eats every meal as if it were his last?"

"And a man who thinks he's a dragon?"

He chuckled. "Aye, we mustn't forget about William."

"And if we did get married, we'd probably have children," she whispered.

"Do ye want children, Eve?"

"When I was a little girl, I always pictured myself having a bunch of kids."

He squeezed her hand. "Our house will be near to bursting, then. If we were to get married."

They broke out of the forest and up onto a ridge, and Eve sucked in a deep breath of surprise. Pine Lake stretch for miles below them, surrounded by spruce- and pine-covered mountains.

"This is too beautiful for words," Eve said.

He led her to a patch of dried grass that had blades of brilliant green shooting up through it, urged her to sit down, then sat down beside her. "That's Bear Mountain," he said, pointing to a long-ridged mountain hugging the east side of the lake. "Can ye see that clearing halfway up the middle, just below that sharp cliff? That's where Matt and Winter are building their new home." Then he pointed toward the shoreline. "Right now they're living in what will become their summer cottage after they move."

"Did you live with them when you lived here?"

He moved his hand to encompass not only Bear Mountain, but the mountain they were on. "The entire forest was my home."

"But where did you sleep?"

"Wherever I wanted. There was one particularly sweet spring that I liked to bed down near, over there." He pointed east of their ridge.

"But where did you sleep when there was snow on the ground and it dropped to twenty below at night?"

He lowered his arm to his lap. "I like being out in the weather."

Eve blinked at him. "So . . . um . . . if we were to get married, you'd still camp out?"

He laughed and pulled her into his arms, then lay

back on the grass, settling her against him so that her head rested on his shoulder. "Trust me, little one, I will be in your bed." He hesitated, then said, "But maybe sometimes we can sleep under the stars."

Eve smiled, figuring she'd never have to worry about getting frostbite since he radiated heat like a blast furnace. She snuggled comfortably against his still-naked chest, threw her arm over him with a huge yawn, and fell sound asleep.

Kenzie stared up at the clouds as he savored the feel of Eve sleeping in his arms, and tried to decide how his marriage proposal had gone. She hadn't exactly jumped for joy as he'd hoped, but she hadn't run away screaming, either.

Though her throwing up on him had certainly given him pause; he'd feared that the thought of marrying him made her physically ill. But she'd been throwing up a lot lately, possibly because the full weight of her mother's sickness was starting to sink in, and her body was trying to purge her worry.

At least Eve appeared to be taking his proposal seriously, asking questions about what their life would be like together. He smiled. It would be chaos, he figured, with several generations living under one roof, surrounded by a farm load of animals. He rather liked the chaos of Gù Brath when everyone was home, and he wouldn't mind if An Tèarmann followed suit.

He could even picture Eve sitting on the front porch, fat and happy in her fourth or fifth pregnancy, shelling peas as she watched their own little heathens chasing an ecstatic puppy around the yard.

On that note, Kenzie drifted off to sleep, a smile of utter contentment on his face.

Chapter Eighteen

Eve breathed a sigh of relief when Kenzie reached Midnight Bay and turned down the road leading to An Tèarmann. She was quite proud that she'd had to stop only once on the entire ride home, and then only for a pit stop. Her stomach seemed to be settling down!

She didn't know if it was because her body was finally getting used to being pregnant, or if Libby MacBain really did have a magical touch.

At first she thought Libby and Michael had come to Gù Brath last night simply to visit with family. But when Libby had asked Eve to go for a walk after dinner, Eve realized Kenzie had trumped her refusal to go see Libby by bringing the doctor to her.

The moment they'd gotten outside, Libby had taken Eve's hand, smiled warmly at her, and asked when she was due. She immediately assured Eve that her secret was safe with her, she just wished to help her get through the first trimester, and would she mind if they simply held hands for a few minutes.

Eve had heard about medical intuitives—people who were able to read a person's body—and didn't see what it could hurt. Though she felt a bit silly holding hands with a stranger in the moonlight, she'd placed her other hand in Libby's.

She hadn't known what she expected, but the only thing she had felt was an overwhelming sense of peace. There wasn't any heat, no tingling or goose bumps, no sudden jolts of anything. After what seemed like only a minute, Libby had let go and given her a hug, then asked if she wanted to know if it was a boy or girl.

Well, of course she did!

So she had learned that on February seventh of next year, she was having a son.

Then they'd simply walked back inside and had dessert.

And Eve hadn't felt sick ever since.

Then this morning, Winter Gregor had handed her precious newborn daughter to Eve, and Eve had discovered she was definitely ready to be a mother. Where she'd been praying for time to slow down while she came to terms with her pregnancy, suddenly February seventh seemed years away. She couldn't wait to hold her baby son in her arms, change his tiny diapers, and put him to her breast.

Some of her eagerness may have come from the warm intimacy she'd felt in the Gregor home when Kenzie had taken her and Mabel to visit them this morning. The whole house had practically throbbed with magic.

And when Mabel had held baby Fiona, her face so relaxed and at peace, a surreal sense of calm had suddenly washed over Eve. In a flash of insight, she knew that whatever may come of her illness, Mabel would not suffer for it. And Eve had decided that she would not suffer *for* her, and that if her mother wanted to teach a dragon to read, she would simply help her make up some lessons plans.

But it was when Matt had placed Fiona in Kenzie's arms that Eve had a complete and utter meltdown. Just seeing that tiny infant in his strong, capable hands had started her heart pounding so wildly, she'd had to excuse herself. She'd sat on the edge of the tub staring out the window, huge tears running down her cheeks, fighting to get her emotions under control.

She hadn't succeeded then, and she still couldn't seem to; because she kept picturing Kenzie holding *their* baby in his big hands, in *their* living room, with *their* home exuding that same intimate sense of magic.

Mabel sighed when Kenzie pulled the truck into their dooryard. "My creaky old bones don't like sitting for three hours straight," Mabel said when he opened her door. "I think I'll take a short walk to stretch my legs."

"Wait, Mom," Eve said, reaching behind her and

grabbing a plastic bag. She leaned across the seat and handed it to Mabel with a smile. "Don't forget William's surprise."

"Oh, gracious, yes," her mother said, clutching the bag to her chest. "Camry said he actually starts drooling at the smell of doughnuts," she confided, looking over her shoulder to see where Kenzie was. "But she told me not to give him more than half a dozen a day, because they make him sick, and not to let Kenzie know I've given him *any*."

Eve wasn't surprised Camry had sent something down for William, since it seemed everyone had seen the dragon man but her. She was beginning to feel discriminated against.

"Do ye love riding in my truck so much that you can't bring yourself to get out?" Kenzie asked, standing by Eve's open door.

She straightened in her seat with a smile. "You don't have to wait for me to get out. I know you're dying to check on your precious horses." She broadened her smile. "And kiss their huge noses."

He leaned in and gave *her* a kiss on *her* nose, then headed for the barn, his laughter trailing behind him. Eve got out and had just opened the rear hatch when Maddy pulled into the yard in Eve's car.

Her friend got out and gave her a hug. "I know you've only been gone three days, but I've missed you." She stepped back and gave Eve the once-over. "Something's different," she said. "Don't tell me. It's not your hair, or your clothes—though I was afraid you'd come back dressed like Paul Bunyan." She snapped her fingers. "I know. You're glowing!"

"What?"

Maddy hugged her again. "You're finally over the morning sickness, and you're into the glow-of-pregnancy stage," she said softly. "Which means that you are now officially 'with child.'"

Eve rolled her eyes and reached in the truck, pulled out her overnight bag, and handed it to Maddy. "He asked me to marry him," she whispered.

Maddy's eyes widened in surprise. "He did?" She set the bag back in the truck, looped her arm through Eve's, and started walking out the driveway. "When? How? What did you say? You'd better not have said yes." She turned down the road toward the ocean. "You'll eventually say yes, of course, but you can't make it easy for him. It's a woman's obligation to make a man sweat for a while."

She stopped and turned Eve to face her. "Did he propose in a fancy restaurant, or pop the question on a romantic moonlight walk?"

"He took me for a horseback ride up the mountain."

"And? So what did you say when he asked?"

"Um . . . I threw up on his boots."

Maddy tossed her head back in laughter. "Oh, that's priceless! The man was a ball of sweat just taking you on a date; I can't imagine what condition he was in when he asked you to marry him."

She let Eve go and started them walking again. "I hope he kissed you *before* you hurled. He did finally kiss you, didn't he?"

Eve nodded. "Oh, yeah. But when I tried to move things along to the next level, he told me he wouldn't make love to me until *after* we're married."

"Is he nuts?"

"No, he's just really old-fashioned. The woods up there are just crawling with throwback highlanders. I swear there must be something in the water in Pine Creek: all the men are as tall as pine trees, all are drop-dead gorgeous, and they all act like they're from the twelfth century."

"Robbie MacBain has certainly been turning heads in town these past few days. Susan tried batting her false eyelashes at him, but when I told her he was happily married, she burst into tears. We really need to find that poor woman a man. So," Maddy said, "after he proposed, did you tell him about the baby?"

"How could I, when he won't even make love without our getting married first?"

"I bet all you have to do is get naked with him again. And you did discover one thing that's very important. Since Kenzie asked you to marry him without knowing about the baby, you know he wasn't asking *because* of it."

"That's true. But when I asked him why he wanted to marry me, he said it's because he *wants* me."

"Wanting's good."

"But then I asked him if he loved me, and he said that

women love their husbands but it's different for men. That men only *need* their wives."

Maddy looked appalled. "Is he for real?"

"But I'm thinking of saying yes, because I've fallen in love with him."

"Even if he might never love you back?"

Eve didn't answer the question. "He wants us to get married on the fall equinox."

"Why then?"

Eve shrugged. "I have no idea. But all the MacKeage girls were born on the winter solstice, and Winter's baby was just born on the summer solstice. They must have this thing about the seasons. Their children are adorable, and all their husbands seem really nice, if unusually old-fashioned."

"How so?"

Eve shot her a grin. "They like to lecture their women."

Maddy snorted. "That's not old-fashioned, it's inbred into all men. I can't tell you how many lectures from Dad I sat through."

"Yet when Camry and I got into trouble in a barroom, Kenzie very nicely refrained from lecturing me."

"You went to a bar? What happened?"

"Two guys got physically aggressive with Camry and me. I broke my guy's nose and fingers, and Camry dislocated her jerk's knee."

"And Kenzie didn't go up one side of you and down the other?" Maddy asked.

"Nope. He just kept hugging me."

Maddy looped her arm through Eve's, and started walking toward the ocean again. "Okay then, I give you permission to be in love with him. Because I gotta tell you, Billy would have killed me if I'd gotten into a bar brawl. And I can't even guess what my father would have done."

Eve stopped and pointed out to sea. "What's that?"

"It looks like a water spout." Maddy pointed to the west. "There's another one. And another one!" She looked at Eve, her eyes huge. "That's weird. I didn't think water tornados formed this far north."

They stared out at the unnatural phenomena, which swiftly grew in number and size a few miles from shore.

"Omigod, that's it!" Eve cried. "They're unnatural! Come on, we have to get back to the house. I have to find Kenzie!" She started dragging her friend. "And Mom is walking down by the ocean!"

"Eve!"

Eve turned at the sound of Kenzie's voice, and saw him running toward them. "Kenzie, look!" she cried, pointing at the spouts.

"I see them," he said when he reached them. He took her hand and started leading her back up the road. "Come on. You both need to get in the house."

"But we have to find Mom! She's walking down by the ocean."

"MacBain went after her," he said, breaking into a jog, forcing her and Maddy to run to keep up. "I want you two to gather some flashlights and blankets, then take Daar and Mabel down to the cellar and stay there."

"Only if you're coming to the cellar with us," Eve said as they reached the driveway. She couldn't bear to think of him in danger again.

"Nay," he snapped, glancing toward the path beside the barn. "There's Robbie. He's carrying Mabel. Come on."

"No! You are not going after whatever the hell that is!"

"Jeesh, Eve, they're just water spouts," Maddy said, walking toward the house. "They'll probably break up the moment they touch shore. "Let's find some flashlights and get in the cellar until they pass. We'll play cards and eat junk food."

Kenzie swept Eve off her feet and into his arms. "And you stay in the cellar until I come get you, understand?"

She dug her fingers into his shoulders. "But . . . I'm afraid you might not come back."

"I'm not alone this time, little one. Robbie MacBain will be with me."

"Why can't we *all* sit in the cellar until it leaves?"

"Because if I do nothing, it will likely kill William."

Eve drew in a shuddering breath, terrified and confused. "*What* will kill him? I don't understand any of this."

He bounded up the stairs onto the porch. "Trust that I *will* come back for you." He gave her a quick kiss on the lips. "And when I do, I will tell you everything."

The door opened and Robbie stepped out of the

house, holding a sword very similar to Kenzie's in his left hand.

"Did Maddy see that?" she hissed, glancing in the kitchen.

"No, she's in the cellar with Daar and Mabel," Robbie said, looking Kenzie in the eye. "We need to go *now*."

Kenzie set Eve on her feet. "Give me your word you'll stay in the cellar. I can't keep my mind on what I'm doing, if I'm worried about you coming after me."

"O-okay. I promise."

"No matter what ye hear, you keep everyone down there until I return."

"I will." Eve pulled down his head and kissed him full on the mouth. "You make sure you come back."

"Aye, I will," he said gruffly, his golden eyes locked on hers.

Then he left, the screen door slapping shut in the rising wind. Eve went to the window over the sink and saw Robbie and Kenzie disappearing down the path to the ocean, heading directly toward the unnatural storm.

She turned, hugging herself tightly. Something dark and sinister had followed Kenzie and William to Midnight Bay, and it seemed determined to stay until one or both of them were dead.

Oh God, she hoped he'd remembered to take his magical burl and pen.

* * *

"Will she stay put?" Robbie asked as he stood beside Kenzie on the island, facing the angry tempest heading toward them. "Or did you have to lock her in?"

"She gave me her word," Kenzie said, stripping off his shirt, then pulling his sword from its sheath just as William came running over to stand beside them. "I thank ye, MacBain, for staying to help."

Robbie shrugged to loosen his shoulders. "I believe it's in my job description, that Guardians have to help protect even bogeymen."

"You're a bully, MacBain," William said, arching his neck to glare past Kenzie at Robbie. "You didn't have to frighten Mabel like that."

"You're a fine one to talk," Kenzie said before Robbie could answer. "Ye terrified Eve the night she came looking for me."

"The woman needed prodding," William snapped. "She was taking forever to get to you." He glared at Robbie again. "But Mabel's not right in the head, and she didn't want to go with you just now because she couldn't remember who you were. You didn't have to carry her home. I almost had her talked into going."

"There wasn't time to persuade her, as she refused to leave unless you agreed to go hide in the cellar with her."

"I hide from no one and no thing," William growled. He eyed the tempest growing closer, then looked at Kenzie. "Where's your fancy pen?"

"In my truck."

He snorted. "That's a hell of a place for it."

"If I use it, the old hag will retreat just like last time. The pen is for protection, and merely protecting ourselves solves nothing. We need to dispatch her and her minions to hell where they belong." He used his sword to point inland. "If ye don't want to face your demons, Killkenny, then go to the cellar with the women."

"Or you could just open your black heart," Robbie muttered, flexing his grip on his sword. "That would put an end to this mess quick enough."

"I don't know what that means!" William roared, the blast causing Kenzie and Robbie to step back. "Don't you think I'd save myself if I did!"

"Christ, you're hard-headed," Robbie said, brushing soot off his chest. He turned his back to face Kenzie, blatantly dismissing William. "Did you ask Eve to marry you, then?"

"I did."

"And?"

"And she threw up on me."

"The pixie threw up on you?" William repeated. He cocked his head. "So would that have been a yes or a no?"

"It was a maybe."

"Did you explain the magic to her?" Robbie asked.

"Nay. But I believe the magic has been explaining itself to her." He nodded toward the approaching storm. "Today she finally asked me what this was about."

"And you told her . . . ?"

"That when I got back, I'd tell her everything."

"Including your own past?" Robbie asked, arching a brow.

Kenzie hesitated, then nodded.

"Well, my friend and our hard-headed nightmare," Robbie said, lifting his sword as he turned to face the howling gale. "Let us fight the good fight!"

No sooner had Kenzie raised his own sword and shouted the Gregor war cry, when the tempest slammed into the island, surrounding the three of them in a vortex of screaming demons.

The battle was fierce, and more than once the outcome was in question. Kenzie knew he was the old hag's true target, since he was the one trying to break her curse on William, but the dragon took the worst beating. And though he'd been born in this modern time, MacBain wielded his own sword with the lethal precision of a true highland warrior.

Robbie MacBain was a Guardian, pledged to protect innocent mortals from getting caught up in the struggle between the dark magic and the drùidhs' work of nurturing mankind, and Kenzie was glad and honored to have MacBain fighting beside him.

William, however, seemed only intent on hacking his way through the demons to get to the hag who had cursed him. Kenzie let Robbie guard the dragon's back, and focused on weakening the witch's dark powers by slaying her minions.

But it wasn't until he saw several of them break off and head to the mainland that he grew truly alarmed. Had the old hag sent them to the farmhouse, suspecting Eve had become his greatest weakness?

He fought harder and with renewed anger, desperate to shorten the hag's reach now that her focus was split between fighting the battle and finding Eve. MacBain also must have realized what was happening, because he left William to come fight beside Kenzie. Together they methodically dispatched the vicious demons to hell, their swords growing black with the vile blood of evilness.

The witch, forced to call back her army in order to protect herself, retreated out to sea with a bloodcurdling scream of defeat and vow of revenge.

Chapter Nineteen

The howling wind had gotten so loud at one point, Eve could have yelled at the top of her lungs and Maddy, sitting beside her, wouldn't have heard it. They'd heard doors banging, windows shattering, dishes breaking, and wood splintering as the century-old farmhouse shuddered on its foundation. At the height of the storm, Eve would have sworn the floor above shook under the weight of footsteps tromping through the house, as if someone—or some*thing*—was searching for them.

Now there was just stark, chilling silence.

Which was even scarier.

"When . . . whenever they interview tornado survivors on TV, they always say it sounded like a freight train," Maddy finally whispered. "But it sounded to me like people *screaming*."

Eve snapped on the flashlight that she'd turned off when she'd heard the footsteps, illuminating the cellar. Mabel and Daar sat beside them, blinking in the sudden light. Mabel was clutching Daar as if she was still afraid he might blow away, and Daar was clutching his rosary beads.

Maddy clung to Eve with equal fervor.

The storm had started weakening about twenty minutes ago, and the house had gone completely, eerily silent five minutes ago.

Still, none of them seemed quite ready to move.

"I don't think we're in Kansas anymore," Eve said, shining the light at the stairs.

Maddy's chuckle had an edge of hysteria. "Do you think there's still four walls and a roof up there?"

"I suppose I should go find out," Eve said, not moving.

At the sound of heavy footsteps entering the house, she snapped off the flashlight.

The cellar door opened. "Eve," Kenzie called down.

"We're here!" she cried, jumping to her feet and running to the stairs. "We're all okay!" She stopped with her foot on the bottom step when he motioned for her not to come any farther.

"I need ye to come up alone," he said, his voice labored. "Ask Maddy to stay with Mabel and Daar a bit longer."

Oh God, it must be bad. She walked back and handed the flashlight to Maddy, who had obviously heard his request—as well as his tone.

"Go on," Maddy said, scooting next to Mabel and wrapping her arm around her. "We'll sit tight until you can get some of the debris cleared away. You stay, too, Father," she told Daar, pulling the blanket over his legs. "We'd just get in their way."

Eve gave Maddy a thankful nod, then ran up the stairs. Kenzie took hold of her arm as she stepped into the kitchen, and her knees nearly buckled when she got a good look at him.

"Oh God," she whispered.

"It's not as bad as it looks," he said, limping away from the cellar door, detouring around the upended table. He stopped by the gaping hole where the porch door should have been, then turned to face her.

He had a cut over his left eye that was still oozing blood, a dark bruise on his chin, and a large welt on his temple. His bare chest, shoulders, and arms were covered in scratches.

Basically, he looked pretty much like he had after the last . . . storm.

"Are ye sure you're okay?" he asked, as if he didn't believe his eyes. "And Mabel and Daar and Maddy?"

"The cellar was virtually untouched," she assured him. "One of the tiny windows blew out when a branch hit it, and some old jars and tools fell off the shelves. But nobody got even a scratch." She touched his cheek. "Is it over? Is whatever was out there gone for good?"

"Probably not," he said, glancing outside. "The house

is uninhabitable, and the barn is no longer sound. We're going to have to camp out until I make repairs."

"Mom and Daar and I can stay with Maddy for a few days. It'll be cramped, but that's what neighbors do for each other."

He tightened his grip on her shoulders. "Nay. We remain together. I'll set up a new camp in the forest, away from the ocean. You and Mabel gather up whatever we'll need and set it in a pile on the porch."

Eve also glanced outside. "Where's Robbie?" She looked up at him. "And . . . William?"

"MacBain only got a few scrapes and is tending to William. Killkenny was hurt, but he'll live."

"The burl! We can use it to heal you and William."

He shook his head. "We're not hurt badly enough to squander what's left of its energy. We'll be fine in a few days."

Eve frowned up at him, then looked out the doorway. "What happened to the animals? My nannies, and Gretchen, and . . . your horses?"

"Robbie turned all the animals loose just before we left, even the hens. Those that survived will find their way back."

Eve buried her face in her hands. "I don't understand any of this. What *is* it?"

He pulled her hands down and held them in his. "It's the dark side of magic, little one." He pressed her palms against his chest. "But ye needn't worry. As long as I have breath in me, it won't come near you."

"But magic isn't real!"

"Shhh," he crooned, running a finger down the side of her face. "Tonight, once everyone is settled in camp, you and I will go for a walk and I'll explain everything to you. Come," he said, leading her to the cellar door. "Bring everyone up and send Maddy home."

"But what do I tell her?" Eve looked around at the wrecked kitchen. "How do I explain to Maddy what just happened?"

"Let her think it was just a freak storm. She already believed the spouts would break up when they hit shore, so she won't be surprised that the damage didn't reach farther inland."

"I-is it going to happen again?"

He placed a finger over her lips. "I will answer your questions tonight."

Eve had spent the rest of the afternoon helping Robbie and Kenzie set up camp, wishing the night would hurry up and get here yet dreading its arrival. Now she was about to take a walk with a man who was as mysterious and undefinable as was her love for him.

She looked around their cozy campsite, and finally realized the rabbit hole she'd fallen into didn't have any exit. The hole she'd slid down was one way, and her only hope of surviving this free fall was if Kenzie was at the bottom, waiting to catch her.

Despite all the mysterious events that had been going on since she'd met him, when she was with him, she felt utterly, perfectly safe. Her mother had called him a gentle giant the day they'd met, and Eve had certainly seen proof of that in the way he handled her, Mabel, Daar, his animals, and even a wild deer. But lurking behind that gentleness, Eve knew there was a dark and dangerous side to Kenzie Gregor—and that was exactly what made her feel safe with him.

He set his plate on the ground and stood up, then settled the leather sheath holding his sword so that it rode diagonally across his back. "Is everyone set for the evening?" he asked, his gaze stopping on Mabel. When she nodded, he looked at Robbie MacBain. "I don't know when we'll be back."

"It doesn't matter," Robbie said, setting down his plate and lacing his fingers behind his head with a tired sigh. "We'll be right here when you do."

"Daar?" Kenzie asked.

Daar grabbed Robbie's plate, which still had some pie on it. "I forgot my pillow, and I can't sleep without it."

"I'll go get it," Robbie said, standing up with a groan. "I need to check if more of the animals came back, anyway."

"I don't think we should leave Mom and Daar alone," Eve whispered to Kenzie.

"Oh, we'll be fine," Mabel said, obviously having heard her. "William's nearby."

"But you said he's hurt," Eve pointed out.

Her mother smiled. "If I scream, he'll come crawling if he has to. He would never let anything happen to me."

Eve looked up at Kenzie, and found him smiling, too.

The first thing Mabel had done when she'd emerged from the cellar was rush up to Kenzie and quietly demand to see her friend—at least having the sense of mind not to mention the dragon in front of Maddy. Mabel hadn't even batted an eyelash at the destruction to her home, but had simply refused to lift a finger to help if she wasn't taken to him immediately.

Kenzie had taken her to William, and when she'd come back, her mother had proudly told Eve what a brave, tough dragon he was. Then she rolled up her sleeves and went to work searching for whatever they'd need to camp out.

Getting Maddy to leave, however, had taken forever. First she wasn't leaving without bringing Mabel and Daar home with her. When she realized that wasn't going to happen, she wanted to help them set up camp. It wasn't until Eve had taken her aside and told her she wanted to be alone to tell Kenzie about the baby that Maddy had reluctantly left—with the promise of returning right after she got out of work tomorrow.

"That was a wonderful meal, Mabel. Thank ye," Kenzie said, leading Eve toward the path to the ocean.

She hesitated, and he stopped and looked down at her. His face was so battered and bruised, and she knew every cut and scrape under his shirt, because she'd tended to every one. She wasn't sure she was ready to learn what had made them.

"Have ye changed your mind, then?" he asked softly.

"No. No," she said a bit more firmly, starting them off again. "I'm just afraid of what you're going to tell me."

"Afraid?" he asked in surprise. "This from a woman who took on a man twice her size?"

"I could see and touch that man in the bar."

They walked in silence for a bit, then Kenzie asked, "And because ye believe something is real only if you can see it, if ye *can't* see something, then it must not be real? Is that how it works?"

"Well . . . no, not always. I can't see radio waves, but they're real."

"Suppose ye substitute the word *magic* for radio waves. Would that help explain what ye can't see?"

She stepped over a broken branch, then frowned up at him. "You're saying magic is like radio waves?"

He took her other hand in his and held them over his heart. "Magic is *energy,* Eve. It's what powers everything: from the sun and stars, to the ocean waves, to my heartbeat. And yours," he said, moving her hands over her heart. "Have ye never wondered what powers *you*?" He cupped her face between his warm, battered palms, locking his gaze on hers. "The entire universe is inside ye, lass, just as you are in the universe. And all of it—everything that you can and can't see—is nothing but pure energy."

"I know that," she said. "It's the doctrine of almost every known religion. But what has any of that got to do with magic?"

He reached in his pocket, pulled out his cell phone,

and held it up between them. "I only have to push one button on this phone, and within seconds I can be speaking to my brother, even though Matt is a couple hundred miles away."

"But that's not magic. It's radio waves."

"It might not be magical to you, because modern science has revealed its secret." He flipped open the phone, making the screen light up. "But not a century ago, if I'd shown this to anyone, they would have called it magic."

He snapped the phone shut and returned it to his pocket, then started walking again. "Most people forget that what someone calls magic today, science will explain tomorrow."

"So those strange storms or whatever they are," Eve said, waving in the direction of the ocean. "You're saying they're magical energy?" She stopped to reach up and touch a cut on his throat. "That *energy* made this scratch? It looks like a claw mark to me."

"It was a claw that made it," he said, covering her hand, "and that claw was as real as the scratch it left." He dropped their hands between them. "But the demon attached to the claw was nothing more than energy that had been manipulated by a ninth-century witch."

"A witch." She started trembling. "Are you implying that people—call them witches or whatever you want—can turn energy into something solid and real, and that this real thing can actually kill a person?" She shook her head. "That's like saying William is really a man who only *thinks* he's a dragon, and suddenly he's ten feet tall and can fly."

He took hold of her shoulders. "And therein lies the answer to all your questions. Everything you can see and touch and feel is nothing more than your mind trying to make sense of what you *can't* see. But modern technology is getting us there, in what Camry calls quantum physics. Scientists are now able to see the energy that makes up a rock, a tree, a bird, and you."

"So I'm just supposed to accept that witches and demons and dragons are real, even if I can't seem them, because maybe a thousand years from now science will prove that they exist?"

"Aye," he said, leading her into a dense thicket of stunted spruce. "In exactly the same way that you've finally come to accept your mother's illness, even though you can't fully understand what's going on in her mind, you must accept that the magic is real. It truly is that simple."

"Or that complicated?"

He lifted a finger to his lips as he led her deeper into the spruce. "Shh. I believe MacBain gave him herbs to make him groggy. He may be awake or sleeping, or somewhere in between."

Eve used his grip on her hand to slow him down as she tried to adjust to the dimming light. She wasn't actually afraid; she just wasn't sure she was fully prepared to finally meet the *him* he was talking about.

They stepped into a small clearing and Kenzie pulled her in front of him, wrapping his arms around her so that her back was against his chest. "This is your mother's good friend, William Killkenny," he said softly, in deference to the softly snoring creature curled up on the grass.

"But you said . . . why is he . . ."

Honest to God, she was looking at a ten-foot-long, scale-skinned, gossamer-winged *dragon*. She pressed back into Kenzie, unable to tear her eyes away from William.

"If he's really a man," she whispered, "then why does he look like a dragon to me? I don't believe in them, so why should I see him as one?"

"Because what *William* believes about himself is far more powerful than what you or anyone else thinks of him," Kenzie softly explained. "And he believes he's a dragon, so he is. When he lived in ninth-century Ireland, an old hag cursed him for burning her home and throwing her off his land. She turned him into the most horrible, feared creature of that time, and William will remain a dragon until he either opens his heart to others in a way he's never been able to, or he finally realizes that the hag's curse is nothing more than a trick she played on his mind."

Eve frowned up at Kenzie. "Then if it's just a trick of his mind, why haven't you simply explained that to him?"

He chuckled humorlessly. "I have, at least a hundred times. But you have to remember what century he's from. People of that time believed witches could either grant them wishes or turn them into nightmares, so trying to change William's thinking is the same as telling him everything he's ever believed in is false."

"I . . . I want to touch him."

Kenzie hesitated only a moment, then led her over to the sleeping dragon. He really was a magnificent beast; iridescent scales covered powerful muscles, his head was a fascinating blend of mythological lore and reptilian nonevolution, and his wings—one of which covered his body like a blanket—were nearly as long as he was, including his tail.

He looked dangerous and powerful and definitely scary: exactly like a ninth-century nightmare. Or a twenty-first-century fairy tale.

Kenzie took her hand and ran it along William's long, muscled neck.

"He feels warm," she whispered in surprise.

"Because he's a warm-blooded man."

"He's magnificent."

"Not to the people of his time, he wasn't."

Eve looked up, arching one brow. "How did he get to *this* time?"

Kenzie led her out through the spruce and back onto the path, heading toward the ocean. "He came here the same way I did. He used the magic to manipulate time."

She pulled him to a stop, then had to tug on his shirt to get him to look at her. "What do you mean, the same way *you* did?"

"According to your modern calendar, I was born in Scotland in the year 1048."

Her heart literally stopped, causing the blood in her head to build to a pounding roar that made her dizzy. Eve took a step back.

She couldn't have heard right.

Or he had to be kidding.

But he certainly looked serious, his gaze locked on hers as he stood as still as a statue, every muscle in his body as tight as a bowstring.

"How can that be? You're not a ghost. I can touch you, so you *must* be real. I even had sex with you." She gasped, holding her belly. "I'm pregnant with our son!"

He also stepped back, his face going pale in the twilight. "What did ye say?" he whispered. "You're with child? But how? When?" He took another step back. "That night you found me on the cliff—" He covered his face with his hands. "Christ, it really happened."

"Look at me," she snapped, pulling his wrists down. "I started it. Do you understand? I was scared and confused and thought I was dreaming, so I just . . . I thought that if nothing about that night was real, then what harm would there be in acting on my fantasy. We were both clearly willing."

He merely stared over her head. "I know what you're thinking, and this is *nothing* like what happened to your sister," she growled. "I started it, Kenzie!" she said, slapping her chest.

When he still said nothing, she reached up and cupped his face. "Tell me you're not going to suddenly disappear back to the eleventh century."

He pulled her into a crushing embrace, lifting her off her feet and burying his face in her neck. "I won't leave you. I promise, I won't disappear." He lifted his head to look at her. "Ye said we're having a son. Ye know it's a boy?"

"Libby MacBain told me he'll be born on February 7."

"A boy," he repeated, burying his face in her neck again.

He was shaking, and she didn't know if he was truly pleased or just badly shocked.

"I—I'm sorry," she whispered into his hair. "I didn't mean this to happen," she rushed on. "I know it's not an excuse, but I really wasn't thinking straight that night, and I was . . . I tried to . . . I couldn't think about anything except feeling you inside me. I'll understand if you take back your proposal, because the last thing I want is for you to feel trapped or tricked into marriage."

He took hold of her hand and started walking to the ocean again. "We'll be married tomorrow."

Eve pulled her hand out of his, crossed her arms against the sudden chill in her heart, and faced the ocean. "No, we won't."

He walked up and stood behind her. "You will not carry my babe without benefit of a ring on your finger and a husband to take care of you."

"I know you're from a different century, but today, babies and marriage don't always go together." She spun around to look up at him. "I will not marry a man who feels he has to marry me."

"I love you."

That warmed up her blood as nothing else could have. "You do not. You already explained that men don't love women, you just *need* us." She turned her back to him again. "This discussion is over."

Eve didn't have to turn around to know he was gone. She stared out at the gently swelling ocean illuminated by the low-hanging moon, tears running down her cheeks.

She had no one to blame but herself.

Other than keeping the mother of all secrets that he truly *was* ancient, he'd been nothing but honest and direct with her.

Except just now, when he'd lied about loving her.

Chapter Twenty

Eve jumped and would have fallen if Kenzie hadn't swept her up into his arms.

"Dammit, quit sneaking up on me like that! Put me down."

"Shh," was all he said, striding up the bluff through the spruce.

"Don't you shush me! I am not some eleventh-century lassie who thinks that a man's word is gospel, and that being barefoot and pregnant and churning butter is the next best thing to heaven."

He set her down on a sleeping bag laid out next to a crackling fire, which told her where he'd gone when he'd vanished. Before she could get up, he straddled her legs and took both her hands in one of his.

He brushed a stray tear off her cheek. "I love you."

She dropped her gaze with a shuddering breath.

He lifted her chin with his finger. "I love you."

"I don't care how many times you say it—I'm not marrying you tomorrow, in September, or ever."

Instead of saying it again, he started unbuttoning her blouse.

"Oh, no you don't," she hissed, trying to stop him. "I don't care if you *are* God's gift to women in bed—you're not going to change my mind with sex."

She managed to free herself, but quickly realized it was only because he needed both hands to undress her. She was quite dizzy by the time she finally found herself flat on her back, as naked as the day she was born, her hands pinned over her head and his leg thrown over hers. And somehow, during their lively little wrestling match, his own clothes had disappeared.

He splayed his hand over her belly, the heat of his palm making her shiver. He kissed her temple, the corner of her eye, her cheek, and then her chin as he cupped one of her breasts—which had grown nicely plump with her pregnancy; she hoped he noticed.

She tried not to respond, even though it killed her. Manipulating her with sex was . . . it was . . . dammit, it was dirty pool she decided, stifling a moan when he brushed his thumb over her nipple.

Watching his head dip toward her breast, his broad shoulders flexing in the moonlight, made her nearly melt with anticipation. When his mouth covered her nipple and he softly suckled, she arched up with an involuntary cry. And the moon reflecting off his finely sculpted muscles was so erotically mesmerizing, all she could think about was licking them.

His fingers began tracing a skin-shivering trail down her belly, over her pelvis, and then . . . She opened up to him, mindless with the need for him to touch her. Just as his fingers found her sensitive bud, he left her breast and covered her mouth, catching her cry of pleasure. His fingers slid over the slickness he was creating, pushing inside her and withdrawing, driving her into a frenzy.

She tightened around him, digging her heels into the sleeping bag, lifting her hips to meet his delicious thrusts. His mouth left hers and returned to her breasts, suckling first one nipple and then the other. And when his thumb started working its delirious magic on her, her focus narrowed and the world receded to a mere backdrop of haze-filtered moonlight.

She came hard and fast and with disgraceful abandon. She shouted her pleasure to the stars, bucking wildly against his hand to capture every last sensation roaring through her.

Afterward, she sucked in ragged breaths, trying to get control of herself. He kissed her face again, gentling her, then ran his fingers through her hair, brushing the sweat off her forehead as his lips caressed her cheeks. His other hand rested on her pelvis, his fingers spanning her from hip bone to hip bone.

She refused to open her eyes, knowing he'd have a smug look on his handsome highlander face, his golden eyes piercing her with a triumphant gleam.

A lingering spasm shivered through her.

Why wasn't he saying anything?

She cracked open her eyelids, just enough to watch his gaze journey down her body. Another delightful aftershock suddenly wracked her, and his hand on her pelvis tightened. His head dipped again, landing on her rib cage and heading . . . south.

"Ohhhh," she moaned when his mouth reached its ultimate destination.

He tucked her hands under her backside, lifting her up as his broad shoulders held her legs open to him. His tongue delved into her, then retreated, then circled her sensitive bud, quickly working her back into a frenzy she wasn't quite sure she'd survive.

She dug her heels into the sleeping bag, lifting toward him, her knees clamping his shoulders as she felt herself coil tighter and tighter. This time it hit her like a nuclear explosion, sending her to the stars and back so suddenly, she didn't even have time to scream before she shot back into the heavens.

She couldn't take much more, but he didn't seem all that concerned at the moment, his mouth working her like a finely tuned instrument. She finally started pleading with him, begging him to make it stop before her heart did. And just when she thought he'd finally heard her, he knelt up, pulled her hips onto his thighs, and poised himself to enter her.

Eve reached up and braced her hands on his shoulders. She was aroused and slick and more than ready for him, but she tightened as he slowly entered her.

"Relax," he crooned against her ear.

"I . . . I can't."

"Aye, ye can. Just breath through it."

A nervous laugh bubbled free. "That doesn't help."

He touched the tip of his nose to hers. "Feel me like you did that night," he continued, his lips brushing hers. He pushed deeper. "Take me inside ye and surround me with your heat."

That *definitely* helped. She used her grip on his shoulders to pull him closer, and since his mouth was so close to hers, she laid a passionate kiss on him. She lifted her hips, her inner muscles pulling at him until he filled her completely.

She clenched around him, tearing a raw sound from his throat, and used her hips to urge him to move. "Don't hold back," she rasped. "I want you deep and hard." She wrapped her legs higher on his back, her tension spiraling into a raw, desperate need for him to slip his control. "I won't break, Kenzie. I need you."

He surged into her like a wave crashing on shore, then retreated and surged even deeper. She met each thrust with moans of encouragement that quickly turned to cries of ecstasy.

His jaw clenched on a guttural snarl, and he shook with the force of his own climax as Eve convulsed around him in waves of pulsating heat.

She panted to catch her breath, which nearly became impossible when he lowered most of his weight onto her, either unable to move or reluctant to pull out of her. He finally lifted his head with a crooked grin, his eyes glowing like golden starlight.

Eve smiled back, running her fingers across his sweaty forehead. Between the shadows cast by the full moon, and the sweat from his . . . exertions, the damage to his face was quite pronounced.

She ran her finger over the bruise on his chin. "You could have been killed."

"But I wasn't."

"But you *could* have been."

He sighed. "I could get kicked in the head by a horse, too. Or slip on a rock and drown in the creek."

"I'm going to talk to William and set him straight so those horrible demons will quit coming here."

"William won't listen to you. He thinks you're just a scrawny little lass who can't even walk down a road in the dark without screaming her head off."

"If that overgrown lizard ever works up the nerve to show me his ugly face, I'll show him how scrawny I am."

His chuckle vibrated through her, and he kissed the tip of her nose. "I think we'd best let Mabel work her magic on William right now." He finally rolled off, snuggled her up to his side, and placed his hand on her belly. "You just concentrate on planning our wedding and growing my son."

"I don't want Mom mixed up in any of this," Eve protested.

"Mabel has made more progress with William in six weeks than I have in six months. Don't worry, she's not in danger."

Eve started running a finger through his chest hair. "And I haven't said I'd marry you yet. But while I'm trying to decide, there's no reason we can't have an affair."

"And what about when you're seven months along and don't have a ring on your finger or a husband in your bed? Who's going to rub your tired feet, and fetch ye glasses of milk at two in the morning?"

She popped her head up to look at him. "You'd do that?"

"Husbands have duties, too."

She sighed. "Yeah. Not the least of which is marrying the women they get pregnant, even when they don't remember getting her pregnant."

His arm tightened again. "If I *remember* correctly, I asked ye to marry me before I knew you were with child."

"But that was when you wanted to marry me only because you *needed* me. Not because you *had* to."

"You're talking in circles, lass."

"I know," she said with another sigh. She pulled the edge of the sleeping bag over her hip, then patted his chest. "Once you get your strength back, just wake me if you want to have sex again, okay?" she said with a yawn, then promptly fell to sleep.

Kenzie wasn't able to fall asleep so quickly.

After battling the last storm of demons, as he'd run flat-out back to the farmhouse, so afraid of what he'd find in the cellar, he had suddenly realized that he loved Eve.

When he'd told her that tonight, she hadn't believed him, and it would do no good to tell her again. It wasn't only that she thought he was lying; he'd sensed something else was bothering her. Her talking in circles now confirmed it.

What was his fearless pixie afraid of?

He smiled up at the moon. Certainly not sex. If she was any more fearless when it came to making love, they'd both be dead right now.

When she'd told him she was having his son, he'd felt like he'd just taken a blow to the gut. How could he not have realized something so basic, considering how attuned he'd become to life since his return to humanity? Her throwing up, her naps, her emotional outbursts—if she'd been wearing a picture of a babe on her forehead, her condition couldn't have been more clear.

But he was too tired to think straight himself, tonight. Battling demons was hard enough, but making love to Eve was even more exhausting. In the most wonderful way.

Kenzie fell asleep with a smile on his face, his hand covering his unborn son.

Chapter Twenty-one

"He won't let you lift a finger to clean the house?" Maddy repeated in disbelief. "Wow, you should stay perpetually pregnant."

Eve shot her a glance as she locked up her store.

Maddy just laughed. "So what was his reaction when you told him?"

"He didn't say much of anything for several minutes, then suddenly announced that we were getting married tomorrow. Which is today."

Maddy looked down at Eve's ring finger, then arched a brow.

"I told him I wouldn't marry a man who felt he *had* to marry me."

"And he said?"

"That he loved me."

Maddy slapped herself on the chest. "That bastard."

"Exactly."

"I was being sarcastic, you idiot. The man really *is* in love with you!"

"That was a mighty huge leap in two days, don't you think?"

Maddy looped her arm through Eve's and started walking down the sidewalk. "Kenzie Gregor is madly, deeply, passionately in love with you. So put the poor guy out of his misery and marry him. You know you're going to eventually, so why torment not only him but yourself?"

Eve looked for traffic, then pulled Maddy across the street. "And just what makes you so sure I'm going to marry him eventually?"

"Because *you* are madly, deeply, and passionately in love with *him*."

Eve pulled her out of the way of foot traffic. "When did you become an expert on my love life?"

"I've had a front-row seat to this entire courtship, remember?" She crossed her arms under her bosom. "Let me guess what happened after he told you he loved you. I bet he pulled you into his arms and kissed you senseless. And you being you, I bet you started undressing him, then made wild, passionate love to him right there on the beach, in the moonlight."

"Wrong. He picked me up and carried me to his old campsite, stripped me naked in two seconds flat, and *he* made love to *me*." Eve shot her a lopsided smile. "Honest to God, he just had to touch me and I exploded. *Several* times."

"Holy shit."

"And you remember how you thought he was an all-nighter kind of guy?"

Maddy nodded vigorously.

"You were so right. I think we made love more times last night than Parker and I did on our entire two-week honeymoon."

"Oh my God," Maddy groaned, fanning her face with her hand. "Dammit, why doesn't he have any brothers who are single! I want my own Kenzie Gregor."

"There's a bunch of MacKeage and MacBain highlanders up in the mountains who are single," Eve told her, stepping back onto the sidewalk and nearly running over Betty Simpson. "Oh, hi, Mrs. Simpson," she said. "Did you find a kid to stack that firewood for you?"

"Hi, Eve. I hear congratulations are in order."

"On what?"

"On your engagement to Kenzie Gregor."

Eve could only gape at her.

Betty gave her a sly wink. "That was quite cunning of you, Evangeline, to take that job as his housekeeper. Best way for a woman to snag herself a rich husband is to keep him well fed, and show him you're more than your pretty blond hair and big blue eyes." She patted her arm. "I guess your engagement took care of all your financial problems, didn't it?"

"Who told you Kenzie and I are getting married?"

"Ruthie, at the bookstore. She said Mabel told her just this morning." Betty patted her arm again. "I was sorry to hear that odd storm destroyed your house. But don't worry, I'm sure Kenzie will build you a new one. Maybe he'll even add on a mother-in-law apartment for Mabel." She winked again. "Newlyweds certainly don't need mothers living with them."

"I'm sorry we've got to run, Mrs. Simpson," Maddy said, dragging Eve down the sidewalk. "I only have half an hour for lunch. Nice seeing you again."

"Bye, Maddy. And congratulations again, Eve!"

"That nosy old busybody," Maddy muttered, pulling Eve around a corner.

"She said almost that exact same thing to me when she found out I was marrying Parker."

"Omigod—are you afraid everyone in town is going to think you got pregnant on purpose to snag him? Don't you dare listen to Betty Simpson. You didn't catch Kenzie—he caught you!"

"But everyone will still *think* I caught him."

"So who gives a rat's ass?" Maddy grabbed Eve's shoulders and actually shook her. "What *you* think and what *Kenzie* thinks is all that matters. But you want to know what I think?"

"What?"

"I think that on the fall equinox, you should have the biggest, fanciest wedding Midnight Bay's ever seen."

"Oh, that'll certainly stop the gossip."

Maddy hugged her. "You can't stop them from

gossiping, Eve. But neither can you let them stop you from marrying a man you truly love." She leaned back to stare into Eve's eyes. "If I survived their whispering when I was only eighteen and seven months pregnant when I married Billy, you sure as hell can."

"I'm sorry if I was one of those people whispering behind my hand," Eve said, pulling her back into an embrace. "I barely knew you back then, but that's no excuse. Will you forgive me?"

"Only if you marry Kenzie. If you don't, I may never speak to you again."

"Liar," Eve said, leading her back toward her store.

Maddy tried to go in the other direction. "Hey, the Port of Call is this way."

Eve took a fortifying breath. "I promise I will face the gossips, but not today, and not in the Port of Call. Let's just go back and eat banana bread until our eyes cross."

"Did they already bring over a batch?" Maddy asked, falling into step beside her. "I can't tell you how excited Mom was when Mabel asked if she could do her baking at our house. Your little cottage industry has given Mom something to fuss over besides my delinquent brother. Hey—will you look at that," she said, pointing up the street.

A tractor trailer rig carrying an excavator wasn't anything out of the ordinary. But a convoy of trucks slowly rolling through town, all of them with tartans painted on their doors and up over their hoods, definitely stopped people in their tracks.

"Will you look at that," Susan Wakely said as she came to stand beside them. "I don't recognize the emblem, but what a pretty design. I wonder who they are?"

"I think that's the MacBain plaid, and I also think I know some of those men," Eve said as the lead pickup stopped in the middle of the road right in front of them.

The passenger's-side window rolled down. "Would you lovely ladies know where the turnoff is to An Tèarmann?"

Susan walked right up to the truck. "It's your very next right," she said, pointing down Main Street.

"Much obliged," the passenger said with a nod.

The driver leaned forward to see past him. "Eve?" he said, his smile widening. "I thought that was you." He nodded toward the trucks behind him. "With a bit of luck and good weather, this crew will have you back in your house in a week."

"Duncan MacKeage, isn't it? You're . . ."

"Callum's son," Duncan said with a grin. "You'd need a really big notebook to keep us all straight." He motioned behind him again. "Most these guys are from Robbie's logging crew, but they also know how to swing a hammer. Two of Morgan's sons, Ian and Hamish, are also with us." He waved her back to the curb when a car trying to pull onto the road tooted its horn. "We'll see you tonight, Eve."

The convoy started off.

Susan immediately grabbed her arm. "You *know* them?" she asked, hungrily searching every truck that drove by.

"They're from Pine Creek," Eve said, extricating herself. "They're cousins of Robbie MacBain, the man who came to babysit the farm while we went away."

Susan sighed. "I suppose they're all married. All the handsome ones are."

"Actually, I think all three MacKeage men are single."

Maddy and Susan both perked up.

"Um . . . maybe I could come over this evening and help you clean out your house so they can repair it," Susan offered. "And I could bring over a double batch of my strawberry shortcake. It looks like you suddenly have a lot of mouths to feed."

Maddy vigorously nodded agreement. "I'll bring some of Mom's beef stew and a few pies. And several jugs of that milk you've got cramming our fridge. I never realized how much milk a cow puts out."

"Poor Gretchen didn't give any milk last night. I think the storm scared her so badly, it'll take a week for her teats to unshrivel."

Susan snorted. "Listen to you, talking just like a farmer's wife." She looked at her watch. "I have to get back to work, but I'm going to see if I can get off early to go home and bake." She stopped and glanced at the convoy turning down the road to An Tèarmann. "Maybe I'll take some of my vacation this week." She smiled at Eve. "After all, neighbors need to help each other when disasters strike. I'll see you this evening," she said with a wave, rushing toward the bank.

"Six to one she arrives tonight wearing painted-on

jeans, a bra that pushes her tits up to her chin, and a blouse cut so low we'll see her belly button," Maddy said with a laugh.

"Oh yeah? And just what are you going to show up wearing?"

Maddy gave her a sidelong smirk. "I intend to wear shorts so short, I'll have two more cheeks to powder."

"I see you're feeling well enough to cause trouble again," Kenzie said, taking a taste of the soup he was cooking over the open fire.

William snapped his tail in agitation. "I haven't moved from this spot all day. And that's your fifth spoonful! Mabel cooked that especially for me, not you. Get your pixie to make you your own pot of chicken soup."

"Ye told Mabel that I asked Eve to marry me."

"Was it a secret? Then maybe you should have made that clear when you told *me*. Besides, Mabel and I don't keep secrets from each other." William sidled closer to the fire, cursing when he put weight on his injured leg. "In fact, she told me a secret about Eve you might be interested to know."

"And that would be?"

"I can't say, because Mabel asked me not to. But I can say that you have me to thank for it."

Kenzie lifted the pot off the fire and held it over the ground, tipping it just shy of dumping it out. "What, exactly, do I have to thank ye for?"

"You wouldn't dare!"

He let some of the soup spill onto the ground.

"The pixie's pregnant!" William growled, moving to stop him.

Kenzie calmly set the soup back on the fire.

William snarled and grabbed his injured leg. "You knew."

"Eve told me last night. But I thought Mabel didn't know. That's what Eve led me to believe."

"Oh, your pixie hasn't told her. But Mabel is her mama, and mothers always know what their daughters are up to." He shuddered. "I can't tell you the mamas I've had come after me with a pitchfork." He grinned. "Mabel's likely to come after you with a chopping axe if you don't make an honest woman of her daughter."

"I'm trying." Kenzie glared at William. "You just keep your ugly nose out of my business."

"So does that mean you're not going to thank me?"

"For what?"

"For your bedding the pixie and knocking her up."

"How did *you* have anything to do with it?"

William puffed out his scaly chest. "You never would have met her if it wasn't for me causing you to move to Midnight Bay. I'm also the one who made sure she found you the night of the storm." He arched his bulbous eyebrows. "Assuming that's when you finally nailed her."

Kenzie just stared at William.

William glanced down at his long curved claws, then polished them on his chest as he looked at Kenzie. "What? Am I being too crude for you again?" He snorted.

"You're turning into one of these modern pansies who hand over their balls to their women to carry around in their pockets. Eve is carrying your babe, and you're following her around like a puppy, begging her to marry you. You're a warrior, for chrissakes! Act like one! Tie her up if you have to, and stand her in front of the old priest."

Kenzie walked toward the edge of the small clearing. "After your soup, if ye feel like taking a little walk to rebuild your strength, ye might want to go watch what's going on at the house. Maddy and another friend of Eve's have come over this evening to help the crew with the repairs."

Kenzie let go of Eve's hand when they came to the shoreline, reached into his shirt pocket, and handed her a ballpoint pen. Eve held it up to the moonlight to get a brief look at it, then carefully put it back in his pocket.

He took it out and tried to give it to her again.

"I don't want it," she said, tucking her hands behind her back. "That's yours, and you need it."

"If you'd held it more than two seconds, you would have realized this one is smaller, made for your hand."

When she still refused to take it, he simply tucked the point of it in the opening of her blouse, then tapped it down into her bra. Eve gasped and shoved her chest toward him. "Take it out before it accidentally goes off!"

He tucked his hands behind his back. "It won't accidentally go off. You can even use it to write with."

Eve stared down at her chest, taking shallow breaths that started to make her dizzy. When blazing light didn't suddenly shoot out, she raised her eyes to his. "Is it an old highland tradition to give a woman you want to marry a *pen*?"

"They didn't have ballpoint pens back in the eleventh century," he said, his eyes glinting in the moonlight. "And whether or not we marry, this pen is yours. You're to carry it with you at all times."

"So if it's a writing instrument, why do I have to carry it at all times?"

"Because it's also a weapon."

She immediately shoved her chest at him again. "I don't *want* a magical pen." She forced a smile. "It's really sweet of you to offer me one, though. It's just that I wouldn't know what to do with it." She suddenly had a thought. "Unless I can use it to turn Susan Wakely into a toad?"

He plucked the pen out of her bra, set it in her palm, then closed her fingers over it. "Ye can't turn anyone into anything with it. This is merely protection from the dark magic."

Eve frowned. "But all you did was push the clicker on yours that night, and light shot out where the ballpoint should have been. If I try to write with it, I'll blow something up."

Still holding her fingers closed over the pen, he used his thumb to push down the clicker. Eve flinched, but only a ballpoint popped out the other end.

"Everything depends on your intention," he told her, clicking it several times, making the ballpoint pop in and out. "If ye want to write, it's a writing instrument. When ye want to protect yourself, it becomes a weapon."

Kenzie turned her hand so that the end pointed safely away, and clicked it again. A pencil-thin stream of light shot out the end and exploded a tiny rock several feet away.

"Holy shit," she whispered, and extended the pen toward him. "I don't want it. I might kill someone."

"Only if ye want to kill them," he said. "It's what your *intention* is, Eve. With just a little practice it will tune itself to you, then carry out your intentions without your even having to think about it."

"So if Maddy were to try to write with it, it wouldn't go off on her?"

"Once it's tuned to you, it won't even work for me."

She looked down at the pen. It really was quite pretty, for a lethal weapon. It was made of some wood she couldn't identify, and felt substantially heavy yet surprisingly right, as if it were made just for her. "Where did you get it?"

"When we visited Pine Creek, I asked Matt to make a pen like the one he made me, sized for your hand."

She looked up at him again. "What's so special about Matt, that he can make magical pens?"

"He's a drùidh. And so is Winter."

"A drùidh? As in a pagan priest?"

"Nay. That's a modern definition. In Gaelic, drùidh loosely translates to wizard."

"Matt and Winter are *wizards*?"

He lightly tapped the tip of her nose. "And *they* can turn people into toads."

No wonder she'd felt like their home had been filled with magic. Boy, this rabbit hole just kept getting deeper and deeper.

"Um, how do I know when the dark magic is threatening me?"

"You'll know. And if ye only suspect you're in danger, your pen will certainly tell ye. It will start vibrating like a modern cell phone."

"Does it only work on dark magic? Let's say I was walking down an alley some night and a man jumped out and attacked me. Could I blast him to smithereens?"

"If that was your intention."

"Holy shit," Eve whispered. She held the pen up in the moonlight.

"But if your intention is only to get away from your attacker, then it won't blast him to smithereens," he said, amusement lacing his voice. "I told ye, once it tunes itself to you, it will be whatever you need it to be at that moment."

"But what happens if our son gets hold of it? Since it's tuned to me while I'm pregnant, would it be tuned to him?"

"It won't work for him. When the time comes, each of our children will be given his or her own pen." He took hold of her shoulders, kissed the tip of her nose, then turned her around so that her back was against him.

"Okay, let's practice a bit. Click the pen, but expect the ballpoint to appear."

Eve held it pointing out to sea, clicked the head of it, and a thin stream of blinding light shot out, sending up a tall plume of steam where it hit the water. She immediately clicked it off and frowned up at Kenzie. "It didn't work."

"Because you didn't believe one word I just told ye, and you expected light to come out." He held onto her shoulders and faced her back out to sea. "Picture the ballpoint appearing, Eve. *Expect* it to appear."

"But if I'm scrambling to protect myself, I'm not going to stop and think *ballpoint* or *light.* I'm just going to point and shoot."

"Ye only have to concentrate on what ye want until it's tuned to you. Then you won't have to think at all. It will know what ye want, because it's an extension of your energy."

"It's not a trick of my mind, is it, like what that witch did to William?" She smiled up at him. "Are you trying to trick me into believing I have a powerful weapon to protect myself?"

He turned her back to face the sea. "Honest to God, I had less trouble teaching the puppies to piddle outdoors instead of in the barn. Can ye at least *try*?"

"To piddle outdoors?" she asked.

He sighed.

Eve stifled a giggle. Teasing him was so much fun, because it was so easy. She couldn't decide which endeared her more: that he'd asked his brother to make a pen especially for her, that he trusted her with the magic, or that he respected her ability to take care of herself and their child.

Or children.

Eve clicked the pen and the ballpoint appeared, then clicked it again and watched it disappear. She pointed it down at a piece of driftwood on the beach, clicked the head of the pen, and didn't even flinch when the driftwood blew to smithereens.

Kenzie wrapped his arms around her with a laugh. "Again," he commanded.

She clicked the pen and made the ballpoint appear, then repeated the action several times.

"Now make that piece of driftwood over there only burst into flames," he told her, pointing down the beach to her left.

Eve aimed the pen, pictured a small flame appearing on the driftwood, and clicked. Light shot from the pen, the wood smoked for only a second, and then a single tongue of flame rose out of it. Eve blew on the end of her fancy pen like it was a smoking gun, and tucked it into her cleavage.

Kenzie kissed her cheek with a laugh. "You put most highland women to shame. Winter started landslides and set half the woods on fire when she was trying to master the magic."

Eve turned in his arms and shot him an arrogant grin. "So does that mean if I practice and practice, I can be a drùidh like Winter?"

"Sorry," he said, shaking his head. "Winter's power was several thousand years in the making. And Matt is descended from the Children of the Mist, and is the most powerful drùidh alive today."

"What exactly do drùidhs do?"

"They guard the Trees of Life."

"And what role do the Trees of Life play?"

"They control the energies of the Earth. If the trees die, so does mankind."

"That's pretty important work."

He kissed her nose. "So is growing a baby. Come on," he said, taking her hand and heading toward the bluff. "It's time for bed."

"But camp is that way," she said, pointing in the opposite direction. She tried to pull him to a stop. "It doesn't look good to all those men if we both disappear until morning."

He finally stopped and turned to her. "Are ye saying you want to share my bed in a camp full of men?"

"Of course not. I intend to sleep next to my mother."

"So ye don't mind embarrassing me in front of my family and friends?"

"How would that embarrass you?" she asked, confused.

"Ian, Hamish, Duncan MacKeage and Robbie MacBain all know that you belong to me now, and they'll question my ability to control my woman."

Eve gaped at him. "And just when did I become *your woman*?"

His grin slashed in the moonlight. "The night on the cliff in the storm." He leaned down so he was looking her directly in the eyes, all traces of his smile gone. "Or more precisely, the moment you decided to jump my love-starved bones."

He didn't look like he was joking.

"So . . . are you saying that as long as those men are here, we have to sleep at your old campsite so you won't be embarrassed?"

He started leading her up the bluff again. "Ye might want to warn Maddy and Susan what they'll be in for if one of the MacKeages takes a liking to them," he said with a chuckle. "Even though they were born in this century, they prefer the courtship practices of their fathers' time. Those lasses could find themselves stolen away to a cabin high on TarStone Mountain."

"That's kidnapping!"

"Only if the woman presses charges."

"And what makes you think a modern woman wouldn't?"

"Because by the time she got free, she'd only be thinking about marrying him," he said, sweeping her off her feet and carrying her up the bluff.

Chapter Twenty-two

In less than ten days, a nearly finished—and bigger—barn sat where the old one had been, and she and Mabel and Daar had moved back into a totally remodeled house four days ago.

Eve suspected magic was involved, but she couldn't prove it.

Both Maddy and Susan had taken two-week vacations, and had worked right alongside Eve trying to feed the men three meals a day—which was much easier once the stainless steel, double-ovened, eight-burners-and-a-griddle commercial range Kenzie had bought was hooked up.

Eve had also noticed there was a new hand-powered butter churn sitting on the porch, but she had refused even to lift the cover and look inside. Mabel was churning their butter over at Maddy's house with Maddy's mom, when both women weren't tending Bishop's Hearth and Home and Bakery, which was now open only from noon to four, five days a week. If people wanted baked goods or to buy a woodstove, Eve figured they could adjust their schedules accordingly.

What a difference a few months made, she mused as she checked the stew in one of four large pots. Only two months ago she'd been newly divorced and looking bankruptcy in the eye, as well as looking for a place where she and her mother could live.

But that was before she *belonged* to Kenzie Gregor, she thought with a smile, touching her belly. She wasn't showing yet, but she'd switched to elastic-waist pants because her belly got softer as it prepared to stretch with her son.

"Have you seen Susan?" Maddy asked, striding through the kitchen. She poured herself a glass of water, guzzled down half of it, and turned to frown at Eve. "She went missing around eleven this morning without saying a word to anyone. Her car's still here, but nobody's seen her."

Eve gasped in alarm. "Are Ian, Duncan, or Hamish missing?"

Maddy finished her water and shrugged. "I have no idea."

Eve started for the door, but suddenly stopped. If one of those highlanders had abducted Susan, who was she to spoil their fun? Susan would think she'd died and gone to heaven if a rugged Scotsman whisked her off to some mountain hideaway.

Eve turned back to Maddy just as her friend was wiping her cleavage with a damp towel. "My God, how many push-up bras do you own? I swear you've worn a different colored one every day this week."

Maddy adjusted her ample bosom back into place with a grin. "Hey, a girl's gotta use whatever assets she has. When was the last time you saw that much unmarried testosterone in Midnight Bay? Never!" she answered her own question. "And Duncan told me he actually owns a kilt *and* a sword. I bet it's a really *big* sword." She grinned. "And thick, and strong, and . . . unbreakable."

Eve nearly doubled over in laughter. "You are sooo bad." She pointed at the door. "Those aren't boy toys out there, and you are playing with fire. What are you going to do if one of them tries to sweep you off your feet?"

"I'm going to blow his socks off," she drawled. "Or anything else I find when I undress him."

"I mean it, Maddy. You are literally playing with fire."

"I like fire in a man. I passed on Kenzie because he scared the bejeezus out of me, but 'once bitten, twice shy' is not how I want to live the rest of my life." She waved her hand at Eve. "My God, the dust hadn't even settled from Parker, and look where you are now. I've been hiding behind my youthful mistake for six *years*! Your courage to follow your heart has given *me* the courage to dig mine out of mothballs, shine it up, and put it back in my chest." She gave Eve a long, fierce hug, and when she pulled away, there were tears in her eyes.

"I'm really just practicing on those guys out there," she softly admitted, "because I'm not quite *that* brave yet." She swiped at her eyes, then shot Eve a lopsided smile. "Sorry for turning all sappy, but it's been a tough week, realizing what a coward I've been and how much work I have ahead of me. And the house seems so empty without Sarah. I swear I didn't know a little girl could take up so much space."

"When are Billy's parents bringing her back?"

"Not for another two weeks. I thought a motor-home tour of every state east of the Mississippi would be good for her, but it's nearly killed me." She looked out the window above the sink, then turned to Eve. "Have you seen Mabel? Mom's out there setting the dinner table under the oak tree, and she's been looking for Mabel to help her for the last half hour."

"She must be out for a walk," Eve said, going out onto the porch.

She scanned the dooryard, but saw only men working. Her mother must be with William again. Sheesh, for a dragon, he sure seemed to need a lot of babying.

"She often loses track of time when she goes for a walk," Eve said when Maddy stepped onto the porch beside her. "If you'll watch the stew, I'll go find her."

"Maybe she's on her island," Maddy suggested, going back in the house.

Eve walked to the barn, and had just reached the door

when Robbie suddenly took hold of her arm and led her away.

"If you don't want to see what kind of damage a dragon can do when he's angry," Robbie said before she could ask about Mabel, "then you might want to tell Maddy to go home and change her clothes. Better yet, tell her to stay home until after my crew leaves."

"What? Why? Maddy hasn't done anything wrong." She suddenly smiled. "Wait . . . angry dragon? Has William got a crush on her?"

Robbie didn't return her smile. "I'm worried it's more than a crush. That beast is very near to exploding, and the next time he sees your friend sashaying by one of my crew, all hell might break loose. I'm serious, Eve: send Maddy home. William's liable to kill the next man who even talks to her."

Eve looked around. "Is he out there watching us right now?"

"No, he's with Kenzie. There's another storm heading this way, and they've gone to investigate."

Eve clutched his arm. "Is it that witch again?"

"No, but it is unnatural. We think another soul like William is trying to reach Kenzie."

Eve gaped. "Another dragon is coming here?"

He shook his head. "Kenzie never knows what's going to show up until it actually does."

"Um . . . does this happen often?"

"Even before he changed back to a man six months ago, he'd already embraced his calling as a soul warrior.

He helped a couple of displaced souls when he was Gesader."

"Gesader?"

Robbie frowned at her. "The panther?" His eyes widened, and he cursed in Gaelic. "Hell, he told me he was going to tell you."

"Six months ago, Kenzie was a p-panther?"

"Ask your husband your questions." He started to walk away.

Eve felt her rabbit hole caving in on her. She belonged to a *soul warrior*?

"Wait—did my mother go with Kenzie and William?"

Robbie shook his head. "No. I haven't seen Mabel for an hour at least."

Eve looked around the dooryard. "Hey, did one of your men take my wood delivery truck to town to pick up something? It was parked over there," she said, pointing to the end of the driveway.

"No, we have our own trucks."

"Then my mother must have!" Truly alarmed, Eve ran up to Robbie. "We have to find her. She could get confused and become lost."

"She's probably just gone to Maddy's house to get something she forgot when she moved back here."

"No, Maddy's mother is looking for her, too. Mom would have told her if she was going after something." Eve started running toward the path leading to the ocean.

Robbie caught up with her and pulled her to a stop. "Where are you going?"

"To find Kenzie. He has to help me find Mom!"

"Okay. You go get him, and I'll send my crew out on the roads looking for your delivery truck."

Eve ran down the path, but slid to a stop when she reached the ocean and saw William wading out of the surf, with Kenzie on his back! William spotted her and fell back into the water with a horrified expression, dumping Kenzie into the water with his own shout of surprise.

"Goddammit, Killkenny," Kenzie growled the moment he gained his footing. He grabbed the retreating dragon's wing and hauled him back around to face him. "She already saw ye, so quit acting like a shy girl."

Eve scrambled down the rocks, right into the surf, and grabbed Kenzie's sleeve, ignoring the fact that a ten-foot-tall dragon was glaring at her. "You have to help me find Mom. She took the truck over an hour ago, without telling anyone where she was going. She might be confused, and could have gone anywhere. I don't know where to start looking!"

Kenzie led her out of the water and helped her up over the rocks. "We'll find her," he promised.

"I'll help," William said, coming to stand beside them.

Eve sidled away so that Kenzie was between William and her.

"I can search from the air in far less time than you can in a truck," the dragon continued, spreading his massive wings. His long neck arched down so he could look Eve in the eye. "Which direction should I go first? If Mabel isn't confused, is there someplace she might have gone? To the food store? Or your store?"

"You can't fly in broad daylight," Kenzie said, leading Eve up the path. "Go to your campsite. We'll find Mabel."

"I want to help!" William growled, lifting into the air and landing in front of them.

"If ye want to help, then go see if ye can't find whoever is coming in with that storm," Kenzie said, pointing out to sea.

"To hell with them—I need to find Mabel!" William roared, smoke shooting from his nostrils. He snapped his tail, mowing down several large bushes like blades of grass. "I fear she *is* confused. When she brought me breakfast, she was talking in French again, as if she thought she was a young woman."

"If you're spotted, a mob will scour the woods for ye," Kenzie said, "and they won't stop until you're hanging from a tree in the middle of town. Now go to sea."

"I can't do nothing, Gregor! What if Mabel is hurt?"

Eve started running for the house. She didn't care if the entire world saw William; she just wanted her mother back home in one piece.

"We'll find her, Eve," Kenzie said, jogging beside her. He pulled her to a stop, put his fingers to his lips, and whistled so loudly that Eve's ears rang.

"What are you doing?"

"William's right. We do need to search from the air."

Eve heard a shrill, piercing screech overhead, and Kenzie raised his arm level with his shoulder. A red-tailed hawk, just like the one on their sign at the end of the driveway, swooped down and landed on his arm.

"Eve, I'd like you to meet Fiona Gregor."

"Y-your sister's a hawk?"

"Actually, she's a Guardian, like Robbie MacBain, but to me she's still my baby sister."

"Your sister's a hawk," Eve repeated. She took a deep breath, then squared her shoulders. The hawk had cocked its head and was studying her with one sharp, perfectly round eye. "Fiona, my mother is driving an old, black truck with a big boxlike rack on the back. She took off about an hour ago. We don't know in which direction, but she couldn't have gotten more than thirty or forty miles."

Kenzie turned Fiona to the rising wind, and the hawk spread her wings and took to the sky with a shrill call. He then grabbed Eve's hand and started running down the path to the farm.

"Fiona will find her," he said, as the first sprinkles of rain started to fall. "In the meantime, try to decide where Mabel might go if she's thinking like a young woman again. We'll get in my truck and start by checking the school she taught at."

"Give me your cell phone," Eve said, holding out her hand as she ran to keep up. "I'll call 911, and have them broadcast an APB on the truck."

* * *

William spun around with a start when Fiona landed on a branch over his head. "What do you want, you accursed bird?" He scowled at her.

"Kenzie and the pixie asked me to go look for Mabel."

William's scowl deepened. "Then why aren't you?" he snapped, flapping one of his wings to shoo her away.

"I might ask you the same question."

William started pacing again. "Kenzie won't let me go search for her because it's daylight. We can't risk my being seen by the moderns."

The hawk gave a decidedly feminine snort. "And when did Irishmen start taking orders from Scotsmen? What I heard must be true: dragons don't have stones."

William's head shot up and he shot a quick burst of fire at her. Fiona merely laughed as she settled her feathers back into place. "Did I speak an untruth, or are you offended because it is true?"

"If the moderns catch a glimpse of me, they'll hunt me down like the monster I am and hang my carcass in the town square."

"Ahhh, we certainly wouldn't want that, would we?"

"I'm not afraid! And I'd take several of the pansy moderns with me, I can tell you that." He snapped his tail, striking the tree she was perched in and making it shudder. "*Go,* you troublesome woman! Mabel might be in trouble!"

"But the soul seeking sanctuary needs me more, Kill-kenny. I truly hope they find your friend." She swiftly flew out to sea, heading directly into the storm.

William roared in anger and in fear for Mabel, who had made him bacon with maple syrup for breakfast just this morning, who talked with him for hours on the island, who so patiently taught him to read.

Then he pictured her lying on the seat of that old truck, her forehead bleeding, and cold rain coming in through the broken window and stealing her life heat.

He used his tail to wipe the drops running down his cheeks, then turned into the wind, spread his wings, and lifted into the sky. He rose into the thick ocean fog being pushed ahead of the storm, then circled back toward land, gaining speed with the wind.

"I'm coming, Mabel," he roared, singeing treetops as he blew his fiery breath to see the ground below him. "They may hang me, but I will save you, my friend!"

Chapter Twenty-three

"Where's your magic now?" Eve whispered hoarsely, staring at the tow truck pulling their battered old delivery truck out of the bay.

Kenzie had tried three times to wrap his arms around her, but all three times she'd pulled away to stand rigidly, her arms crossed under her breasts and tears streaming down her cheeks. He'd also tried to at least set a jacket over her shoulders, but she'd only shrugged it to the ground. So all he could do was stand behind her in the pouring rain, the blinding strobes of the sheriff's car and the tow truck lights intensifying the tension humming through the air.

"The magic has nothing to do with life and death, little one, but how we embrace both," he told her.

He motioned for Maddy to stop her advance, and shook his head when Eve's friend tried to hand him an umbrella. He inched closer until his chest barely touched Eve's back, and fought the pain squeezing his heart when a shudder wracked her body. "I have lived and died hundreds of times, Eve, and I give ye my word, Mabel is right now on a journey you would envy. She's where she needs to be, little one," he offered, his hands hovering over her trembling shoulders.

"Yeah, well, I prefer she was here with me."

He finally clasped his hands behind his back, his own gaze locked on the truck as it emerged from the water. Several men rushed to the hole where the door used to be and looked inside, then looked at the sheriff and shook their heads.

The retreating tide had revealed the truck a little over an hour ago, when one of MacBain's crew had driven down to this desolate boat launch—that was over thirty miles from home—in his search for Mabel. The man had waded out and dove in the water, but had found the door opened like it was now and the cab empty. He'd called Robbie first, then 911.

The sheriff's department had deputies suiting up to dive, while others checked the surrounding woods and shoreline for any sign that Mabel might have made it to shore on her own.

So far, they'd found nothing to indicate that she had.

"Please let me take you back to the house," Kenzie pleaded. "There's really nothing more to be done here, and the search could go on well into the night."

"No."

"Then would ye at least change into the dry clothes Maddy brought ye, and stand under an umbrella?"

"I don't want her to be dead," she whispered. "She's all I have left."

"Nay, ye have me. And you have our son."

Eve turned, and his knees buckled at the abject sadness in her eyes. Her lower lip quivered as she sucked in another shuddering breath. "I-I didn't get to tell her about the baby," she cried, throwing herself at him. "She didn't know!"

"Aye, but she did," he said, clutching her to him and kissing her wet hair. "William told me just today that Mabel told him you are expecting."

She looked up at him. "She knew?"

"She was your mother, little one. She likely knew before you did."

She buried her face in his chest with a wracking sob, and Kenzie pulled the edges of his jacket around her, trying to warm her up.

Yes, where was the magic now, he wanted to roar. What good was his knowledge of life and death and his understanding of the mystery and magic of both, if he couldn't console Eve? Because as her heart was breaking, so was his.

If only there was some way he could persuade her, or better yet *show* her, that Mabel was right now mingling with stardust, floating in those raindrops falling to earth, and whispering in her tiny grandson's developing ear how much he was loved.

If only he could explain that Mabel wasn't here because she was *everywhere*.

Kenzie saw Robbie MacBain brush his foot over the ground near the edge of the boat launch, as if to obscure a track in the mud. He then looked directly at Kenzie with a slight smile, and headed toward him.

"We need to get home," Robbie said softly as he strode past, gesturing at the sky with his eyes and silently mouthing the word *William*.

Kenzie swept Eve off her feet and carried her to his truck. "Get the blanket from the back," he told Maddy. "You can sit with her."

After Kenzie tucked the blanket around Eve in the backseat, Maddy wrapped her arms around her.

He got behind the wheel, and Robbie MacBain opened the passenger door and got in beside him.

After turning the heater on high, Kenzie headed toward home, Eve quietly sobbing.

He was stopped by a roadblock of police cars and fire trucks when they reached Midnight Bay. Kenzie rolled down his window as a sheriff's deputy approached.

"You folks might as well turn around and go back the way you came," the officer said. "I can tell you an alternate route to Ellsworth, if that's where you're going."

"We live here in Midnight Bay," Kenzie said, looking up the street. Several men leaned over the hoods of trucks, all pointing rifles at something. The hair on the back of his neck rose, and he looked at the officer. "What's going on?"

"You've probably heard rumors about some sort of creature roaming about, and it seems we've got it holed up in the library. It came striding down Main Street clear as day, carrying a woman in its arms." He shook his head. "I swear the thing looked like a damned dragon. It's got wings and everything. Hey," he said, ducking lower to look in Kenzie's window. "Wasn't there a man in the passenger seat?" He straightened, looking around. "Where the hell did he go? I didn't see him get out."

Kenzie opened his door and the officer stepped back, his hand going to his gun.

Kenzie lifted his hands for the officer to see them. "There wasn't anyone in front. Just two women in the backseat."

Eve scrambled out just then and immediately started running toward the library.

"Hey!" the officer shouted.

Kenzie caught up with her just as she reached the lawn. The men aiming their guns at the library all shouted, and he raised his hand to them as he wrapped his arm around Eve and lifted her off her feet.

"Mom!" she screamed at the library. "He's got Mom!"

"Shhh, easy, Eve," he growled, dragging her out of the line of fire. "Ye can't go running in there."

"But she must still be alive! What if he was trying to get her help when they chased him in there? Where's my pen?" She frantically searched her pockets. "I'll *make* them let me go in!"

"Nay," Kenzie snapped, plucking it out of her hand.

"MacBain is in there with them, and if Mabel is alive, he'll bring her out."

Someone shouted, "The door's opening!" and the actions suddenly worked on several rifles.

"Don't shoot," Robbie called from the top of the library steps. "We're coming out. Please lower your weapons."

Eve gave a shuddering sob when he walked down the steps . . . without Mabel. MacBain had left the huge double doors open. A shimmering white light suddenly filled the library, shooting out through the doors and the windows on all three floors.

Then a bare-assed naked man walked out, carrying Mabel.

Kenzie grabbed Eve's hand and started running.

"She's concussed, but she's awake and talking," Robbie said when they reached him. "Let him bring her to you." He shook his head. "I wish you could have heard those two in there just now."

"That's *William*? He's a man again?" Eve stared toward the library.

Kenzie squeezed her shoulders. "He must have finally loved someone more than he hated himself, and the ugly shell surrounding his heart finally fell away."

Robbie touched Eve to make her look at him. "Your mother told Killkenny to dump her on the steps and escape by way of the roof, but he said the only place he was dumping her was in Kenzie's arms. He cared more about her welfare than he feared the mob out here waiting to kill him."

He looked over his shoulder at William walking toward them, then at Kenzie. "I don't know if we've just witnessed a miracle, or gotten *ourselves* cursed." He slapped Kenzie on the shoulder and grinned. "I fear the man is going to be more trouble for you than the beast."

"Gregor, take this woman to the doctor!" William demanded.

"Mom?" Eve gently touched her face. "Are you really okay?"

"I'm fine," Mabel said. "But William is a hardheaded pain in the ass!"

"Mother!"

Mabel blinked, then reached out with a shaking hand and touched Eve's arm. "I was trying to go to our old home, Evangeline. I thought that if I could just get there in time, Jens would be waiting for me."

Tears rolled down Mabel's cheeks. "But I got confused, and then lost. And the road suddenly stopped, and the next thing I knew the truck was filling with water." She looked over at the naked man standing beside them. "And then William swooped out of the sky, breathing fire to light his way, and plunged right into the water. He tore open my door and dragged me out, and . . ."

Mabel clutched Eve's sleeve. "And then he flew off with me. I *flew,* Evangeline," she whispered, her voice filled with wonder. "This great, noble beast carried me to safety. But the closer we got to town the less he was able to fly, because his wings started to shrink. He ended up walking right down Main Street, carrying me." She looked at William and smiled. "You are my hero, William Killkenny."

William stepped back when several men rushed up wheeling a gurney, as several other men, rifles in hand, ran toward the library. Kenzie set Mabel on the gurney, then pulled Eve into his arms as the medical people tended to her mother.

"Psst," Maddy whispered from beside them. "Eve, who *is* that man?" she asked, nodding toward William. "And why is he naked?"

William strode directly up to her, clasped her face between his large hands, and kissed her full on the mouth, not letting up even as she pounded his naked shoulders. When he finally pulled back, he said, "If I ever see you wearing short bloomers again, Maddy Kimble, I'll make sure you can't sit on your pretty little ass for a week. Understand?"

"Who the *hell* do you think you are? Eve!" she said, trying to turn her head. But Killkenny just held her facing him.

"Maddy?" he said very, very softly.

"*What,* you lunatic?"

"Boo."

Chapter Twenty-four

Eve sat on her porch in the early morning sun, her hands folded on her lap, as Kenzie—*his* hands tucked behind his back—paced back and forth.

"To begin with, ye don't ever take out your pen when you're angry. It's only for when ye feel threatened, or when one of our children or someone else is threatened."

Eve nodded agreeably.

"Now, about your refusal to marry me." He stopped and folded his arms over his chest. "Doing things your way isn't working for me. I find I'm uncomfortable with our sleeping together every night, virtually under the noses of a priest and your mother. Father Daar will marry us this evening, and tonight I am sleeping in my house, in our bed."

Eve added a smile to her nod this time.

His jaw slackened slightly, he frowned, then he started pacing again. "And about your mother's near death," he continued. "I've been thinking of how I can show ye that death isn't the end of someone. So I've decided that this fall we'll go back to Pine Creek, and ye can talk with Jack Stone."

"What can he tell me that you can't?"

"Stone is a North American shaman, and from what I've read on shamanism, he helps individuals have visions of what we can't see. Now, about Maddy and William."

Eve jumped to her feet. It was one thing to sit through a lecture about herself, but she refused to sit through one about Maddy and William. She ran up to Kenzie, wrapped her arms around his waist, stood on tiptoe, and kissed his chin.

"I'd really love to continue our little chat, but if you expect us to get married this evening, I have a lot to do."

He kissed the tip of her nose, then rested his forehead against hers. "I love you," he said softly.

"I love you, too."

"I wasn't just saying it the first time so you'd feel better about marrying me," he said. "I realized I loved you when I was running back to the house to get you out of the cellar, afraid the storm had harmed you.

"And," he continued in a rush when she tried to pull away. "I was a black panther when I came to this century. And Fiona really is my sister and a hawk, and she didn't go look for Mabel because she knew William would.

"*And*," he continued when she started fidgeting. "I'd like to name our son Kyle, after Fiona's son."

"Anything else?" Eve asked. "Because your son is pressing on my bladder, and if you don't finish fast, it's not going to be pretty."

He immediately let her go.

Eve waited until she reached the bathroom before she started laughing. First thing tomorrow, she was going to e-mail the MacKeage women that she'd found another way to shorten a lecture.

And so it was that on the plain-old-ordinary day of July thirty-first, Eve found herself standing in front of Father Daar in the dooryard of An Tèarmann, surrounded by a menagerie of farm animals and a red-tailed hawk, about to pledge her troth to the man of her dreams.

Who also just happened to be a soul warrior.

And though she thought it was a very noble profession he'd been called to, she wasn't sure *every* soul was worth saving. Case in point: William Killkenny.

He was standing on Kenzie's right—no less imposing for being fully clothed—and was casting lecherous glances at Maddy, who was standing on Eve's left.

Utterly scandalized at being publicly kissed by a very naked man yesterday, Maddy had spent the day avoiding William. And this evening she was wearing pants so baggy it was a wonder they stayed up, and a blouse buttoned all the way up to her neck, even though it was eighty degrees and humid. Maddy thought William was disgustingly uncouth, obsessively full of himself, and only okay good looking, and she was obviously trying to discourage any further interest from him.

As for Susan . . . well, she was still missing.

And so was Hamish MacKeage.

Mabel sat beside Father Daar, holding the wedding bands and the vows she and William had composed during one of his lessons.

Eve couldn't wait to hear them.

When Father Daar started the ceremony in Gaelic, Eve interrupted. "Wait—is this actually legal?"

"Why wouldn't it be?" Kenzie asked.

She whispered in his ear, "You told me Daar is almost two thousand years old, so he likely isn't licensed by the state of Maine to marry anyone."

"He's presided over every MacKeage and MacBain wedding for the last forty years. I believe Grace got him a justice-of-the-peace license so her daughters would be legally wed."

"Okay. Sorry, Father," she said, shooting the scowling priest a smile. "But could you marry us in English?"

"It's Gaelic or nothing, girl."

"Okay," Eve said with a sigh.

Several soft, pathetic barks came from the barn, and *Kenzie* sighed.

"Oh, go get her," Eve said. "I don't know why you thought the seal pup would stay in there with Fiona out here."

Kenzie headed to the barn, and Fiona swooped off Daar's shoulder and followed.

"You realize that if Marine Fish and Wildlife finds out you're keeping a seal pup without a permit, they're going to fine you up the whazoo," Maddy told Eve. "Why haven't you taken her to the rehabilitation center?"

William snorted. "Because that blasted pup doesn't need rehabilitating. She's all drama and tears."

Maddy leaned past Eve to glare at William. "How many more days is it before you head back to Ireland?"

He shot her a smirk. "I'm purchasing the land surrounding what everyone in town now calls Dragon Cove," he said, puffing up his large chest. "Want to come sit on the cliffs with me and watch for the dragon those kayakers claimed they saw? Our best chance of spotting it would be at night, under a full moon."

Maddy straightened so Eve was blocking their view of each other again. "No, thank you."

Kenzie came striding back with the seal pup in his arms.

"I'll take her," Mabel said, helping him settle the young animal on her lap. Then she had to hold the vows out of its reach when it tried to eat them.

Until a breeze suddenly blew them out of her hand.

William gave chase and had to wrestle them away from the four baby goslings that had immediately pounced on them.

Eve expected Kenzie to either start laughing or growling as he wondered if he was *ever* going to get a ring on her finger. But when she looked up at him, he was looking out to sea.

He suddenly turned and faced forward. "Forget the vows, Killkenny. Proceed, Father. The *short* version, please."

Eve tried to glance back to see what he'd seen, but he wrapped his arm around her shoulders and held her facing the priest.

Daar quickly started speaking in Gaelic, and after what seemed like only three sentences, he nodded at Kenzie. Kenzie kissed her full on the mouth, slid a wedding band on her finger, took his from Mabel, shoved it on his own hand, and then swiftly moved toward the house.

"Get everyone inside and close the storm shutters," he said.

"Where's your pen?" Eve asked.

"In my pocket. And yours?"

"In my bra. And your sword?"

"On the island," he called, running toward the ocean path as William fell in behind him.

Eve walked up the porch stairs, stepped inside, and looked out at the approaching storm, seeing Fiona soaring after her brother. She flipped the switch that lowered the storm shutters over every window in the house, then shut the three-inch-thick steel-and-ballistic glass door and seated the bolts.

Maddy came over to look out the door window, which was their only view outside now. "We need to call NOAA and asked them what in hell's up with this bay. We keep getting these freak storms, but only in this one spot! It's unnatural, I tell you."

"I prefer to think of them as supernatural. And you know what? I'm sort of getting used to them," Eve said.

She glanced at the wooden butter churn in the kitchen corner, poured the cream warming on the counter into the churn, sat down, and started rocking it back and forth. Then she stopped with a grin, slipped off her sandals, and started rocking again, watching her wedding band glitter in the last rays of sunlight.

She was barefoot, pregnant, and churning butter, but she'd discovered she loved farming, and Eve decided all those generations of women hadn't fought only for equality, they'd also fought for *choice*.

And she chose to deeply and passionately love a very handsome, very brave soul warrior, who loved her so deeply and passionately that, together, they could weather any storm.

Letter from Lake Watch

Dear Reader,

If you took a moment to read my dedication at the front of this book, you might realize that my mother and Mabel had quite a bit in common and that, like Eve, I had a few lessons of my own to learn.

My mother's slow withdrawal from everyday life lasted nearly twelve years. It took my family—my father, my three brothers, my sister, and me—quite a long time to accept that our strong, anchoring matriarch's decline wasn't something that at first blush we could deny, then hope to reverse or even slow down. It wasn't until several years passed that we collectively realized her downward spiral wouldn't be stopped.

And it was only then, when we finally accepted Mom just as she *was*, that the magic truly began.

Ella was blissfully happy in her unawareness

of what was happening to her, seemingly content just . . . being. She laughed a lot, and we laughed with her. She smiled graciously and nodded attentively at visitors—though she didn't have a clue who anyone was—and sighed in relief when they left. She engaged in an ongoing battle of wills with my then toddler son, rushing to hide her precious bananas when she saw him heading across the lawn to her house. And since she had been born in Quebec, we all had to bone up on our French when she eventually regressed to her native language.

Mom found such delight in birthday parties and Sunday family dinners that *everyone's* birthday was celebrated at her house. My dad shortened the legs on one of our heirloom chairs to fit it with casters when Mom stopped walking, and she would sit at the head of the table and unabashedly eat enough ice cream and cake to make a lumberjack blush—and she never gained a pound! (Note to dieters: happiness seems to burn an inordinate amount of calories.)

I believe it was on her seventy-eighth birthday that I asked Mom how old she was, and after a moment's contemplation she declared she was thirty-one—even though I, her youngest child, was several years older. (Apparently happiness not only burns calories, it's also the fountain of youth!)

Having my parents living right next door for

the last ten years of my mother's life was a rewardingly intimate experience. It is my belief that we all come into this world to teach life lessons as well as to learn them, and I can attest that my mother continued teaching all of us many valuable lessons right up to and through her death. In fact, my most vivid memory of her funeral is that I couldn't stop smiling. I felt so *blessed* to have been part of her life, and regretted nothing—not even her illness.

My son the banana thief eventually moved into my parents' house, and his son—Ella's great-grandson—slept in her bedroom for the first three years of his life. And if you don't quite believe in the magic, then I ask you: Why to this day does little Alex say *oui* when asked a question that should be answered with Yes? No one has ever spoken French to the boy, yet he continues to use the perfectly inflected *oui* of his *grand-memère.*

What was it Kenzie wanted Eve to understand when they thought her mother had died? That *Mabel was right now mingling with stardust, floating in those raindrops falling to Earth, and whispering in her tiny grandson's developing ear how much he is loved. If only he could explain that Mabel wasn't here because she was EVERYWHERE.*

So as Eve eventually did, it is my hope that as you travel down your own life path, you, too, will recognize the magic surrounding you. It is there in the first breath of life and in the last, in the intimacy of cradling a sleeping child or holding the hand of an ill or dying loved one, in the simple joy of waking each morning to discover what oft-disguised blessings the day will bring.

Which is why, when asked, I recall one of my mother's more endearing lessons, and say, "*Oui*, I believe in the magic."

Until later, from LakeWatch,

Janet

And now,

turn the page

for a sneak peek at Janet Chapman's

upcoming Christmas novella!

Available November 2009 from Pocket Books

Camry MacKeage woke up to a wet tongue slobbering in her ear and the smell of doggie breath. She rolled away with a groan, pain throbbing in her temple.

When she rolled into a body that wasn't canine she sat up with a start, grabbed her head to keep it from splitting wide open, and fell back against the pillow with a louder groan.

"What is licking my face?" Luke Pascal rasped from beside her. "I know it's not your tongue, MacKeage, because it's way too friendly."

"That's Ruffles," she muttered. "And she's a shameless hussy. Is there a reason you're in my bed, Pascal? Because if you're not out of it in two seconds, I'm going to blacken your other eye."

"Give me a minute, would you? My head is killing me, and I'm afraid a rib will pierce my lung if I move right now."

"What are you doing here?"

"I heard you whimpering in the night, so I came in and checked on you. I must have fallen asleep before I could leave."

"That's a flat-out lie, because I never whimper."

"What in hell did they give us at the hospital?"

"Obviously some very powerful pain pills. Um . . .

you don't happen to have any spare ones in your pocket, do you?"

"Boxers don't have pockets."

"I have some for both of you. Max, get down," Fiona said, walking up to Camry's side of the bed. "You too, Ruffles. Go on, shoo!"

Camry felt the bed dip, and cracked open her one good eye to see Fiona holding a pill and a glass of water. Cam opened her mouth and the girl popped in the pill, then lifted her head to give her a drink. As soon as she was done, Fiona headed around the bed to do the same for Luke.

"The doctor warned me that you'd both be pretty sore this morning. Max! I told you to go in the living room!"

"Whisper," Cam whispered.

"Sorry."

"Why is Luke here?" Cam asked.

"The nice EMT from the ambulance called his wife, and they both hung out in the waiting room with me. Then they gave us a ride home and helped me get you both settled in for the night. John put Luke in my bed, and his wife, Glenna, helped me put you in yours. I slept on the couch, so I don't know how you two ended up in bed together," she finished, sounding way too delighted.

"No, I mean why is Luke in my *house*?"

"Oh, that. When the doctor gave me instructions for both of you, I figured Luke should come stay with us for a few days." She smiled at Cam's one-eyed glare. "After he so gallantly came to my rescue last night, I thought it was the least we could do."

"*He* doesn't care to be talked about as if *he* isn't here," Luke said. "And thank you," he muttered, only to groan when Tigger jumped up on the bed, jostling them both. "How the hell many dogs do you own, anyway?"

"None," Cam told him. "But I babysit four."

"You babysit dogs? Why?"

"To pay the bills."

Camry heard Fiona sigh. "She's still trying to decide what she wants to be when she grows up."

"Excuse me?" Luke said.

"Right now she's torn between being Suzy Homemaker or president of the United States. I told her she's smart enough to be a rocket scientist if she wanted, but she doesn't think that would be very exciting."

Apparently Luke was so impressed, he couldn't comment.

Cam felt her arm being patted, and found Fiona standing beside her again. "Don't worry about the dogs. I'll take them for their runs for the next few days. The doctor said you need to stay off that ankle."

She looked over at Luke, then back at Cam. "And Luke's got some badly bruised ribs, and Doctor Griswell said they'll probably hurt worse than if they were broken. But don't worry; he sent you both home with plenty of pain pills."

"Can he at least walk back to his own bed?" Cam asked.

"*He* can, just as soon as Fiona leaves," Luke said. "Because *he* is only wearing boxer shorts."

Fiona swept Tigger into her arms, spun around with a giggle, and left.

Luke still didn't move.

"She's gone."

"I know. How about giving me enough time for the pill to kick in?"

"You get five minutes, Pascal."

"So, you babysit dogs and wait tables for a living?"

"No, I babysit dogs through the week and tend bar on the weekends. I was just waiting tables last night so I could keep an eye on Fiona."

"How long has she been . . . missing?"

"I found her on the beach this past Friday. She told me she'd run away from home four days prior to that."

"And you can't get her to tell you anything about her family?"

"No. And I don't dare push her, because I'm afraid she'll run away from *me*."

"Christ, her parents must be going out of their minds. Did you call the police to see if they have a missing child reported?"

"First thing Friday, while she was taking a shower. They said no one fitting Fiona's description had been reported missing. Um . . . thank you for rescuing her last night. A lot of men wouldn't have gotten involved, especially considering there were four of those drunken jerks. There were plenty of other men sitting there last night, but I didn't see any of them jump out of their seat."

"I have a half sister about Fiona's age."

"Fiona said you're on sabbatical. From what?"

He was silent for several heartbeats, then softly chuckled. "Would you believe rocket science?"

Camry didn't even dare to breathe as she tried to calculate the odds of two physicists getting into a barroom brawl and winding up in the same bed the next morning.

"And you know what?" he continued. "I happen to believe it's an exciting profession."

"How can crunching numbers until your eyes cross be exciting? Especially if those numbers suddenly stop making a lick of sense?"

"You know something about mathematical physics, do you?"

"I know it must be frustrating as hell."

"And babysitting other people's dogs is exciting?"

"The dogs don't question every damn thing I say in an email, or *kindly* point out my mistakes."

"I didn't know dogs used email," he said, amusement lacing his voice.

Camry gave him a shove. "The pill's obviously working now."

"Ow, my ribs! It definitely *isn't* working yet."

"Sorry."

She felt the bed dip again, and cracked open her eye just enough to see that he'd rolled toward her, propping his head on his hand. "So, you babysit dogs because they think you're the smartest thing since sliced bread, is that it? You don't care to have an engaging argument with a worthy opponent once in a while?"

Camry pulled the blanket up to her chin and tucked it down between them. "I like a good argument when the person I'm arguing with isn't so full of himself that he insists on coming to America to set me straight in person."

"I'm a little lost here. I thought we were talking about arguing in general, but you seem to be talking about something a bit more specific. Mind elaborating?"

"No. Go away, Pascal."

He eased back onto his pillow and sighed. "I'm hungry. I never did get supper last night."

"There's some mayonnaise in the fridge. You're welcome to it."

"That's it? You don't cook?"

"Why bother, when I can just go to the Go Back Grill?"

"Maybe you should lean more toward being president when you grow up, instead of Suzy Homemaker." He sighed again. "I don't suppose anyone delivers in this half-deserted town. Maybe Dave or one of his waitresses could bring something over to us."

"Dave brought Cam's SUV home last night," Fiona said, walking back into the bedroom carrying a tray of food and setting it down between them.

Cam slowly sat up, the smell making her mouth water. "He brought food, too?"

"No, I drove to the grocery store this morning, and was able to get back before the mutts arrived." Fiona placed the pillow behind Cam against the headboard.

"You have a driver's license?"

"Almost," Fiona said, going around to set Luke's pillow in place. "And since those pills will knock both of you out soon, I'll wait until then to run to Luke's hotel and get his stuff. Is your room key in your pants, Luke? What's your room number?"

"You can't drive with *almost* a license," Cam told her. "You're supposed to have an adult with you."

"Don't worry that I'll crash your truck, Cam. I've been driving on tote roads since I was ten," the girl said.

"Tote roads?" Camry said, perking up. "That means you live in western Maine."

"They have tote roads in Aroostook and Washington counties, too." Fiona caught Tigger mid-leap as the dachshund tried to jump onto the bed, and headed toward the door with the dog. "I'm going to leave Max and Ruffles here, and I'll take Suki and Tigger with me. Luke, your room number?"

"He's going back to his hotel this morning," Camry told her.

"It's room seven," he said, picking up a piece of toast. "And I haven't unpacked, so you'll find my suitcase on the bed."

"You are *not* moving in here with us."

"You heard what the doctor told Fiona. I'm going to be in a lot of pain for the next few days, and it's not safe for me to take powerful drugs if there's no one around to make sure I don't maim myself. I need supervision, and since you do, too, we might as well be supervised together."

"That makes perfect sense to me," Fiona said from the doorway. "And I certainly don't mind taking care of the both of you. In fact, it will let me know if I want to be a nurse when I grow up." The young girl, who appeared to be enjoying herself way too much, arched her brows at Camry. "Unlike *someone* around here, I want it all: a career *and* a husband *and* children before my biological clock starts ticking down."

Camry grabbed an orange off the tray to fling at her. "You little brat!"

Luke snatched it out of her hand before she could throw it. "Not the food!"

Camry pointed at Fiona. "You just wait until your daddy gets hold of you, young lady. I intend to be standing right beside him, helping him lecture you. And as soon as I can walk, I'm going through all of your belongings to find out his name."

"Too late. I burned everything with my name on it in the fireplace this morning."

Camry gasped, sincerely hurt. "You don't trust me?"

Fiona stepped closer. "Of course I do, Camry. It's Luke I don't trust," she said, rolling her eyes. "After all, he *is* a man."

Luke started to hurl the orange at her, but Camry snatched it out of his hand, then began peeling it. Fiona spun away with a laugh, shooed the three other dogs out ahead of her, and closed the bedroom door.

"She's been living with you only a few days and you've already corrupted her opinion of men," Luke accused, and took a bite of his toast.

"I'm pretty sure Fiona had you men figured out long before I found her. She told me she left home because her father wouldn't stop lecturing her."

"Because he loves her."

She stopped eating the orange and looked at him. "Why can't men love their wives and daughters without lecturing them to death?"

"How should I know? I've never had a wife or a daughter."

"How about a girlfriend?"

"Not at the moment," he said, staring down at his toast. "I don't seem to have any problem *getting* a girlfriend, I just can't seem to keep one."

"Because you lecture them to death?"

"No, that's not it." He picked up the plate of eggs and started eating, talking between bites. "They never stick around long enough for me to reach the lecture stage." He looked over at her. "Assuming there even is one," he said, returning to wolfing down his food.

Camry found herself quite intrigued. She could see why Luke Pascal didn't have trouble getting girlfriends. He had the body of an athlete—which really didn't go with the physicist thing—and his eyes were a beautiful deep blue. As for his hair, well, she had to admit she did like it long, as it gave him a rugged, rebellious look—which also didn't match his profession.

His chest wasn't anything to scoff at, either. His shoulders were broad, and his well-defined pecs, liberally sprinkled with soft-looking hair, certainly rang *her* bell.

"So why can't you keep a girlfriend?" she asked. Maybe he bombed in the bedroom. He was a nerd, after all, even if he did have a good deal of brawn.

"According to the women who were still speaking to me when they packed up their toothbrushes, I'm boring. Apparently you ladies need a guy's undivided attention," he said, sounding more confounded than resigned.

Camry almost burst out laughing, but caught herself

when she realized he was serious. "So you spent all your time working instead of with your girlfriends?"

"If they wanted to be with me, why didn't they come hang out at my lab?"

Okay, the guy truly was clueless. "Maybe you should try dating other physicists. You know, another scientist who would understand being ignored?"

"Have you *met* many women scientists?" He actually shivered. "They scare the hell out of me."

"How?"

"I can name you three right off the top of my head who pull their hair back so tight, they look like they've had botched facelifts. And two come to mind who could probably knock me on my ass in three seconds flat." He snorted. "And a lot of female scientists have the personality of lab rats."

Camry didn't know why, but she found that hilariously funny. "And most of the *male* scientists I've met," she said through her laughter, "couldn't dance their way out of a wet paper bag!"

"Hey, *I* can dance."

"And I've met fish with more personality than most of them have."

Luke started laughing, too. "Okay, you've got me there. So have I."

Camry threw back the covers and started to swing her legs off the bed.

"Hey, where are you going?" he asked, grabbing her arm. "You can't walk."

"I have to use the bathroom."

"Hmm. Me, too. Okay, here's what we'll do. You wait right there, and I'll walk around and help you since I don't have a bum ankle."

"Okay, but I get the bathroom first."

Luke set his plate on the tray between them, then walked around to her side.

Camry nearly fell over, tilting her head to look at him. "You're a lot bigger when you're half-naked." Her eyes stopped halfway up, and she reached out and touched his ribs. "Wow, that's one hell of a bruise." Her gaze finally made it to his battered face. "Are you sure you're a physicist? You certainly held your own last night."

"I've been working out," he said, puffing up his chest, only to let it sink with a groan as he cradled his ribs. "Okay. Give me your hand, and don't put any weight on your nakle."

Camry giggled. "I think your pill's working."

"Nope. I can still feel my ribs."

She pulled herself out of bed—thankful that Fiona had put her in flannel pajamas—then clutched his arm as she balanced on her good leg. "My pill isn't working, either. Both my head and nakle hurt. Don't let me fall."

"I won't. You know why, MacKeage?" he asked, leading her to the bathroom.

"Why?"

"Because you're downright pretty when you smile."

She smiled up at him. "You're not so bad yourself, for a physicist."

They reached the bathroom, and Camry transferred her weight from his arm to the sink.

"You won't take forever, will you? I really have to go, too," he said.

She waved toward the bedroom. "Pee out the window, or something. I don't have any neighbors."

Cam closed the door and hobbled over to the toilet.

"You know what I think?" Luke called through the bathroom door.

"I don't have a clue. What?"

"You know that guy you were having the email argument with? I think you should meet him in person."

"So I can cram his laptop down his throat?"

He didn't answer right away. "Did you really think he was full of himself?"

"He was a know-it-all, holier-than-thou, arrogant son of a bitch."

"He really pissed you off, didn't he?" Luke said softly.

Done taking care of business, Camry hobbled to the sink, looked in the mirror, and screamed.

The doorknob rattled. "What's wrong? Did you fall?"

"No, I just looked in the mirror," she said with a slightly hysterical laugh, carefully touching her swollen eye.

It sounded like Luke thunked his head against the door. "Dammit, you just scared the hell out of me!"

"I just scared the hell out of myself." She washed and dried her hands, ran her fingers through her rumpled hair, and opened the door. "Your turn," she said.

"I just need to wash my hands."

"Why?"

He grinned crookedly. "I peed out the window."

"I was *kidding*."

"You were taking too long," he said, stepping around her to use the sink.

He didn't scream when he looked in the mirror, but he did gasp. "Aren't we a pair?" Camry said, smiling at him in the mirror. "At least we've got two good eyes between us, and you can walk and I can . . . I can . . ." She hung her head. "I can never go into another bar. Every time I get into trouble, it's in a bar."

He lifted her chin with his finger. "You can go with me. I won't let you get into trouble."

"Said the spider to the fly."

"Smile again."

"It hurts my face."

"Because of your shiner, or when you're around men in general?"

"Hey, I am a *happy* person, dammit."

"Wow, that pill sure wore off fast. Should I ask Fiona to give you another one?"

Camry reached up and pulled down his head, then kissed him full on the mouth. "Is *that* happy enough for you?"

He pulled her into his arms, cradled her head against his shoulder, and kissed her back—a bit more forcefully, quite a bit longer, and definitely . . .

He sure didn't keep losing girlfriends because he bombed in the bedroom. This guy could *kiss*.

Camry went weak in the knees, and sagged against him when his tongue started doing delicious things to hers. She nearly burst into tears when he suddenly pulled away.

"Christ, you're scary," he rasped, his blue eyes locked on hers.

"Scary?" she repeated in confusion, running her fingertip over his jaw. "How's that?"

He tilted her head back again and started kissing her cheek, then trailed soft, shivering kisses down her neck.

Camry trembled with blossoming passion. Yup—he *definitely* rang her bell.